THE WISE ASS

D0875137

TOM McCAFFREY

Black Rose Writing | Texas

ISBN: 978-1-68433-635-7
PUBLISHED BY BLACK ROSE WRITING
www.blackrosewriting.com

Printed in the United States of America
Suggested Retail Price (SRP) $18.95

The Wise Ass is printed in Garamond

*As a planet-friendly publisher, Black Rose Writing does its best to eliminate unnecessary waste to reduce paper usage and energy costs, while never compromising the reading experience. As a result, the final word count vs. page count may not meet common expectations.

Cover Photo courtesy of Kathy Fronsdahl

THE WISE ASS

PROLOGUE
EARLY DAYS

I promise not to bore you with a tedious recitation of my formative years. But as you will see later, this one thing is important, so pay attention.

I've always had an affinity for animals. As I think back on it, at an incredibly early age I formed a subconscious connection between animals and women. When I was four, Kathy Brown, a cute five-year-old brunette with large green eyes— who lived in the next apartment of our building in the High Bridge section of the Bronx—took me down into the alleyways to assist her in playing doctor to what I later realized were dead pigeons that we found there.

I was an orderly who scoured the labyrinthian alleyways the length of the block with a wagon and collected and returned with the birds to the designated spot. There Kathy would wrap them in tissue paper and place them in shoe boxes lined along a wall as if they were sleeping patients in a hospital ward. She squirted a few drops of some liquid she carried in her pocket into the beaks of each of these lifeless animals. The apparent efficacy of her treatment was reinforced by the fact that, when we returned to the same spot the following day, the birds and their beds were nowhere to be found. I spent a lot of time trying to match up the living pigeons I would later spot on the street with the patients we had cured the day before. On a good day, we saved a dozen patients.

At the end of each arduous shift in the avian medical ward, Kathy Brown would lead me by the hand out of the subterranean darkness, and before my eyes had adjusted to the daylight, peck me on the cheek and skip off towards her apartment. The resulting tingling was worth the risk of catching any of the numerous diseases I encountered each shift. Both kisses and germs did wonders for my immune system. You never forget your first crush.

This method of hard-wiring wasn't without its problems, which I proved later that same year while my poor, very-pregnant mother walked me and the rest of her animated brood home from McCoombs Park. My preternaturally responsible older sister led our Irish caravan, holding my older brother's hand while I grasped tightly to the street-side of the pram carrying my younger brother. I remember being fascinated by his bobbing mop of bright red curls, since the rest of us were all brunettes and my older brother had told me that ginger's have no souls. Time would tell.

My mother herded us along, heading South under the El on the park side of Jerome Avenue with her alternating combinations of threats and promised treats. My older brother, who I now suspect fell somewhere on the Asperger's Scale, brought the caravan to a sudden halt when he squatted down in the middle of the sidewalk and studied an army of ants that had commandeered the last of a Baby Ruth bar that someone had dropped.

Having grown bored watching my ginger sibling, my attention shifted to Jerome Avenue and the overhead squealing of a southbound No. 4 train pulling into the Yankee Stadium Station. At the ding-dong-ping sound of its opening doors, my eyes followed the disturbed descending flock of pigeons gliding down from the guano covered steel girders of the El to sample the last of a patch of flattened Crackerjack on Jerome ten feet away. I scanned the group to see if any of them were recent patients. With a firm "stay put," my mother locked the pram's wheels and advanced to the front of the caravan where she reached down and lifted my older brother back to standing position and gave him and my sister a slight shove on the bottoms to propel them past this latest distraction.

My ears perked up at the swelling engine roar of an enormous Mack Truck approaching from behind us. The bobbing circle of the pigeons continued unfazed to peck and pry at the tacky mass of caramel-covered popcorn as if they were searching for the famous prize. Without thinking—a recurring issue in my life—I released my grip on the pram and raced out into the southbound lane of Jerome Avenue towards the birds, waving my arms frantically as I tried to shoo them out of harm's way. I barely noticed the banshee wail that rose from my mother's lips or the screeching metal of the Mack truck brakes mixed with its sonorous horn behind me. The pigeons defiantly held their ground until I stuck a two-footed landing in the middle of their feeding scrum, at which point they rose in unison back towards their overhead steel perches, encircling me in a feathered magician's curtain. Having saved the flock, I turned towards the family caravan, who had all turned their faces away from me.

As I turned back toward the street, I noticed—in what my memory recorded in slow motion—that the oncoming traffic in the north-bound lane had slowed to a crawl and I fixated on the horror in the eyes of the cabbie passing to my left. The heat of a steam blast furnace on my back and the hissing sounds of releasing air brakes brought me eye-to-eye with a dirty-white metal bulldog and an oversized cursive group of letters I later learned had spelled 'MACK' rocking to a slow stop. The slam of a heavy truck door prefaced the large black man who appeared from around the front end of the truck, tapping his chest while wiping rivulets of sweat from his face with a large white handkerchief. He leaned against the truck, as if about to faint, and stammered, "Are you okay?"

Before I could respond, I heard my mother alliterate, "I'm soooo sorry sir," before yanking my collar backward with such force that my feet rose like a kite's tail traveling in the air behind me. I landed on my backside and continued skidding backwards until I came to rest against the oversized wheels of the pram. I looked up to see the contorted face of my mother, who now grabbed me by my front collar and lifted me with a strength I never knew she possessed, confirmed by a powerful swat to my backside that propelled me through the air into the waiting arms of my sister at the front of the pram. "Now move!" my mother commanded. My older brother had replaced me by the ginger, so my sister grabbed my wrist and tugged me forward while the pram wheels squeaked. I heard my mother mumble her most threatening mantra, "Wait 'til your father gets home."

By Christmas that year we had moved far away from the rundown apartments near Yankee Stadium to a delightful house in an upscale residential community where I would be less tempted to save what my Dad called "flying rats" on busy streets.

As I grew older, I nurtured my empathy for animals by adopting stray dogs and cats, and whatever injured, more exotic, suburban wildlife I would come across in my adventures in the neighboring wooded areas. The more grievously injured beasts were patched up by my father, who had been a medic in the Navy during the Korean War and put more than a few stitches in me and my siblings, which explains my lifelong aversion to doctors. If my feral patients survived, they convalesced in a large wooden box in the corner of my room. The multigenerational family members that inhabited the large house begrudgingly accepted the dogs and cats who, with few exceptions, lived out long and happy lives as domesticated additions to our clan. However, as soon as the recuperating wild-life were well-enough to escape my room and explore the rest of the house— always seeming to surprise my poor mother in the process—I was forced to discharge them from my infirmary and back into the wild. During their extended runs, squirrels, raccoons, mice, rats, birds and even snakes passed through my surgery, taking years off my mother's life.

Being that this was the Bronx in the 1960s, I never had much contact with the larger species of animals, with one exception. An old man that the kids in my neighborhood called 'Junkie', drove the last of the large wooden Weber wagons, led by an old mule, through our neighborhood on the weekly garbage pickup days. The mule wore cracked leather blinders to mask his view of the mechanized traffic, and his thick brown coat carried a patina of oily grit that spewed from the exhausts of passing automobiles. The melody from the long string of rusty tin cowbells along the front of the wagon kept syncopated time with the base sounds of the mule's metal horseshoes clopping on the asphalt.

Junkie was thin and diminutive in stature, and his skin leathered from a lifetime of exposure to the sun. He wore the same tattered brown suit over a stained, long-sleeved shirt, buttoned to the collar. The frayed creases in his trousers barely reached the tops of his scarred military boots. His face, framed by a floppy old grey fedora, was angular and creased, and his eyes had epicanthic folds that made him look Mongolian. His exotic derivation was reinforced by the undecipherable litany of what had to be curses streaming past the ubiquitous Marlboro in his lips whenever the rambunctious neighborhood urchins, myself included, would spring out of some driveway and run along-side of his wagon, taunting Junkie and his mule.

That all ended one garbage day when my paternal grandfather, we called him Spaghetti, forced me to help him drag an old dead Frigidaire from the back of our garage out to the front of the house. He could have done this by himself, as he was a beast of a man who hauled hundred-pound tins of tar up onto rooftops well into his eighties, but he had an ulterior motive that day. We sat on the old white fridge while he smoked Prince Albert in his pipe until the growing cacophony of cowbells and horseshoes signalled Junkie's pending arrival from around the corner.

Spaghetti stood and waved familiarly to Junkie and, as the wagon drew along the front of the house, my grandfather addressed Junkie in his strange guttural language. Junkie smiled for the one and only time in my memory, displaying a couple of faux-gold teeth, tarnished by a lifetime of tobacco juice. They laughed together like Easter conspirators, and Junkie pointed towards where I remained frozen on the fridge. Spaghetti nodded, and Junkie hooked the reins and leaped off his clapboard perch with the agility of a squirrel monkey. Before I could flee, he grabbed my biceps, gently lifted me off the fridge and set me down on my feet beside it. I was in fourth grade at the time but was already his height. Without a word, Junkie snatched the top end of the Fridge and dragged it towards the back of his wagon. I looked over at Spaghetti, who waved me off and walked toward the front where the mule had turned to face him.

I looked back as the imp of a man deftly tilted the Fridge against the dropped back gate of the wagon and, reaching down with one fluid movement, heaved the heavy metal monolith from the street deep into the wooden cargo bed. When I turned to see if Spaghetti had witnessed this herculean effort, I saw him gently stroking the animal's muzzle and whispering something unintelligible in its ear while the animal nodded. Then Spaghetti kissed the animal on its snout before chucking it affectionately under its chin. The animal stole one final glance at Spaghetti before responding to the tug of its reins by the remounted Junkie. After another short indecipherable exchange, Junkie waved to Spaghetti, lightly shook the reins and the mule carried them off.

"I didn't know you spoke Mongolian?" I said incredulously.

"That's feckin Irish, you wee moron," he said with a laugh. "And one more thing, don't let me catch you or your idjit friends bothering that man or his mule again or I'll cut your feckin heads off."

After Bozzy McCarroll's near decapitation by Spaghetti's stealthy shrub-shears the summer before, my friends and I took my grandfather's threat very seriously, so Junkie rode out the remainder of his days through my neighborhood in peace.

Once puberty struck, my interests understandably shifted away from childhood fantasies to the more mundane and legitimate pursuits of girls, drinking and fighting. Despite these sophomoric distractions, over the next two decades I surprisingly managed to meet and marry the woman of my dreams and maintain decent enough grades to find my way through upper academia and into law school. There I graduated close enough to the top of my class to land a lucrative job with a prestigious Wall Street law firm. And that's where my problems really started.

CHAPTER ONE
PROFESSIONAL CONFESSIONS

I'd like to tell you that my success as a lawyer came because of my superior intellect, but that would be bullshit. I've always been an average guy with a penchant for procrastination. The truth is that for some strange reason, throughout my professional life, the Universe has always stepped in and provided me with whatever legal information—cases, statutes, theories—I've ever needed, whenever I have needed it. It's like I'm a permanent contestant on 'Who Wants to Be a Millionaire' and my lifeline is Clarence Darrow.

It wasn't always like that. I didn't have the gift back in law school. I suffered from 'imposter syndrome,' and so I worked my ass off 24/7 for three years to avoid a daily panic attack. I worked harder than most of the trust-fund legacies that I followed through the law school door that first year. They never broke a sweat, because they knew they belonged there and would graduate and take their place in their professional legal pantheon no matter what they did. Their success was genetically preordained.

I, on the other hand, was born with dirt under my fingernails. I was the first one in my family to complete college, never mind go on to graduate school. My grandparents were raised on farms on the other side of the pond and were lucky to complete grade school. They came to this country at the turn of the last century to work as supers, doormen, housekeepers, nannies and cooks for the ancestors of my law school classmates. Hell, the only book I ever saw my grandfather,

Spaghetti, read was Steinbeck's *The Red Pony*. So, I entered law school five rungs down on society's evolutionary ladder and was hanging on for dear life.

My reward for pure tenaciousness was landing a second-year lottery interview with the Wall Street version of Pygmalion's Henry Higgins. He was a senior partner at a white-shoe law firm who, in an apparent fit of whimsy, decided that my obvious Neanderthal DNA might come along with a heightened killer instinct. He was right.

Once employed, I was the rookie who—right out of the gate—was sent all over the country to take and defend the toughest depositions. I didn't give a shit who was sitting across the conference room table from me. If I wanted information from their witness, I kept at them until I got it. If I wanted to prevent the other side from prying information out of our witnesses, I shut them down. I once reached under the table and thumped my own witness in the nuts to keep him from completing what was starting out to be an unbelievably bad admission. Before long, I second sat a couple of trials, because I was always able to whisper the right thought in the ear of the white-haired partner I was squiring. I didn't care that they got the accolades.

I was also the associate my law firm trotted out to discretely spring their high-power clients' children, spouses and valued employees from jail. Having gotten to where I was on luck and sweat, I had no professional ego, and innately understood that the Criminal Courthouse is really run by the Clerks and the Court Officers, not the Judges, and certainly not the lawyers. In fact, I grew up with many of these plebeians, so we spoke the same working-class dialect. If you could connect with them on their own level, that was half the battle. Many white-shoe lawyers learned the hard way that you pissed them off at your peril.

It was during one of my Friday night runs to arraignment court that I first met Dan Pearsall. He was a huge black man in his late thirties who resembled Isaac Hayes. He was sitting alone reading a copy of the Hollywood Reporter in the back-bench area of the courtroom bleachers filled with the usual Friday night crowd of worried parents, spouses and children, stage whispering with their respective defendant's legal-aid or 18 B lawyers, waiting anxiously for the calendar call. Dan Pearsall looked remarkably cool sitting there amongst the damned.

Luckily, my boy Mike Moulton was the Clerk on duty in the court room that night. Mike was sitting at his industrial desk stage right in the front of the gallery, studiously ignoring the gathering line of attorneys impatiently waiting to learn if their client's file lay somewhere in the two-foot stack on Mike's desk. They knew that if the file wasn't there, their client was spending the rest of the weekend as a guest of the State in the Manhattan Tombs or Riker's Island.

Mike saw me approaching down the center aisle. He stood up and met me at the court rail, while the other waiting attorneys mumbled their haughty displeasure.

"Who do you got tonight, Jimmy?" Mike asked.

"Jonas Williams the Third, a little pussy from Greenwich who got pinched in a buy-and-bust this afternoon trying to score some coke. His dad is a major client of the firm."

Mike was a bit of a savant when it came to his job, and I watched with amusement as he closed his eyes for a few seconds and placed his left hand to his forehead, mimicking the Amazing Kreskin as he ran the names in his stack of files through his prodigious memory bank.

"Yeah, I got him. Hold on—" Mike returned to his desk and reached into the stack about three quarters down and deftly retrieved Young Jonas' file without causing the precarious pile to topple. He quickly scanned it, gently placed it on top of the stack and returned to me.

"They are charging him with possession under 220.03." He whispered.

"Shit. This is his first offense and his daddy's heart is set on seeing his boy graduate from law school. Any chance the ADA will drop it down to a violation if we plea tonight?"

"I doubt it." Mike said. "That douchebag Douglas is handling the calendar."

"Damn it." I replied.

Samuel Douglas was a little prick of an ADA whose vindictiveness was only surpassed by his bitterness at being relegated to regularly handling night arraignments. Once a rising star in the Manhattan District Attorney's Office, he got caught by a Judge withholding exculpatory Brady material in a homicide case. Since they couldn't prove enough intent to warrant his firing, Douglas' penance was to suffer a year in night court purgatory. Since misery loves company, 'No-Deal' Douglas made sure that nobody was happy when he was handling arraignments.

Mike leaned in. "How important is this kid to you?"

"Personally, not at all. Professionally, very."

"Leave it with me," Mike said as he tapped the side of his nose with his forefinger. He walked back towards his desk, still ignoring the now lengthy line of lawyers vying for his attention, grabbed the file off the top of his stack and walked through the large bronze door directly to the left of the Judge's bench.

Before I could find a seat among my legal brethren on the first bench, the bronze door flew open to the sound of Mike's baritone commanding "All Rise!", while the spectators and shysters all complied in in unison. Following directly behind Mike was Justice George T. Silver, an elderly jurist who was on senior status and enjoyed keeping his hand in the mix by working a few calendars of night arraignments. The Judge was carrying my client's file as he assumed his throne on the bench while Mike retrieved his remaining stack of files and took his place immediately to the Judge's left. Stage left of the courtroom, a door quietly opened, and a court officer led a nervous little dipshit in handcuffs into the well of the Court. I checked him against the photo I was carrying and confirmed that it was Jonas, while the officer removed his cuffs and directed him to a spot at the defense table. I headed towards my spot beside him as Mike shouted, "People versus Jonas Williams III".

Judge Silver looked over at Douglas, who was fumbling with his files, and nodded at me.

"Counsel, approach," he commanded, gesturing with his right hand.

I was the first to arrive at the bench and went right into my spiel. "Your honor, this is Mr. William's first offense of any kind. He's a good kid, from a great family, with an excellent future ahead of him. Any hint of a criminal record would ruin that".

Douglas interrupted. "The jails are full of good kids your honor, and this one was caught in a clean bust."

Judge Silver cut Douglas off: "Was he picked up as part of the annual NYU graduation sweep of Washington Square Park?"

"As a matter of fact, Your Honor, he was," I chimed in, smiling over at the flustered Douglas.

"Didn't you graduate from NYU, Mr. Douglas?" Judge Silver asked.

"Yes, your honor," Douglas responded, puffing his chest out just a little.

"What a waste of taxpayer's money," Judge Silver said dismissively, waving us back to our positions. "Okay, I've heard enough."

When we returned to counsel's table, the Judge addressed my client directly.

"Mr. Williams, will you promise me that I will never see your face in court again?"

My client was startled. I leaned over and whispered, "Say, 'yes, your honor'."

"Yes, your honor," he stammered.

The Judge jotted something in the file and handed it off to Mike, who took a quick look at it and made his own notation on its jacket before he placed it as the first in a new stack before him.

"Well then," the Judge continued, "I'm going to adjourn this case in contemplation of dismissal. Mr. Williams, if you can keep your nose clean for the next six months—and I mean that in all aspects of that term—I'll dismiss the case and seal your record."

Douglas objected. "But your honor -"

"Enough, counsel. We have a long night ahead of us," Judge Silver turned to Mike, "Mr. Moulton, call the next case."

Jonas looked at me, confused. "What just happened?"

"You're done here, go home," I said, leading him by his elbow out though the swinging gates and down the center aisle towards the exit at the back of the courtroom. Once outside, I handed him a twenty. "Use this to buy your ticket back to Greenwich. Do not use it to score drugs because trust me, this was a onetime Christmas present. Next time, you're fucked."

He nodded, "I won't, I promise. Thank you, um, er, Mr...?"

"McCarthy. Jimmy McCarthy," I said, patting him on the shoulder.

"Well, thank you Jimmy McCarthy," he said, smiling for the first time. He rubbed his wrists and gazed around with a newfound appreciation for his freedom before heading off into the Manhattan night. I could only hope that he had learned his lesson. Most of these spoiled pricks don't until it's too late.

As I turned around to leave, I almost bumped into the massive chest of Dan Pearsall.

"Mr. McCarthy," he said, extending a hand that could have doubled for catcher's mitt.

My hand disappeared into this hydraulic compressor and I was pretty sure his fingertips reached my elbow before one formal shake lifted me to my toes.

"You demonstrated some slick moves in there," he said, smiling with a set of pearly whites that would have made a piano proud.

"Just another night at the Circus," I replied, "Mr...?"

"Pearsall. Dan Pearsall," he said.

"Jimmy," I said with a slight nod and began scanning the street in search of a cab. "Well, Dan, I'm glad you enjoyed the show. It was a pleasure meeting you."

"Hold on a second, Jimmy," Dan said, his smile losing a little of its lustre. He slid his large frame between me and the curb with an unexpected agility.

Night Court isn't a tourist attraction, so Dan's spot among the courtroom spectators meant that he had some business with the penal system. "My boy Donnie got swept up in the same Washington Square Park bullshit as the white kid in there."

I tried to cut to the chase. "Listen Dan, I'm an associate at a big firm who does what his partners tell him to do. Tonight, they told me to get that rich brat out of jail. I can't freelance."

"Well, what if I retain your firm?" He pulled out his wallet and removed two grand in Benjamins.

The first rule of survival I learned at my law firm was that you never took a call on a Friday from any partner after five pm if you didn't want to work the weekend. I wasn't about to tempt fate by calling the managing partner on a Friday night to clear this retainer. Funny how small-time bullshit can lead to life-altering decisions.

"Fuck it. Put your money away. I'm treating this as a one-shot, pro bono matter. No guarantees, arraignment only, but if I don't get the Judge to adjourn it in contemplation of dismissal, then you have to find someone else to take the case over."

"Done," Dan said, almost carrying me back through the doors of 80 Center Street.

Much to Sam Douglas' consternation, Mike Moulton and I repeated our tag team magic before Judge Silver and an hour later Dan and Doug Pearsall were happily reunited on the Courthouse steps.

"Thank you so much Mr. McCarthy," Doug, a thinner, fairer clone of his dad, gushed. I got the sense that unlike the earlier Greenwich brat, he really meant it.

"No problem, Doug," I said. "Good luck."

I turned to Dan. "Listen, it's been real, but I gotta go."

"Wait, Jimmy," Dan said, "Can't I at least buy you dinner?"

"Nah, my wife's waiting dinner for me at home," I said, this time quickly heading out to intercept a northbound taxi. *Fool me once.*

"I'll call you then," Dan shouted. "We can have lunch."

"Sure thing. Anytime," I said as an afterthought as I hopped into the cab and quickly slammed the door behind me. I half expected his iron grip on my shoulder before I got away and shuddered with a bewildering sense of relief as the driver pulled into traffic. It wasn't the last time I underestimated Dan Pearsall's tenacity. It turned out that like Horton the Elephant, when Dan Pearsall said something, he meant it.

CHAPTER TWO
LUNCH ANYONE

Big firm practice is basically a gilded cage for an associate. In exchange for signing your life away to toil endlessly from one case to the next, the partners throw so much stupid money at you that it makes it impossible to walk away voluntarily. That doesn't mean associates don't leave. The culling starts with the first annual review and those few that make it to year eight face the final 'up-or-out' decision of partnership or the door. There may be two partners in each entering class of 45 new associates. But with egos the size of their pay checks, each novice enters the race thinking they are the front runner. I never suffered from that illusion. The imposter in me always knew that my bell would be rung long before I was offered a seat amongst the Brahmins.

The professional futility of life at a Wall Street mega-firm isn't as obvious as you would think. That first summer working between second and third year of law school is a textbook example of masterful handling. The work the talent overseers give you is interesting, with flexible enough deadlines that they can constantly interrupt your day with breakfasts and luncheons. They always end it early enough so the youngest, coolest partners can take you to dinner followed by either a museum exhibit opening, a play, a ballgame, or a ballet. The mid-eighties Yankees were in a bit of a rut, so my wife and I opted for the culture immersion route. We even got orchestra seats to see Baryshnikov dance at Lincoln Center. Who could believe a human could have a three-Mississippi hang-time for one grand jete? LeBron James, eat your heart out.

New York hardens you. Most people can walk three blocks in midtown Manhattan and literally step over a dozen homeless people without blinking an eye. You know they are there, but you force yourself to ignore them or risk repeated heartbreak at their suffering. That same emotional conditioning allows summer associates to ignore the silent anguish of the real associates. The partners make sure to limit any of your exposure to only those star associates that are clearly on partnership track, to ensure that no one tells you the truth. The rest of the drones keep their heads down and get on with feeding the litigation machine and collecting their large pay checks. Their go-to trick is never to make eye contact with the 'summers' when they pass in the hallways or library. The 'summers' sense in their gut that something's not right, but they force themselves to ignore it and get on with being courted by the best and the brightest. It's a heady experience.

Of course, once having accepted the law firm's offer for full-time employment after graduation, you get to drink the Kool-Aid on the very first day of work. Partners race to dump the heavy lifting for their cases on as many bodies as they can wrangle, knowing each body represents a new source of billable hours that get tallied onto their respective scorecards when the firm's profits are divvied up amongst the chosen at the end of each fiscal year. Each new associate provides at least eighteen billable hours a day, seven days a week, including most holidays. Partners don't care how those eighteen daily hours are allocated, as long as their projects come first. By the end of your first year, you find yourself immersed in your own quiet desperation, callously ignoring the smiling 'summers' passing you in the hallway. As I mentioned before, misery loves company.

My advanced skill sets made for more interesting work fare and provided me the perks of being out of the office for extended periods attending depositions all around the country. At a time before emails and ubiquitous cell phones, constant traveling facilitated the avoidance of the most onerous partners. After all, it's hard to hit a moving target and why try when you can page any name off the associate list and summon them from the bowels of the library to your office on the 26th floor. That page went through the receptionist, who always had a list of those associates absent for business reasons. I was a regular on that list. After a while, most of the partners didn't even bother asking to page me.

One Monday afternoon I was hunkered down at my favorite carrel at the farthest recesses of the firm's library preparing for a horrid death bed deposition of a plaintiff in an asbestos case. One of the firm's newest partners represented a conglomerate that had purchased a cement company that turned out to be the most recent addition to the growing list of targets for the monolithic asbestos bar—that's right, the same ones you see during daytime television commercials. My family's background as tradesmen in the construction industry allowed me to detect the difference between a well-coached plaintiff reciting a laundry list of product names belonging to each of the forty defendants at the deposition, and those who actually hauled the sixty pound bags of poison on their shoulders and sucked in its deadly dust. I was a Judas goat who could ensure that most of these wretched bastards did not properly identify our client's brand of toxin and force them to pony up millions into the settlement kitty. I hated every second of it. It killed my soul.

I was startled out of my misery by the sound of my name over the firm's page system. In fact, it was so unexpected I thought I misheard it and ignored it until the second "James McCarthy" page told me to report to the main reception area. Expecting to see some harried partner holding the elevator with a cab downstairs waiting to whisk us away to some emergency shit-storm, I rehearsed my litany of excuses for avoiding new work as I raced the three flights of stairs that led from the library to the 17th floor reception area. Upon spotting me coming around the corner from the internal stairwell, the matronly receptionist professionally announced, "Your two o'clock is here." She nodded slightly towards the luxurious couch to the left of the reception desk.

"Jimmy McCarthy!"

Dan Pearsall's basso profundo reached me before I spotted him spring powerfully from the comfy couch. As I reached to take his outstretched hand, he threw his other arm around my shoulder and skilfully guided me towards the elevator bank. "C'mon. I'm buying you that lunch I promised."

Looking back on it, I can see now that Dan had used that same move on several people. For many of them, it was a final exit.

CHAPTER THREE
AN OFFER I CAN'T REFUSE

The town car Dan had waiting downstairs took us north to Mulberry Street. During the short ride, I exchanged polite pleasantries and asked about how Doug was doing.

I hadn't pegged Dan as a pasta kind of guy and when the car pulled up in front of Angelo's, it must have been obvious from my expression.

"What? Can't a brother hunker for a little 'Chicken Scarpariello'?" He laughed.

I could see through its front window that the eatery was crowded with the usual mix of tourists and wannabe wise guys, and a sizeable queue of hungry replacements extended out the doorway. I did not want to prolong my time with Dan any further than necessary waiting to be seated.

I gave the universal signal of 'bad idea' by anxiously glancing at my watch, but Dan ignored it, motioned for me to follow, and walked past the bottleneck. I hesitated long enough to draw some glares from the others waiting in line, then quickly followed Dan into the restaurant.

A large, bald Italian American approached Dan and the two men embraced and exchanged subtle and respectful pecks on the cheek. They spoke *sotto voce* while Dan pointed back to where I stood. The bald man looked at me, nodded and led Dan and me to a private dining area on the second floor. As we were seated a busboy arrived with some warm bread and fresh olive oil pesto.

"Okay," I said once we were alone, "I gotta ask. What's with the VIP treatment?"

Dan laughed and waved me off. "The owner's a friend of my uncle."

"Is your uncle in the restaurant business?" I pressed.

"Uncle Ty is into a lot of things," Dan said.

"Uncle Ty?" I asked.

"Tiberius, like the Roman emperor," Dan said. "In fact, that's one of the reasons I wanted to take you to lunch."

The waiter arrived with the menus, and Dan ordered some Chianti and antipasto.

"But first we eat."

The conversation during our meal reminded me of those job interview dinners with the partners at the firm. Dan elicited a lot about my background and after a couple of glasses of wine, I was more than willing to share. However, whenever I countered with my own questions about him, Dan ignored them and placed another forkful of pasta or bread into his mouth. After I while, I gave up and finished my gnocchi Sorrentino so I could be done with this strange guy once and for all.

While we waited for dessert, Dan asked me, "What are you doing Saturday?"

"Working."

"Fuck that," he said, "I want you to meet Uncle Ty."

"Listen," I said, "I'm sure Uncle Ty is a great guy, but I really don't have the time."

"Make the time," Dan said, leaning imperceptibly towards the table. Then he smiled. "It's his homecoming party. I've told him about you, and he wants to meet you."

"Why?" I asked.

"He's starting up a new operation, and he needs a good lawyer," Dan said, as his Panna Cotta arrived with his espresso.

"I've got a job, thanks," I said. I dug into my tiramisu to end the conversation.

"Whatever you're making, Uncle Ty will double it. And that's just for starters. You'd be your own boss, do your own side shit," Dan said with the patter of a used car salesman.

As I mentioned, the firm was paying us stupid money to strip the litigation mines, but they owned me. I thought about the next death-bed asbestos deposition coming down the pipe. My face must have betrayed my indecision as Dan quickly closed the deal. "I'll send a car to your house, Saturday morning, ten a.m."

I finished the last of my latte and nodded. "Okay, I'll go. But no promises."

CHAPTER FOUR
WELCOME HOME UNCLE TY

What does one wear to a 'welcome home' party? Luckily, my wife, Gina, having realized that since I was raised in worn jeans and rumpled t-shirts, always had some nice casual outfit that you would normally never catch me wearing, stashed away for more formal social occasions. She never told me when she bought them or where she hid them, but whenever the moment of desperation arrived, they appeared like magic, and always fit perfectly. The day of Uncle Ty's welcome home party was no different. For the first time in my life I wore white linen slacks and a pale yellow shirt. Until then I had only experienced linen used as my grandmother's Sunday tablecloths. Turns out, linen ensembles were *de rigueur* for this welcome home party.

By this time of my life, I was used to limousines, one of the many client-funded perks for all associates leaving the office after midnight. The partners wanted to make sure you got home quickly so that you could be as fresh as possible for your next eighteen-hour day. I was always asleep by the time the car passed the Christopher Street Pier heading north on the West Side Highway. During those warm summer nights of the pre-AIDS eighties, I'm sure I missed some magnificent spectacles among the '*avant garde*' denizens of the dark that like to congregate there.

The limousine that arrived that Saturday morning in May was a whole new level of transport. Gina was watching for it out our sixth floor living room window while I pondered how to pull-off wearing my new beige loafers without socks.

Gina called out, as a metallic, midnight blue, late model Cadillac Fleetwood Brougham, with all-around tints, pulled up in front of my apartment building and a burly Mediterranean-looking man in a dark suit hopped out of the driver's seat and approached my building. By the time I reached the intercom, the buzzer sounded, and a deep accented voice stated, "Car for Mizder Mac Car Tree".

Gina sent me packing with a quick kiss and "good luck." By the time I reached the curb, a small crowd of neighbors had gathered. One of them raised a laugh from the others by calling out "Hey look, Jimmy's finally going to the prom." I still smile when I think of it.

I had no idea where this party was taking place, and the driver ignored all attempts to engage him in conversation on that issue beyond the monosyllabic "yes" he was taking me to the party, and "no" he couldn't tell me the address. We headed north on the Saw Mill River Parkway to the Major Deegan Expressway and across the Tappan Zee Bridge. From there we took the Palisades Parkway North to New City. We finally arrived at South Mountain Road where we passed a couple of athletic looking security types and entered a walled-and-gated, six-acre estate with all the trimmings. The winding driveway ultimately led to a colonial mansion where similarly expensive cars were parked valet style along the edge of a beautifully manicured lawn. I found myself whispering "Welcome home, Uncle Ty" as two more security clones met the car at the front steps and opened the door for me. As I hopped out, I heard one of the clones tell my driver, "Vito, Mr. Valachi wants you to stay close so you can take Mr. McCarthy home."

Vito nodded, and I watched as he pulled away and swung the car around the far side of the house.

"Right this way, Mr. McCarthy," the larger clone said as he led me into the house. "The party is in the back by the pool."

The interior of the house was as tastefully beautiful as the exterior, and I had only seen similar furnishings on episodes of Robin Leach's Lifestyles of the Rich and Famous. The only things seemingly out of place were a row of idiosyncratic movie posters that included a well-known porn movie and a blood-and-guts horror gore fest.

I exited through a back entrance onto a large flagstone patio filled with a pantheon of beautiful people, all appearing to enjoy the alcohol and hors d'oeuvres from the passing trays of the waiters circulating freely through the crowd. The scene was framed with ubiquitous Tiki torches and scored by easy listening music playing in the background. Two wet bars were manned by stunning young women.

Scanning the crowd, I found myself surprisingly relieved to spot Dan Pearsall over by the pool. He was dressed in a pastel linen ensemble and would have looked right at home on the set of Miami Vice. His short-sleeve shirt exposed arms that had spent a lot of time in the gym.

Dan was engaged in an animated conversation with an older man bearing the vestiges of a career in the boxing ring. His nose was a bit flattened against his face and his brows thickened from too many blows. His fists were that of a tradesman, calloused and scarred, and his wavy black hair was laced with silver. His body was solid, if not quite fit, and his Guayabera shirt lay flat against his stomach. Notwithstanding the roughness of his physical features, he was meticulously groomed, well-tailored and accented by enough strategically placed jewelry to indicate wealth.

I lifted a beverage off a passing tray and made my way over in Dan's direction. He looked up with the challenge of a pit bull sensing an approaching intruder. His defensive posture instantly relaxed into inviting once he recognized me.

"Jimmy. You made it!" He seemed to clear the remaining few feet of scattered guests between us with a sweep of his arm to allow me to enter his circle with the older man.

"Ty. This is that lawyer I was telling you about."

I could tell by the look the old man gave me that he didn't impress easily, and that he wasn't going to be swept up by anyone's hype, including Dan's. Shakespeare was right, the eyes are the windows to your soul, and the old man had a permanent "vacancy" sign flashing behind his peepers.

I reached out my hand and said, "Jimmy McCarthy. Nice to meet you, Mr. Valachi."

My hand hung there for an awkward moment before he loosely clasped it without really engaging in the effort.

"Dan speaks very highly of you, Jimmy," he said without conviction. I could sense the calculations he was making as he sized me up. "However, I like to do my own homework before I enter any relationship, business or personal. You understand, don't you, Jimmy?"

"Completely," I responded, hoping my face wasn't flushing. "I feel the same way."

"Good," the old man said, "next time we meet, if there is a next time, then maybe we'll talk further." He turned to Dan, who did his best to mask his helpless embarrassment at my dismissive treatment.

"Dan, have Vito take Jimmy wherever he needs to go," Valachi continued.

This time the old man reached out his hand to signal that our conversation was over. I grasped it with as much force as my once laborer hands could muster, short of attempting to inflict injury.

"Welcome home, Mr. Valachi," I said curtly as I shook off his grip. "I hope you enjoy the remainder of your party." I turned to Dan, "tell Vito I'll be out front." When I looked back at the old man, I could see his expression had morphed into one more inquisitive. I nodded respectfully and turned back towards the house.

Vito was equally loquacious during our return trip to the City. That was fine, as I spent the time trying to figure out what had happened back there while vowing never to speak with Dan Pearsall again. But as they say, *the best laid plans*.

Gina met me at the door of the apartment as I entered.

"Dan Pearsall, called. He wants you to call him as soon as possible. It's important," she said, handing me a slip of paper. "Here's his number."

"Fuck him," I grunted, crumpling the paper and tossing it across the room. "What a waste of my day."

"What happened?" Gina asked.

"Nothing," I replied, as I poured myself a scotch. "It was a total disaster. That old prick Valachi couldn't give a rat's ass if I was there or not. And don't get me started on that moron Pearsall. Uncle Ty, my ass."

As was her way, Gina reflexively went into support mode. "Don't worry about it. It's not like you wanted the job, anyway."

And then the phone rang.

"I'm not here!" I called as she went to answer it. As she picked up the receiver, I could hear her saying, "no, he's not here... All right, I'll give him the message... Goodbye."

She looked unhappy as she hung up the phone.

"That was Steve Hevlin from your office. Some emergency. They need you to come in this afternoon. They said to bring a change of clothes."

I polished off my drink. "Can this day get any fucking worse!"

Steve Hevlin was the biggest douchebag who ever made partner at the firm. He had the bitchiest clients with the shittiest problems. It was always an emergency, and every time you killed yourself to bail them out, Steve took all the credit and put his thumb on the billing scale to ensure a larger slice of the profits when the partners' pie was divvied up each year.

The phone rang again. This time I grabbed it, "look Steve, I just got in," I shouted into the receiver, "I'll be there as soon as I can."

"Jimmy, it's Dan, not Steve, and I'm really sorry about this morning," Dan Pearsall said.

"Not now Dan, I'm too busy for this bullshit. I gotta go," I said.

"Wait, wait, wait!" The awkwardness of his plea betrayed its novelty. "Listen, I'm not sure what happened today but after you left, Ty told me he wants to bring you on. Full retainer. Name your price."

"Bullshit," I responded.

"If you don't believe me, ask him yourself. Look out your window."

I covered the receiver with my hand. "Gina, look out the window and tell me what you see."

She walked over and took a quick half look and then leaned in completely with both hands on the glass. "Another Limo, Jimmy. Some old Italian guy is standing outside looking up at us. There's a big black guy with him," she said as she waved back to him.

I crossed to the window and spotted Valachi and Dan. Valachi spotted me, crooked his finger and motioned for me to come out.

"What are you going to do, Jimmy?" Gina asked.

"With any luck, I'll soon be telling Steve Hevlin to go fuck himself."

CHAPTER FIVE
A LAST BIT OF BACKGROUND

Valachi never fully explained what changed his mind that Saturday beyond his comment when I arrived downstairs at the Limo that first afternoon: "You crazy Irish prick, you almost broke my fucking hand back there." Which confirmed one of the many truisms my Dad used to tell us. "You can tell everything you need to know about a man by his handshake." I was never sure where that left my sister, who probably had the strongest handshake among his brood, but that's another story.

Dan later explained that Valachi had my background checked by some ex-Mossad types he keeps on retainer and I was given a clean bill of health. However, that call didn't come until after my dismissal. Surprisingly, it was Valachi's idea to make the trip down that day. He told Dan that he liked that I didn't blink when he crapped all over me at the party.

Dan had a stack of paperwork waiting in the Limo which included a retainer letter from a company named Sleeping Iguana Films, based in Grand Cayman Island, addressed to me individually at my home address that provided for a monthly retainer of U.S. $21,000.00. He also had a bank cashier's check drawn on the Cayman International Bank Ltd for U.S. $63,000.00 as a three month's advance on the retainer. I had to focus to keep my hand from shaking as I held the check because it was more than my annual salary at the time. Finally, Dan removed two large, heavy litigation bags from the trunk of the Limo and placed them on the sidewalk. I learned over time that those huge Caddy trunks didn't discriminate as to their contents.

"These are some film deals Uncle Ty wants you to review. Once you are up to speed on these, we'll talk further," Dan said. "He thinks he's been screwed by these companies while he's been away. Says their accountings are bullshit."

I popped the catch on the closest bag and started thumbing through its contents. I was wondering if I was biting off more than I could chew here. However, one thing I learned immersed in the firm's litigation mines; contracts may differ in complexity and subject matter, but a deal is a deal, and it all comes down to the language in the document.

Fuck it, I thought. Gina and I had not been blessed with kids, and she had a solid job as a nurse. We could fall back on her income if things went south, so if there was ever a time to roll the dice, this was it.

"So, Jimmy McCarthy, you ready to have our talk now?" Valachi asked.

"Sure," I said. "But first I need to call an asshole about a job I'm quitting."

Valachi smiled. "Just remember," he said shaking a gnarly finger at me, "once you cash that check, you don't get to tell this asshole you're quitting."

I laughed, and Dan joined in, although a little more nervously.

* * * * *

I used part of the advance as a down payment on a nice house in the Riverdale section of the Bronx and converted its separate basement apartment into a spacious home-office, with all the necessary upgraded phone and fax lines. In the beginning, I had access to the County Law Libraries in the Bronx and Manhattan and their copy machines. I had become used to doing my own typing at the firm because my handwriting was so atrocious that it took longer for a pool secretary to decipher it and make all of many the corrections than if I typed it from scratch myself. I became handy with a Dictaphone to get down my longer documents and sometimes Gina would pitch in to help transcribe in a pinch. My suits stayed in the closet unless I had to go to court or meet with opposing counsel or a witness. All my meetings with Dan or Valachi occurred at the estate in New City and for those, Vito remained my taciturn transport. By the end of the first month I had a smooth routine all locked down.

Valachi was right, he had been screwed while he was away, and I quickly focused my efforts on successfully recovering substantial amounts of royalties and other contractual bonus payments due his production companies. They mostly involved his investments as executive producer in several b-movies. The strange thing was that I rarely had to file an action against the potential defendant. I would go over each matter with Valachi and Dan up in New City and explain to them my findings from an analysis of the files and then send off a nasty letter laying out the potential claim and threatening swift legal action. In less than a week, I would get a call from Dan explaining that Valachi had recovered his funds in full and that the matter was resolved to his satisfaction. I knew I was good, but this was too easy.

After I had cleared up most of his old matters, Valachi and Dan began bringing me in to negotiate the new projects he was now investing his ever-increasing pool of funds. Those funds were always located in numerous offshore accounts and there were some larger transactions that involved money transfers from as many as ten different sources. And the funds never came from the same account twice. Once a payment came out of an account, anything left was transferred into a new account, usually in another offshore bank. When money from a deal came in, it was split among dozens of newly opened accounts, which then went to fund other deals. Dan Pearsall handled these financial transactions, but I knew where all the skeletons were buried.

I was making amazing money, and the work was interesting and not too challenging. Valachi brought me in to handle more of his 'legitimate' business deals, and I continued to protect his interests by running everything through cut-out corporations. When I was forced to go to court to litigate on his behalf, I either won outright or settled in a way where he wasn't really impacted. I always got something back out of the deal. However, most disputes got settled once the opposition learned that Valachi had a financial stake. As months turned into years, in addition to my annually increasing monthly retainer, Valachi started to pay me cash bonuses on some of his more lucrative deals. As a result, I started to open my own accounts in various Cayman Island banks under fictitious offshore corporations and amassing my own piece of the pie.

Just like with the homeless people and the summer associates, I didn't want to know the truth. The more successful I was in protecting Valachi's interests, the deeper he pulled me towards the core of his empire. Suddenly, there were new faces at my meetings with Valachi, and he became more open about the nature of his business dealings with them. But these guys weren't businessmen in the traditional sense. These guys were part of Valachi's crew, and they treated him like a king, including by delivering massive amounts of cash to Dan Pearsall when they arrived at whatever meeting place we would use that night.

Once I crossed the ethical Rubicon, I also began to get calls from Dan Pearsall asking me to appear at arraignments in state or federal court on behalf of one or more of Valachi's associates. I never had to take these cases to trial, as my primary function remained protecting Valachi's 'legitimate' business interests, so I was always able to hand them off to Valachi's regular criminal retainer, a flashy and ballsy lawyer named Robert Meloni. However, as my sphere of influence increased over Valachi's non-legitimate matters, and those other men got to know me, they started asking for me by name once they were arrested. Most of the time, I arranged their bail and sprung them after arraignment. If it was a more serious felony charge that resulted in remand, I got the details and relayed instructions from Valachi which always ended with "and keep your mouth shut."

By the end of the nineties, there was no more kidding myself. I was a mob lawyer who helped launder millions of dollars a week and I didn't care.

CHAPTER SIX
THE OTHER SHOE DROPS

I hate all prosecutors. There is something in their genetic makeup that makes them believe in the darkest reaches of their tiny hearts that they remain above all temptation and thus are qualified to punish the rest of humanity when they surrender to theirs. Truth is that most of them were the biggest pussies growing up who spent their free time extricating themselves from some variation of having their underwear pulled up over their head by the bullies of the world. Now that they have the unlimited power of the government behind them, they went out of their way to fuck with the rest of us.

I mentioned earlier that my family were all tradesmen. That is, except my sister, who also went to college, got her doctorate in Education, crossed the pond, and went on to run the most exclusive private school in London. She then came out of the closet, married the love of her life, and pretty much disappeared from her Irish-Catholic family's Bible. Rumor has it that during my mother's one visit to London she threw Holy water, procured from Lourdes, on my sister as she slept, but since no miraculous conversion occurred, that was the last time they ever spoke. I love that girl. She had the biggest balls in my family. Unfortunately for me, my sister's post-baptismal severance was universal and complete, and she shunned contact with everyone in our family from that point on.

You see, my sister was the lucky one and her hasty fade into Clan obscurity surely saved her life.

My three brothers all rose through their respective trades to own a successful contracting company. In New York, that can't happen without getting bloodied and dirty, and my brothers wore their hard-earned scars defiantly with pride. Over the years they, individually and collectively, fought off extortionist incursions, first from the Italians and later from the Russians. I once watched my older brother send an Italian local union emissary to the hospital for seventy-five stitches in his face for refusing to remove his foot from my brother's gang-box. No one touched my brother's equipment after that. On another occasion, my youngest brother 'accidently' removed the thumb from a gesturing Russian bricklayer who had the audacity to tell him to take a hike rather than return to work after an extended coffee break. The thumb was reattached at the hospital, but the job ran seamlessly from that point on. My middle brother, the soulless Ginger, was the hardest of the three. Rumor had it that the cement pylons in some buildings he raised in Manhattan, on time and under budget, have more bones than rebar supporting them.

My brothers were smart. They never looked for trouble and never flinched when trouble came knocking. The Italians and Russians ultimately learned that you can't win a fight with a crazy man and went after the lower hanging fruit among the New York based contractors. It didn't hurt that my brothers also paid off all the right people in government.

Despite several investigations, the New York feds couldn't figure out how my brothers managed to stay in business, given their respective aversion to playing ball with the more organized criminals. But then the same government douchebags thought they had broken the back of the felonious New York Irish when they sent Jimmy Coonan, the leader of the Westies, to jail. You see, the true Irish perfected the subtleties of terrorism generations before their diaspora set foot in this country. Those ruthless genes that ran through all our veins, though recessive, could be easily activated with the right provocation. Otherwise those genes lay hidden behind the blarney from our lips and the twinkle in our eyes. Moreover, while the Irish loved nothing more than to scrap with their own, they would readily kill the first non-Celt that tried to do so. My father used to have a funny cartoon taped to the bathroom mirror that showed a nervous roman centurion reporting to an angry superior during a stalled execution *ad bestias* in the Roman Colosseum. It bore the caption "Sorry Sir! The Irish are fighting amongst themselves and the Lions refuse to come out." Enough said.

My brothers were not happy when I decided to become a 'scumbag shyster,' even after they offered me a piece of the family business. To them I was 'soft', and they were right to a relative extent. My epiphany came when I was seventeen years old and laboring for a local Irish contractor who liked to hire non-union locals at a time before OSHA had really caught on in this country. I was working a new building, seven stories up with no safety equipment, and had to move a palette of tiles across an open 12-foot expanse along a narrow I-beam. I have always hated high open spaces and when exposed, suffer from a mild form of vertigo. But my hormone driven machismo and a desire to earn more money than the local grocery chain was paying stock boys, drove me onward.

During my first trip across the I-beam while precariously carrying a stack of tiles, I was half-way to the other side when a steelworker suddenly appeared and scampered towards me. Without missing a beat, he stepped off the beam, caught himself with one arm and waved me past him with the other. I almost shit myself as I stepped over him. On another trip across, to avoid slipping, I had to kick some burned welding rods off the beam in front of me, and as I watched them fall below, I was transported back to those Wily Coyote cartoons where you follow his fall from a great height until it ends badly with a puff of dust at the bottom. I knew in that moment that I couldn't walk steel the rest of my life. Hence law school. The hazards in this choice proved far more subtle, but equally deadly.

My brothers became remarkably successful, buying up an entire industrial block in the South Bronx where they maintained their offices and machinery. I became the pariah, and soon our social contacts were limited to the occasional birthday or Christmas card sent by one of their wives. But I was as stubborn as they were, so I didn't really give a shit until it was too late. And that's on me.

The feds came for me during the early morning hours of March 17, 2018, which I'm sure was no accident. I remember bolting up in bed at the sound of splintering wood and glass from somewhere in the front of the house. My mind raced to comprehend what had dragged me from the depths of a deep sleep while my panicked wife shook me into full consciousness. As I placed my foot on the floor, the bedroom door sprung open and heavily armed and armored figures flew into my room. Before I could do anything, I was face down on the floor with my hands behind me in flex-cuffs. I could see my wife being led out of the room as I was lifted into a sitting position on the end of the bed, thankful she was not in cuffs, which meant they were only there for me.

"Call Meloni," I yelled.

The first suit that appeared was solid blue and draped around a six-foot, stocky, Irish American who appeared in the bedroom doorway and introduced himself as Special Agent John Frawley. He looked to be in his early forties, but his Celtic genes had already converted his once black mane to salt-and-pepper, which he wore stylish but short. He held what I could see to be an arrest warrant in his left hand while flashing his F.B.I. credentials in his right.

"Sorry about your front door Jimmy, but the bosses insisted," Agent Frawley said almost authentically as he glanced around the room. "Nice place you got here."

I suppressed my knee-jerk desire to tell him to "fuck-off" and recalled the mantra I had repeated to hundreds of felonious clients over the years, "Say nothing."

They transported me to the Metropolitan Corrections Center in lower Manhattan for processing. Having only been on the witnessing end of this procedure before, I was blind-sided by overwhelming anxiety as I formally entered the system. It's one thing to visit a client behind bars, knowing that you were always able to walk out the door when the interview was over. I remembered the words of my law professor, a tough anti-establishment Israeli named Abe Abrams, who taught Criminal Procedure, "First they take your freedom, and then they take your soul."

They shuttled me to a separate cellblock in the basement and isolated me in a holding chamber.

After an hour, a federal corrections officer led me to an interview room on the same floor, where I was met by a worried looking Robert Meloni. As soon as the officer left the room, Robert pulled out a stack of papers from his briefcase and began speaking in almost a whisper.

"They've picked up Valachi, Pearsall, and most of the crew," Robert said, as he reviewed the indictment. "They've named everyone, including you, as actors in the R.I.C.O. enterprise." He slid the indictment across the table to me. "They are citing the murders of those two heroin dealers in Washington Heights as the primary predicate acts."

I scanned through the Indictment to the allegations relating to my involvement and was surprisingly relieved to see that it related to only general charges of money laundering. The allegations against Valachi were far more detailed and placed him as titular head of the enterprise who gave the orders through Pearsall to, among other things, carry out the 2013 executions of Joey and

Phil Santiago, whose bodies were found in a dumpster outside a restaurant in Fort Tryon Park. To me, the Santiago brothers were a couple of ruthless sociopaths and the world was a better place without them. I noted the signature of Peter Donoghue, the U.S. Attorney for the Southern District of New York, at the end of the Indictment.

"Who is lead counsel on this?" I asked.

"Some AUSA named Mark Lafayette," Robert answered, making some notes on the back of one of the documents. "He's with the Organized Crime Strike Force. I'm getting some background on him as we speak."

While the work that I performed for Valachi didn't involve me in those kinds of decisions, I was aware of them and arranged for their payments through a series of dummy corporations. I also knew that only a few people were present at the meeting where that order was given. I was one of them.

Robert must have read my mind.

"Valachi thinks there's a rat," he said, avoiding my eyes as he glanced towards the door of the interview room. "He says he's not going back inside, no matter what."

"Well, where does this leave me?" I asked.

"The feds seem to be keeping you safe and sound for now," he said, taking the indictment back from me and slipping it into his case. "Don't worry about it. Valachi said he's going to take care of everything."

Robert rose to leave. "The feds have frozen everyone's assets, so I'm working with some people to put up security for whatever bail the Judge orders at the arraignment tomorrow." He walked over to the door and knocked on the glass, "until then, sit tight and don't talk to anyone."

I knew that there was no way that the feds had found the millions sitting in my overseas accounts, but I also knew that I couldn't access them while they had their scope up my ass, and that Robert was feeding me bullshit because no judge in his right mind would be granting bail in a mafia R.I.C.O. case.

I also knew that I was a loose end that could connect the paper trail that would tie Valachi and Pearsall to the Washington Heights murders. The feds may be idiots, but I was sure that they had come to the same conclusion. I did the math and didn't like where this was going.

The correction officer arrived and opened the door. Robert went to step past the guard, hesitated and looked back at me over my shoulder. "Oh, and don't worry about Gina. We'll take good care of her."

That sealed the deal for me. As soon as I was sure that Robert had left the area, I shouted out to the correction officer, "I need to speak with Mark Lafayette. Right now."

Mark Lafayette arrived a short time later. He was young, tall and trim, with limp black hair and a thick black moustache that went out of style in the last century. While he didn't wear glasses, his rhythmic blinking led me to believe that he was breaking in contacts. He was the cat that had eaten the canary.

"What can I do for you Mr. McCarthy?" He said without sitting down.

"You can give me full immunity and put me in the witness protection program," I said.

"And why would I want to do that?" He said.

"You know what," I said impatiently, "fuck it. You're either an idiot or a douchebag. Either way, I'm not wasting any more time on you. I want to speak with Peter Donoghue directly."

Mark realized he had overplayed his hand and was in danger of losing the bragging rights on the biggest case in his career.

"May I sit down?" he asked. I gestured to the chair, and he tentatively took his place at the table.

"I speak for Peter on everything relating to this case," Mark said with a new tone of earnestness. "I can make the deal, assuming–"

"Let's cut to the chase," I said, leaning impatiently across the table, "I can give you the entire Valachi operation, including those two murders. But before I say another word, I need you to send your goon squad out to pick up my wife and stash her away somewhere safe and sound. Once that is confirmed, I'll give you what you need."

An hour later Mark returned looking like he was about to vomit. Fearing the worst, I shouted, "Did you find Gina?"

He nodded, and whispered, "She's okay. We have her."

"Then what's the fucking problem?"

"Your brothers are dead."

CHAPTER SEVEN
YOU CAN'T GO HOME AGAIN

I'm not sure what I expected, but by morning Gina and I were in the company of two beefy federal Marshals in a black and tinted SUV hurtling down I95 South towards Washington D.C. to our 'processing center.' The hardest part that morning was when they told me was that I couldn't attend my brothers' funerals, unless I wanted to end up next to them in Gate of Heaven cemetery before the funeral flowers on their graves have withered. To tell you the truth, I was so happy to have Gina safe beside me that at the time I really didn't process the extent of that loss. Months later, when the survivor's guilt fully registered, it was a motherfucker.

Once we were safely ensconced in the Washington safe house, the Marshals told me that to everyone's surprise, Valachi and Pearsall managed to post the ten million dollar bail the Judge had imposed that morning, although they had to surrender their passports and wear ankle bracelets as part of their release conditions. I guessed the Feds didn't find all their offshore accounts after all, and I wasn't about to help them on the chance that it would lead them to my own.

They also mentioned how upset Robert Meloni appeared when I wasn't produced at arraignment. If there was any question about my loyalty in their minds, it was resolved at that moment. Luckily, I had resolved all questions as to their loyalty to me the moment Robert walked out of the interview room.

It surprised me how much paperwork went into transitioning into the Witness Security Program, or WITSEC as the Feds like to call it. The lawyer in me was interested in the detail that went into preparing Gina and I for our new lives, which started by a comprehensive examination of our existing ones. Of course, being the Feds, they already had a substantial head start on our personal information, including all our reportable financial information, banking, academic, medical and dental records. They even knew all our hobbies. I wasn't thrilled when one of the Marshall's pulled me aside to show me my internet browsing history. So, the next time the neighborhood paranoid-survivalist tells you that Big Brother is watching, believe him, it's true. They presented all of this to us for vetting to make sure they hadn't missed anything. They almost hadn't. I wasn't about to mention those offshore accounts, so Gina and I signed off on what they presented and moved on to the next step.

When it comes to issuing new identities, WITSEC likes to follow the KISS (keep it simple scumbag) formula. They explained that experience had taught them that it was best that we stick with our first names and select new surnames that kept our existing initials. So, the McCarthys became the Morans, which is the name the Marshals addressed us with from that point on. We spent hours that first night repeatedly signing our new names until it became automatic.

Then we were given our new biographies. I was an independent Insurance broker from Warwick, in Orange County, New York, who had also done well as a Day Trader and decided it was time to make a move to a more tax friendly environment. Gina was a retired nurse, who was happy to trade in those twelve-hour shifts for a life of leisure. At least that last part was true, Gina had spent the last twenty-five years working as an RN on a telemetry unit at a major metropolitan hospital, and it would explain her detailed knowledge of the medical world should it come up in conversation. The town that was chosen was close enough to New York City to explain any inadvertent slips that would demonstrate our authentic knowledge of City life. We had to study the surrounding geographic locations, the schools, shops, hospitals, transportation routes and hubs, just in case someone asked. Gina, who had a unique ability at rote learning, took the lead on responding when we were quizzed by our handlers, and I was simply good enough, when pushed, to get by.

They promised us that our new passports, driver's licenses, social security cards and any other necessary legal documents would be delivered to us just before we disappeared for good, to protect against that information leaking out beforehand. They also assured us that all the necessary leases, utilities, bank accounts and credit cards would already be in place at our new location.

During this time, I was also fully debriefed by members of the FBI and assistant U.S. Attorneys from the Southern District of New York. I took Mark Lafayette and his team through every nook and cranny of the Valachi criminal enterprise and drew them the road map that tied Valachi and Pearsall to the Santiago murders. I submitted sworn affidavits which initially became part of the sealed trial record until defendants' batteries of trial counsel managed to force their disclosure through contentious and repeated motion practice. I had to sign my first affidavit a second time because I had signed it 'Jimmy Moran.'

When the time came for me to testify, I was spirited out of the safe house in the middle of the night by a team of heavily armed U.S. Marshals to Potomac Airfield and flown by private jet to Teterboro Airport in New Jersey. Another heavily armored SUV convoy transported me to Lower Manhattan and by the time the sun rose, before the Federal Courthouse at 500 Pearl Street had opened its doors to the public, I was sitting in a small room adjoining Judge Herman Bolger's Chambers, armed Marshall's in tow.

The prosecution had provided their opening statements the day before, which took most of that first day. In a surprise move, the defense reserved their right to make their opening statements until after the prosecution rested, immediately before they presented their defense. I was going to be the government's first witness that morning. I wasn't nervous about the idea of testifying. In fact, after what they did to my brothers, which I knew they would never be charged with, I was looking forward to putting the knife to all of them. And that's exactly what I did.

The prosecution had successfully moved to clear the courtroom of all spectators, including the press, during my testimony. My direct examination by Mark Lafayette was polished and devastating and over in two hours. It ended in a crescendo with my descriptions of transferring the final payment for the murder of the Santiago brothers from one of Valachi's offshore accounts to two of his co-defendants sitting at the defense table.

The cross-examination was expectedly aggressive and personal, but I was unwavering. It continued for six exhausting hours, with just a half hour break for lunch, which I ate with the Marshals in the same side room. I took all their best shots, and at the very end copped to the fact that I was the worst kind of rat. But I fired back that they turned me into a rat, and at least I wasn't a killer. I knew I shouldn't have done it but at the conclusion of my testimony, as I stepped out of the witness box, I couldn't help but add "If you bastards hadn't killed my brothers I might have kept my mouth shut."

The defense lawyers rose in unison, objecting all at once about my insertion of unproven facts into the record that tainted the jury and mandated a mistrial. Judge Bolger did his best to regain control of the courtroom while Lafayette argued over the defense counsels' chorus that their objections were meritless. In the end, Judge Bolger reserved decision on the defendants' mistrial motion and exited the bench in a huff. As I left the courtroom through the side door, Valachi and Pearsall, along with their other four co-defendants, never took their eyes off me. Neither did the jury.

While I waited for my Marshal escort to appear in the side room, Mark Lafayette entered shaking his head with a pained expression. I knew I had fucked up. "Sorry, man. I never should have lost my cool," I said. "But I just couldn't leave it unsaid."

Mark nodded understandingly. "Don't worry about it. You gave us everything you promised. Now get out of here." Surprisingly, he reached out and shook my hand. "Don't take this personally, but I hope I never see you again," he smiled and quickly exited the room. Maybe Lafayette was the exception to the 'all prosecutors are pricks' rule.

The Marshals took me through an internal hallway the Judges use to a private elevator which took us directly to the basement. We traveled back through the same labyrinth of tunnels we had come in through that morning to the garage three blocks away, where we had left the armada of SUVs and armed occupants.

By ten p.m., I had rejoined an extremely anxious-looking Gina in the D.C. safe-house. I could see that the place looked sanitized and that our personal items had been stowed away in a suitcase. One of the Marshals handed me an accordion file with some freshly minted legal documents. I rummaged through it and pulled out my new driver's license. It was the same ugly mug in the picture, but the license itself was much prettier than the New York style license I had been carrying for decades. But the information just didn't feel right.

Mr. James P. Moran

4714 Beverly Drive

Berthoud, Colorado 80513

Gina removed hers from the file and held it closer to the nearest lamp for inspection as she said to no one in particular, "Where the fuck is Berthoud, Colorado?"

CHAPTER EIGHT
WELCOME TO OZ

Whenever I have traveled outside of New York City, it has always been to other major cities like Chicago, Los Angeles, Miami, San Francisco and even overseas capitals like London, Berlin and Paris. While each of these places are uniquely beautiful, not one of them, in my humble opinion, provided the complete package presented by the Big Apple. What can I say, I've had a New York City bias since the cold night in 1956 when my mother's gynecologist slapped my ass in the delivery room of Women's Hospital, on 109th Street near Amsterdam Avenue. And like all real born-and-bred New Yorkers, you take your city for granted, until you can't.

That thought weighed heavily on my mind as the wheels of the small jet, ferrying us to our new life, contacted the asphalt tarmac at Northern Colorado Regional Airport. The sun was peeking over the eastern horizon as I exited the plane, trying to remember if I had ever disembarked onto an open tarmac before. One of the Marshals, a young man who introduced himself only as Brian, was doing his best to sell Gina on the wonders of life in Northern Colorado. Unfortunately, he did so with the passion of someone reading the ingredients off the back of a cereal box.

I couldn't tell if it was the stress of everything that had been happening over the past six months, but there was a tightness in my chest and a mild headache danced around the back of my skull. I was also parched.

"I'm fucking dying for some water," I whispered to Gina.

The Marshal closest to me must have noticed my discomfort, which wasn't surprising, given that they watched our every move like their life depended on it. Unfortunately for them, it did.

"It's the altitude," he said nonchalantly. It surprised me he had a voice, as this was the first words I had heard him utter the entire trip. "You'll get used to it." He did his best to smile, but it was forced and uncomfortable.

One of the other Marshals snatched the suitcases from my hands just as a black SUV appeared. Brian moved close beside me and, without taking his eyes off the approaching vehicle, said, "This will be your contact agent, Mark Lenahan."

As the SUV came to a stop in front of us, Brian circled to the driver's entrance and started speaking to its occupant, while handing a packet of documents through the window. I could not make out the driver through the deeply tinted glass. Another Marshal quickly stowed our bags in the rear of the SUV and opened the passenger rear door and motioned for us to enter. Brian, who had returned to where we were standing, extended his hand.

"Good luck, Mr. Moran," he said. I watched over his shoulder as the other Marshals scurried back onto the plane with the pace of an Indy 500 pit crew.

"Where the fuck are you going?" I asked, reaching for his hand, and suddenly feeling very vulnerable.

"Back to D.C.," he said as he turned and headed toward the jet stairs. He looked back over his shoulder and shouted, "Don't worry, Mr. Moran. Mark will take great care of you. He's a legend."

By this point Gina had entered the SUV and scooted across the seat to give me room.

As I moved to join her in the back seat, a deep baritone voice with an east coast accent commanded, "Up front with me, Jimmy. This isn't a fucking cab."

Six months in the company of the U.S. Marshal's service had taught me that their ranks were composed of mostly young, educated, fit and extremely polite men and woman. Even the upper echelon resembled extras from a G.Q. magazine shoot. Their hair was meticulously styled, their shoes shined, and their suits tailored and pressed. Not once during that time did one of them curse. Of course, that only made me want to curse even more, and I did, as often as I could.

I pulled open the passenger door and locked eyes with a grizzled-maned, Sam Elliott look-alike, right down to the blue jeans and burgundy gator Lucchese boots. He appeared to be in his early fifties, far older than any of the other field Marshals I had met, and while he was not in the same level of gym fitness of his younger

D.C. counterparts, he had a gnarly toughness about him. Definitely a horse of a different color.

"Welcome to the Garden Spot of Colorado," he said, as I lifted a manila file off the passenger seat and slid into its place. He reached over and grabbed the file from my hand and tossed it into the back seat right beside Gina.

"You're welcome to thumb through that file if you like sweetie," he said, making eye contact with Gina in the rear-view mirror, "it's the real estate paperwork for your new home."

He made a hard U-turn and headed back the way he had come. I watched as our jet started to taxi down the runway and lift off, taking my old life with it.

"It's an older house on a nice piece of property," Lenahan continued, glancing at Gina in the rear-view mirror. "One of my clients is a real sociopath," he paused a moment for dramatic effect, "he reinvented as a real estate agent named Randy T who finds me the right house for the job, each time, every time, as long as I don't ask any questions. The one he found you needs a bit of work, but you'll have plenty of time to get it in order."

He turned to me and flashed a smile. "You're not afraid of a little hard work, are ya Jimmy? You don't mind me calling you Jimmy, do ya? My friends call me Lenny."

"Nah, Jimmy is fine," I said, "and no, hard work doesn't bother me, Lenny."

"That's good," he said with a chuckle. "You know, I had to ask because rumor has it you were a lawyer in your past life."

Gina laughed from the back seat. She was going through the house file. "Despite having the hands of a prince," she said, "he still knows how to swing a hammer."

She tossed the file on the seat beside her, "and with all this new free time on my hands, I'll find plenty of things to keep him busy."

"Now that's what I'm talking about sweetie!" Lenahan shouted. "You guys are going to be fun."

We were racing south doing seventy-five on interstate I-25, while still being passed by several eighteen wheelers with such force that our large SUV rocked. I could see the foothills to the Rocky Mountains on my right, and in the distance much taller mountaintops. Given that we were well into June, it surprised me to see that they were still snow-capped. Lenahan followed my gaze.

"The snow disappears for a few weeks at the end of July," he said as he maneuvered the SUV onto the Loveland exit ramp.

"Loveland?" I noted. "Sounds like a fun place."

Gina smacked my shoulder. "Don't get your hopes up."

"Just passing through," Lenahan countered. "Too popular a town to hide you in."

Twenty minutes later, after lots of long and barren county roads that passed through open farmland with the occasional washed-out farmhouse visible in the distance, we finally pulled into Beverly Drive. The name 'Beverly' seemed out of place among the other signs like 'Goose Hollow,' 'Shepherd's Circle' or 'Windswept Lane.'

The first house on Beverly didn't appear until we navigated a couple of hilly turns and the next one appeared after a few more. The road then straightened a bit to reveal a stretch of distantly consecutive houses each on their own large parcels of property. They were nicely maintained and their vast front lawns freshly mowed, with clean, white, three-rail fences, set back about six feet from the road and running the entire front perimeter of each property. Gates blocked most of the driveways. They all maintained their own version of horse country chic, and for the first time I saw horses scattered among the properties. Each of the houses were of similar size and various shades of earth-tone colors. A couple of the properties had smaller buildings set off on their back acreage.

"This is an older estate, one of the first subdivisions of the farmland in this area. Each house is set on a minimum of four-acres of property," Lenahan said, pointing. "That's yours up there on the right."

The first thing I noticed was that the grass on my property was uniformly overgrown above the second rail of the weathered split-rail fence that bordered the front property line. As the wind kicked up, the only thing that kept the flexible hay from looking like a free-range prairie was the half dozen tall metal tubes topped with various wind-propelled, spinning sculptures. Each consisted of a combination of bicycle parts, license plates, and even elongated oil funnels. A twelve foot-long, four foot-high, mound was set about a dozen feet before, and parallel to, the front of the house. Peeking out from its apex were numerous cone-capped faces of various sized and colored garden gnomes.

We pulled down the large gravel driveway that ran along the right side of the property and ended at the two-car garage. Another split-rail fence with a long metal gate opened on the right onto a smaller enclosed paddock immediately followed by a large open property in the back. A smaller gate attached to the side of the garage opened onto a fenced path that wound down an incline and around behind the house into the back yard. High grass covered the entire property. There was a three-year-old Toyota Rav 4 parked at the end of the driveway.

"That's yours," Lenahan said, pointing at the Toyota. "Stay put for a second."

He reached into his center console and removed a large handgun which he stuffed in the back of his belt as he stepped out of the SUV, all the while glancing furtively around before closing the car door and heading towards and into the house. He returned a few moments later and opened the back door of the SUV for Gina.

"All clear," he said, "welcome home."

"What's with the gnomes?" Gina asked, pointing towards the mound as she exited the vehicle.

"Why, gnomes are the keepers of family secrets," Lenahan said with a wink. "What sort of Celt doesn't know that?"

"Well these guys better be good at their jobs," Gina said with a chuckle as she pulled her suitcase from the back of the car and headed towards the front door. "And for the record, I ain't Irish!"

"So then, what's with the spinning thingies, are they Irish too?" I asked. "Don't recall hearing anything about them from my grandparents."

"You mean the whirligigs?" Lenahan replied. "The last owners of this place were a couple of hippy artists who wanted to make their property interactive with the natural and constant wind that rushes down off the Foothills."

"I would have settled for a couple of wind chimes," I said.

"They got those too," Lenahan replied.

"They must have used their lawnmower as parts for their exhibits," I said looking back at the overgrown lawn as I followed Lenahan into the house.

The exterior of the house was in decent shape, but badly in need of a coat of paint.

A large Blue Spruce as tall as the house stood directly before the small front porch, shielding a view of the front door from the roadway. As I followed the pathway between the tree and porch, I was startled by a large and foreboding dark green face anchored on the wide tree trunk, which stared directly across the short expanse at the front door.

"That's Jack in the Green," Lenahan said, as he held the front door for me. "He keeps an eye on the place and makes sure only the invited cross your doorway."

"Well he must be slipping," I winked as I entered past him. "He let you in."

Gina had already gotten the coffeemaker brewing and was examining the contents of the fridge.

"Not too shabby, Lenny," she called over her shoulder.

I'm a bit of a food snob," Lenahan said. "Actually, a gourmand, and not a bad chef."

"Well then, Mrs. Lenahan is one lucky woman," Gina said.

"Sure is," Lenahan removed coffee cups from one of the cabinets, "She divorced my sorry ass when they shipped me out here ten years ago."

He placed the cups on the raised bar countertop and poured the coffee. Gina shot me an 'awkward' look from across the kitchen.

"Sorry I brought it up," she said.

"Best thing that ever happened to me," Lenahan replied as he grabbed the milk out of the fridge. "She said I was married to my job, and she only stayed as long as she did because she liked living in D.C." He poured some milk into one of the cups and took a long draw.

"She was one hell of a bitch," Lenahan said as he stopped to savor the aroma from his cup. "But she was right, I do love my job." He stared absently out the kitchen window that faced the front of the property just as a white F150 slowly drove past on the distant road.

"And on that note," he said, placing his coffee cup on the counter, "How about I give you the cook's tour of the place and then we can sit down and review the 'do's-and-don'ts' over a little pasta primavera I'm about to whip up as your first meal here. Then I'll leave you to settle in."

CHAPTER NINE
HAPPY IN YOUR NEW SELF

Over a wonderful dinner, Lenahan explained that he was attached to the U.S. Marshal's Office in Denver but that he lived in the city of Boulder about half an hour away from where we were in Berthoud. He said he oversaw WITSEC for all Northern Colorado. As far as I was concerned, he could have told us that he lived in Alpha Centauri, because I hadn't a clue as to the geography of Colorado, or my place in it. As a matter of fact, I was even terrified of the thought of trying to drive to the actual town of Berthoud, which he told me was only fifteen minutes away by car.

"Just use your GPS," Lenahan said.

"I've lived in New York all my life," I said incredulously, "by the time I could drive I had memorized every road my father had driven in the five boroughs. I've never had to use GPS."

"Come with me," he said, leading me out of the side door onto our wrap around deck that offered us a beautiful view of the foothills. He pointed due west.

"You see those three mountain peaks?" He said.

I followed his line of sight to three closely set, snow-capped mountain tops peeking over the horizon. They still reflected the evening sun that had already passed over the now shaded foothills.

"That tall one in the middle is Long's Peak. It's one of more than fifty Fourteeners in Colorado," he said admiringly.

"Fourteeners?" I asked.

"Mountains over fourteen-thousand feet," he answered.

"Fifty of 'em! Fuhgetaboutit!" Gina bellowed from inside the house in her best Bronx accent.

Lenahan ignored her. "I've heard some locals call the set the 'Three Sisters'. Others call them the 'Three Witches'. I call them the 'Three —.'"

"Bitches?" Gina interjected as she joined us on the deck, her second glass of Josh Cab Sav in her hand.

"–Ladies!" Lenahan completed his thought and then laughed. "But all you need to remember is, if you ever get lost, just find those three magnificent mountains on the horizon and head towards them. They'll get you close enough for you to locate enough local landmarks to find your way home."

"I miss the New York grid," I said wistfully. "Too far west and you're in the Hudson. Too far east, the East River. Everything in between, a short cab ride away."

"Speaking of home," Lenahan said, turning back towards the house. "I better head out."

I was overcome by a sudden rush of separation anxiety that I hadn't felt since my first day of Kindergarten. Being in protective custody for the past six months, I had developed a form of Stockholm syndrome with my vigilant caretakers. I could sleep soundly knowing they had to keep me alive. It didn't matter which Marshal it was as long as there was one of them present. That attachment had passed that morning from Brian to Lenahan as quickly as it took to pass them my luggage. I didn't feel ready to be suddenly left to my own devices, and I sure didn't feel like I could protect myself and Gina from the local wildlife, never-mind anyone looking to settle a score.

"You sure you don't want to stay for some coffee?" I asked, my voice cracking just a little.

"I really have to go, but I will be back bright and early to show you the lay of the land," he said.

I looked to Gina for some support, but she seemed perfectly comfortable as she poured herself another large glass of wine. Then again, she was always tougher than me. "Okay, Lenny," she said, "We'll see you then."

"Goodnight Gina. Walk me out to the car, Jimmy," Lenahan said as he headed towards the front door. I followed him out, half-hoping he would take me back to Boulder with him.

Dusk had set in, and the brighter stars appeared in the night sky. Lenahan motioned for me to wait on the porch as he continued towards the SUV, his feet crunching on gravel the only sound. His head rotated slowly as he carefully surveyed the surrounding area. Then he walked around to the back of the SUV, motioned to me to approach, and then popped the tailgate and reached under the back seat. As I arrived at the rear of the SUV, Lenahan removed a small locked metal case the size of a lunch box and half as thin. He retrieved a tiny key from his pocket, opened the box and withdrew a small handgun.

"Ever use one of these?" he asked.

I had seen a few handguns passed among my mafia colleagues over the past ten years, and before that, as evidence on some criminal matters I had worked on. Dan Pearsall had even shown me the basic functions on his favorite nine-millimeter. But I never fired one.

"Sure thing," I lied.

"Good," Lenahan said, returning the gun to the box and handing it and its key over to me. "Keep this with you tonight. Tomorrow we'll get you your own."

"Do you think I'm going to need this?" I asked nervously as I delicately accepted the box. He closed the tailgate and headed towards the driver's door.

"As I told you at dinner," he said without looking at me, "the Judge denied their motion for a mistrial. The Jury has spoken. They are going away for good." He turned one last time and patted me—double tap—on the shoulder before he slid onto the driver's seat.

"I heard about the 'dead brothers' speech. Ballsy move," he nodded towards the silver box in my hand, "that's only in case some Black bear decides it wants to raid your kitchen in the middle of the night. They can smell food for miles."

He winked, closed his door and a second later I was watching his taillights disappear at the end of the driveway. During the few moments that had passed, darkness had quickly descended upon us.

I walked back to the front door, making sure to say hello to Jack the Spruce as I passed. The entry door was oversized, heavy, and made of solid oak. There were no peepholes or glass, which made the interior entry foyer very dark. Lenahan explained during dinner that he installed that door for safety reasons. He added door armor by the locks and hinges to prevent anyone from kicking it down. He also installed a Ring security system around the exterior of the house, including an interactive, video-doorbell, which he had already synched with the new iPhones he provided us. He mentioned that he would also have access to our security camera stream.

Once back inside, I locked the heavy bolt behind me. I carried the small gun box extended before me as if it was a tray of shit, out onto the deck where Gina sat in a sun chair with her feet resting on the metal railings. She was sipping the last of the wine.

"What's in the box?" She asked.

"Bear repellent," I replied, placing it gently on the small deck table and taking my place in the chair beside her.

We sat in silence for a while. I strained my eyes against the darkening night trying to make out the terrain. The distant wire fencing I had noticed earlier that bordered the back of our property had now vanished with the sunset. The foothills had faded into a shrouded backdrop that established the entire western border of the subdivision. Faint lights peppered the distant properties and I could just make out an isolated silhouette of a house or barn. If I focused, I could hear a muffled horse whinny or dog barking carried on the ubiquitous breeze from the neighboring properties.

Then the coyotes started. At first it was a distant, lone wail, more crackling and higher pitched than the sonorous howl of the wolves I had heard on the Discovery Channel. Others joined in, but more like a free-for-all cacophony than a synchronous harmony. It reminded me of the horns of Manhattan cabbies fighting through midtown traffic on a busy weekday afternoon. The chorus ended as quickly as it began.

It was a new moon, so the stars had the night sky all to themselves. They didn't squander their opportunity. I had never seen these numbers or depths of stars in New York, even in the northern suburbs. It was like witnessing the light show in the New York Planetarium. Soon I was leaning back in my seat to get a better perspective to identify the primary constellations.

"You know those fucking Greeks must have been on crack," I whispered to Gina.

"How so," she replied softly.

"Because no matter how hard I try, I can't see the figures they saw in those constellations."

She leaned her head closer to mine and began to scan the sky with me.

"Look," I said pointing, assuming my most impressive courtroom voice. "That one there is called 'Lupus,' but if you can draw a wolf out of those eleven stars, I'll give you a million bucks."

She laughed. Gina got my sense of humor.

"And that one there," I said indicating another spot. "That's 'Ursa Minor,' the 'Little Bear.' But it will always and only be a 'little dipper' to me."

I turned and gazed directly at her. "And don't get me started on 'The Herdsman'."

"You really need to drink more," she said, pecking me on the cheek before standing up and stretching. "C'mon, let's call it a night. We're still on east coast time and I'm fucking exhausted."

I stood to join her. "Speaking of bears," she said, pointing to my box on the table, "don't forget the repellent."

Gina climbed the long front hallway stairs to what Lenahan had referred to as 'The Tower' but was actually a small second living room loft which opened onto a master bedroom suite on the one side and overlooked a large atrium living room below on the other. Well-placed high windows and skylights throughout the house allowed enough natural light, and tonight, even starlight, which reduced the need for interior lighting.

I went around the house double-checking all the locks on the windows and doors, including on the basement level, which was a separate living space accessible through an interior stairwell. It had a living room, kitchenette, office space and separate laundry room.

The basement opened out through sliding glass doors onto a backyard deck with a hot tub, and then through another gate onto our back property. Lenahan had shown me how to work the industrial security bar he had installed on the basement doors during the initial tour. I followed his instructions to the letter.

This house now seemed exceptionally large, empty, and eerily quiet as I made my way back through its bowels to the third-floor bedroom. I had to run back down the long stairway to retrieve my 'gun-in-a-box' from where I had left it on the kitchen counter. By the time I again reached the third-floor landing, I was experiencing the same oxygen deprivation I had at the airport and had to pause momentarily to catch my breath. I heard Gina snoring softly as I finally reached our king-sized bed. I placed the small box and key on the nightstand beside me then opened my iPhone and ran through each external camera on my Ring App. The night vision lenses made everything look unnatural, but secure. Jack the

Spruce looked particularly haunting as he stared at the front doorbell. As I lay there rehashing everything from my past that led to that moment, I don't remember making a conscious decision to go to sleep, but physical exhaustion ultimately won out.

I hadn't dreamed since the day I was arrested, but that night I dreamed of my brothers. We were kids again eating breakfast around the large oak dining room table in our family home. There was an empty chair where my sister usually sat. "Where is she?" I asked.

My brothers ignored my question and continued eating. I could hear running water and the banging of pots and pans in the adjoining kitchen. I left the table and followed the sounds, thinking I'd find my sister there. When I entered what was clearly my family's kitchen I saw Dan Pearsall standing at our old Westinghouse stove scraping some food from a pan into a garbage pail while Ty Valachi stood over at the sink washing dishes and carefully placing them to a wire rack directly beside him. I was Fellini-confused as I realized that I was now an adult.

Valachi looked over at me and said, "We're cleaning up. Go get your brothers' plates, they're done."

"But they are still eating," I said.

"No, they're not," Pearsall said with a smile, "they're done!"

At that moment, a loud explosion from behind me sent me hurtling forward as the kitchen was engulfed in flying debris and flames. The fear and pain that followed was overwhelming as I lay in the darkness screaming. Suddenly, two hands reached through the choking dust, gripping my shoulders, and lifting me to my feet. I expected to see Dan Pearsall but instead it was the little Junkie-Tinker from my childhood. He led me by the hand past the shattered bodies of Pearsall and Valachi and out through the rubble onto an isolated country road, where his clapboard wagon stood, bells and all, along with his trusty mule, who watched me carefully as we approached. Junkie lifted me onto the driver's bench and handed me the reins.

"Find your sister," he said in a voice I had never heard before.

"How?" I asked.

"The mule will show you," Junkie said, flashing me that gold tooth smile.

The wagon lurched forward, and the bells started to chime, then nothing.

CHAPTER TEN
LAY OF THE LAND

True to his word, Lenahan was back at the house at the crack of dawn. I know this because, being hard-wired from a lifetime of school and work based upon East coast time, I was awake for the day at four am here in Colorado. I was to learn that this wasn't a fluke. My circadian rhythm never made the transition. Gina, on the other hand, continued to sleep like a local.

Being almost mid-summer, the spectrum of the sky was already changing from pitch black to purple to blue. I spent that hour sucking down some desperately needed caffeine while I walked the house, taking my first undistracted inventory of my new surroundings. I hadn't realized that first day, just how much exposed wood there was. Huge oak support beams ran along every ceiling in every room and hallway. The floors were hickory and the entire open kitchen and dining room area and cabinetry was mahogany. The house was nicely maintained but dated looking. I couldn't help but miss the modern McMansion we left behind with all its polished stone, marble, and stainless-steel appliances.

"I bet you never saw yourself in a place like this," Lenahan said as he materialized in the front foyer.

"How the fuck—" I shouted, almost spilling my coffee.

"I have my own set of keys," he replied, waving them to make his point, "but you really need to be a bit more vigilant, Jimmy," he continued, as he circled the high kitchen counter, grabbed a cup from the cabinet and poured himself a large cup of coffee. This time, he drank it black.

For a large man he moved gracefully, but what was more striking was that he crossed the hard-wooden floor in his cowboy boots without making a sound. Whereas I sounded every creaking floorboard even walking in my bare feet.

"I usually keep a set of keys for the first six months, just in case of emergency," he said. "But if you are uncomfortable with that," he tossed me the key ring, "that's okay too."

I thought about last night's anxiety and tossed him back the keys. "No, you hang onto them."

He peered out the large dining-room window toward the overgrown front of the property, and his eyes seemed to fix for a moment on Gnome Island. He took a long draw from the coffee cup.

"I picked this place for you because—given how modern and beautiful your last home was—no one would believe you'd live here."

"You saw my old house?" I asked, surprised.

"Everything about your past life is in your file," he said. "And don't worry, Uncle Sam is keeping the deal you cut."

He poured a second cup of coffee and took a seat in the barstool beside me at the kitchen counter.

"As far as the rest of the world is concerned," Lenahan continued, "we've seized the house and everything else you own under the forfeiture provisions of the RICO statute. I've been told that when it's all said and done, they hope it will clear two million, net, on a quick sale."

He studied me for a moment. "I heard you were a good lawyer, but you must be the fucking King of Bullshit," he said, almost appreciatively.

"Normally, the government takes the lot and gives guys like you a modest stipend to help you get set up in your new life."

He withdrew a large envelope from his jacket pocket and slid it over to me.

"But in your case, they had me drop a half a million on this house, which you and Gina now own outright, and then spread the remaining one and a half million in about fifty different accounts in your name, including a couple of forex accounts."

I opened the envelope and rifled through the financial information reflected there. Lenahan was right, I made the deal of the century with the feds, but I gave them the Mafia's Moby Dick on a platter. In exchange I got to keep the sale price for the real estate while letting them keep the two million I had been maintaining in my domestic bank accounts.

My plan was to work with the money in these new accounts until the feds got bored watching me and then slowly open some new ones and use them to launder in some serious money I still had hidden in my overseas accounts, especially through foreign currency trading. I had to admit that I learned a lot over the years watching Dan Pearsall move Valachi's money around. He was like those Manhattan curb side, three-card-monte hustlers fleecing the tourists. Once his hands were moving, you could never spot the red queen. I knew that as long as James Moran paid Uncle Sam a nice chunk of taxes every year, I'd be okay going forward. Everyone likes a winner.

Lost in thought, I didn't quite register the first sound in the distance. As it repeated, it seemed to draw closer and louder. It made me think of the advancing sound of the Imams' call to prayer I once heard when I was meeting a friend in Astoria, Queens.

"Go wake your wife and get dressed," Lenahan said suddenly. "Hear those roosters? This is the country, brother. Once the sun rises, we got to make some moves!"

Gina wasn't having my Green Acres, get up at dawn, welcome to the country bullshit, and told me in not so many words that she needed her sleep and that I should fuck off with Lenahan.

By the time I had returned to the kitchen, Lenahan appeared at the front door with an enormous, white, American Staffordshire, with a large, studded, pink collar on a thick leather leash. Think of a pit-bull on steroids. I almost shit myself as he dropped the leash and the dog lumbered towards me and knocked me backwards against the countertop. The beast forced a couple of drool-laden licks of my face with her sandpaper tongue before Lenahan interceded.

"Maeve, down," he said softly. She obeyed mid-lick and dropped to the floor in a crouched position. "She must like you," Lenahan continued and pointed towards the stairway. "Gina didn't sound too enthusiastic, so I'm just going to leave Maeve here with her while we do the grand tour."

"Where'd she come from?" I asked, going to the sink to wash the dog spit off my face.

"Most days she rides with me," he said, rubbing her head tenderly "I rescued her three years ago from a kill shelter in Mesa County. We've been inseparable ever since."

"She's not going to eat Gina?" I asked, only half kidding.

"Nah," he said, chuckling. "She'll sit right by this door until I come back. But if anyone but me comes through this door without saying the code word 'banana,' it will be a shit storm for them."

"Banana?" I heard Gina's voice from the top of the stair. "You're fucking kidding me, right?"

She slowly made her way down the stairs rubbing her eyes while clinching her bathrobe closed in front of her. Maeve looked up at her and her tail wagged heavily, making a loud thumping sound on the wooden floor.

"You guys gotta get yourselves a dog!" Lenahan said enthusiastically. "You are natural pet parents."

Once Gina and I came to terms with not having children, we didn't want to become one of those couples who substituted animals in their place. At least that's what I thought. I was about to say something to that effect, when, to my surprise, Gina squatted down next to Maeve and began to pet her head gently. Maeve rolled on her back and Gina obliged by rubbing her belly more vigorously.

"That sounds like a great idea," Gina said, as she punctuated her rubbing with cutesy, baby words for Maeve. "You guys can take off; Maeve and I will be just fine. As long as you left me some coffee."

I looked over at the empty coffee pot and gestured to the door. "Let's get out of here, or 'banana' is not going to save us."

Despite the remnants of early morning chill in the air, the rising sun instantly warmed my exposed skin as I made my way from the house to the SUV.

Lenahan drove, humming what sounded like a country tune. I scanned the horizons, not really paying attention to the route we were traveling. I had gotten used to the government babysitters moving me around like baggage, so I learned to sit back and enjoy the ride.

The morning sky had emerged a uniform light blue punctuated with small iridescent white clouds. To my left I saw open land with smatterings of farm equipment and as the car proceeded along there were herds of horses, cows, sheep and goats gathering on the different properties. To my right, I could see the green foothills and white dusted mountaintops in the distance, so I knew we were heading south. The Rockies had become my Hudson River.

"So, what's first on the agenda?" I asked.

"A hardy breakfast," he answered.

"Where?"

"Hygiene."

"Get outta here!"

"Now don't go making fun of our small-town monikers," he said. "Hygiene is named after a local Sanatorium where they used to treat patients with Tuberculosis."

"You missed your calling," I said. "You would have done well leading one of our Big Apple Bus Tours.

"I do have an eye for details," he said, playing along.

"TB, eh! Sounds like just the place I want to have breakfast. I hope they wash their hands around here."

He smiled and continued humming his country song.

"My first day of law school, I was standing at the urinal next to this preppy looking kid," I said. "The kid finished up, walked over to the sink and began to lather up like a surgeon before a heart transplant. After a demonstrative final shake, I strolled past the sink area, gave myself a glance in the mirror, patted my hair, and headed towards the door. Before I reached for the handle, the prepster said in a perfect Brahmin accent, 'Where I come from, they taught us to wash our hands after urinating.' To which I replied, 'No kidding? Where I come from, they taught us not to piss on our hands!'"

Lenahan guffawed.

"You are a wise ass!" he said.

"Better than a dumb ass," I quipped.

Having established my personality marker with my new babysitter, I resumed sightseeing. The next herd of cattle were jet black with a wide white band around their middle. The white band was uniformly painted on each cow, making them resemble Oreos, the double stuffed kind.

After a few minutes, I spotted an immense bull guarding a smaller herd of brown cows on the next property. I wouldn't have noticed him among the others grazing in the tall grass if he hadn't raised his head and taken a long gaze at his perimeter while he finished chewing a mouthful of hay.

"Look at those fucking horns," I muttered as I jabbed my index finger across Lenahan's line of sight. I must have sounded like I was six.

Lenahan glanced over at the bull. "Oh, that's 'Methuselah' the Watusi,'" he said, returning his eyes to the road. That bull is as old as his name and mean as cat shit! A bit of a celebrity among the locals. And the heifers."

"I pity the asshole—man or beast—who tries to screw with his cows," I said, continuing with my sightseeing. I thought of the stories about hayseeds that had lost their virginity to local livestock and shuddered. No one would be tipping these cows.

The county road finally reached a major crossing called 'Route 66', and I wondered if it was part of that famous stretch on which they based the 60s television show. The cars passing along it were the first I had seen since I left the house.

While we waited for the light to change, I spotted a couple of very animated twenty-something's hurrying from a nondescript brick building on the corner to their car. It was the first non-farm I had seen along the route and looked a bit like a restaurant. Each of the young men carried a small paper bag. One kept looking in his bag and commenting excitedly to the other. The sign on the building read "Dispensary".

"Not sure what the doctors are handing out in that dispensary, but the locals look pretty happy," I said.

Lenahan looked over and smiled. "Happy is what happy does," he said. "That's one of Colorado's ubiquitous pot shops."

I thought of all the clients' kids I had appeared for over the years in New York courtrooms, just for buying a small quantity of herb. Then there was that one lead singer from the 80s I got off with only an adjournment in contemplation of dismissal in exchange for some autographs and photos with the court personnel. I guess Colorado had figured out a better way of getting its piece of the pie through taxes on a popular product rather than legal fines. Good for them. Prohibition had taught our country nothing.

After another couple of miles of more farms and their animals, a small sign on the road announced that we had arrived at a town named 'Hygiene.' It was a bucolic little number that was almost New England quaint and literally had one stop light in the middle of its four-block radius. A sign prominently advertised a local Feed Store and another the 'Colorado Horse Rescue.' A little art studio sat kitty-corner from a gas station at the intersection. Embedded train tracks ran through the town just on the south-side of the stoplight.

Lenahan seemed unimpressed by the charm as he made a left at the light onto another county road heading due east. After less than a New York City block he made another sharp left into a small gravel parking lot, at the end of which sat a large white wooden country farmhouse with a 180-degree wrap-around porch. There were more vehicles parked there than I had seen on my trip that morning. Shit, more than I had seen since arriving in Colorado. They were all pickup trucks, each American made. I double checked to see what brand of SUV Lenahan was driving. Luckily, it was a Ford Explorer.

I looked up at the wooden sign over the entrance to the porch— 'Oracle of Pythia'. I definitely wasn't in Kansas anymore.

CHAPTER ELEVEN
SIRENUM SCOPULI

Lenahan slid into the first open spot in the parking lot and threw open his door.

"C'mon," he barked as he slammed the door and headed towards the front porch, taking the stairs two at a time.

As Lenahan reached the front door, two enormous men exited in tandem and held it open for him. He passed through with a wave, never breaking stride.

The men, twenty-something twins, were both wearing faded green, Carhartt overalls, raggedly sheared with what must have been a box cutter into knee-length shorts. Their matching grey, short-sleeve shirts barely stretched over their tattooed biceps, and the exposed body art continued down to their wrists on all four of their arms as intricate and multicolored sleeves. The images were a smorgasbord of nature and religious motifs.

The twins' matching ensemble was completed by pairs of huge, black 'Doc Martin' boots, open at the top, from which leapt matching coy fish tattoos. Each man sported a coarse bushy beard that extended to the top of their respective bibs. I could see the stairs flex as they slowly descended together in lockstep towards the parking lot. The food inside must have been amazing because they shared a look bordering on orgasmic.

Suddenly realizing that I was sitting alone in public for the first time in six months, I sprung from the car and bee-lined along Lenahan's path up the stairs and through the large wooden double doors, arriving at a long center hall that divided the interior of the house. Immediately to my left, a large living room had been converted into a country-style dining room with about a dozen, four-seater, wooden tables, each one covered by a red-and-white, checkerboard, linen tablecloth. The room was filled with the sounds of clanking cutlery on plates and the buzz of friendly conversation. There wasn't an empty seat in the house. As I scanned the crowd for Lenahan, I realized that the patrons were all men. While I tried to get my head around this, I dodged a hustling, beautiful young waitress carrying a loaded tray. Her gentle "excuse me, sir" as she passed was hypnotically melodic.

I couldn't take my eyes off her. She looked to be in her early twenties. She stood about five foot nine and I'm guessing about one hundred and twenty pounds. This was all attractively packaged in a clean, crisp, tailor-made white shirt and comfortably fitted black slacks. Her fair skin glowed with an essence of fitness that doesn't come from a gym, but from a life of being outdoors in fresh country air. Her light brown hair was tied in a loose ponytail that hung to the middle of her shoulder blades and swung like an inverted metronome that kept time with her confident strides and matched the alternating creases in her pants line that winked just below her ass at the top of her pants legs.

As she approached the center of the room, I could see that the eyes of every man in the place lucky enough to be facing her direction had locked on her, without notably shifting their faces. Every unfortunate soul whose back was to her studied the expressions of their tablemates in vicarious appreciation. As she circled around the outside perimeter of the fortunate table whose food she carried, all faces at the table lit up and their bodies shifted like sunflowers in unison as they each gave her their full attention. Her name tag said it all: Calliope.

It was at that moment that she glanced up across the room to where I was standing, and I was instantly entranced by her generous smile and amber eyes. I watched her full, rose-colored lips move in engaging conversation with the men at her table and strained just to hear the sound of her voice again.

I was jarred from my revels by a firm grip on my shoulder.

"Jimmy, Jimmy, Jimmy... now what would Gina think if she could see the look on your face?" Lenahan said with a chuckle. He glanced appreciatively, yet resolutely, at Calliope as I turned to him and fought to control the flush ascending from my neck to my face. "I see I got here just in time to save you from the rocks. Let's go, breakfast is waiting. This way!"

He placed his hand on the center of my back for good measure and guided me reluctantly towards the arching entrance to the room across the hallway. As we marched those six feet, my eyes caught sight of another equally beautiful young Latina carrying another full tray though the swinging wooden doors at the far end of the hallway. Lenahan noticed the slight hitch in my stride as I tried to get a better look and almost shoved me forward through the awaiting entranceway.

This dining room was only half the size of the other, but its décor was less country and more formal. The seven circular tables of various sizes were covered with white linen clothes. Red taper candles anchored the floral centerpieces on each. It was darker, given, I imagined, that the morning sun had not yet crossed the top of the house. The tables were all empty except one, a small disk in the furthest corner of the room from its entranceway.

A tall, young, African American waitress, dressed as the other two, stood in profile speaking with two figures at the table. They all turned to watch us approach, and the person sitting closest to the waitress leaned towards her and said something amusing *sotto voce*. The responding sound of the waitress' laughter in response was enchanting and exposed a perfect ivory smile framed by stiletto cheekbones which defined her flawless, ebony skin. But it was her unexpectedly indigo eyes that really stole the show. Her name tag said Mel.

"Jimmy, these are my dear friends, Helen and Bobbi," Lenahan said from somewhere beyond my peripheral vision. A moment later, I heard another husky voice. "Nice to meet you, Jimmy."

The flush again rose above my collar and I forced myself to turn away from the waitress, who stared awkwardly at the tray she was holding.

The person whose outstretched hand was now reaching for my own was dressed similarly to the waitresses but was uniquely androgynous in her physical characteristics. She was also tall and fit, but there was no softness about her form. It radiated strength of body and will. Her golden hair was worn in a short, tousled pixie cut and was belied by thick dark eyebrows which sat above hazel colored eyes. She wore only a tasteful hint of green mascara that made her eyes pop, and her full lips sat unadorned on a strong jawline that was smooth and sharp. She wore perfect, one-carat diamond studs in each ear and expensive gold rings on both hands. Her nails were trimmed and nicely manicured with clear polish.

Her tailored shirt was open to her solar plexus and I could see the faded words 'I AM' tattooed in large Arial font across the exposed olive skin of her chest. Her shirt sleeves were rolled to the elbow, displaying the words 'Blessed' and 'Grateful' separately running along the exterior of each forearm. The strength of her handshake only added to my confusion, but luckily snapped me out of the fog I was in.

"Helen LaLousis." she said, before gesturing to the woman standing next to her. "And this is my partner, Bobbi Angelini."

"Nice to meet you, Helen, and you too Bobbi", I said—politely extending my slightly throbbing hand towards the other woman without really looking at her.

"And of course, you've met Mel," Helen said, turning back to the waitress with a showman's smile. "She'll be managing our breakfast. Lenny has already given Mel your order."

"Belgian waffles with homemade, vanilla ice cream," Lenahan said, as he slid into one of the empty chairs. "Can't find them anywhere else in this state as good as here."

Before I could turn back to look at Mel, she had scooted past me and out of the room.

I realized then that Bobbi was now holding my hand in both of hers. She had a peculiar look on her face. "What did you say your name was?" Her voice was soprano, to Helen's contralto.

I turned to study the woman who had captured my hand but didn't try to free it. Her touch was soft and comforting, as were her eyes. Her one-piece, floor-length dress was jet black, like her hair, and covered a full but attractively curvaceous body. The top sat just off her shoulders, exposing indulgent, porcelain skin. Her lips were full, pouty and burgundy and her green eyes encased in a rich brown eyeshadow. Her only jewelry was a Draconic pendent on a simple silver chain. It was an understated, inviting, Goth look.

"Jimmy, Jimmy Moran," I said, gently withdrawing my hand from her grasp and sitting in the chair beside Lenahan.

"Well," she said softly as she returned to her seat. "That's almost true."

"Now Bobbi," Lenahan cautioned, "What did I tell you about doing that?"

"Sorry, Lenny," Bobbi said wickedly. "Couldn't help myself." She looked over at Helen and gave her a sly wink and Helen shook her head with an exasperated smile.

I was the only singer in the chorus who didn't know the song. Helen threw me a lifeline.

"Bobbi is a very powerful psychic-medium," Helen said with just a hint of pride. "She is the 'Oracle' in my 'House of Pythia."

"She's a goddam witch, is what she is!" Lenahan countered, but this time with a broad smile that belied the tone of his voice. "And she's no Glinda."

I rubbed the fingers and thumb of my right hand pensively out of sight beneath the table. "Don't worry, Jimmy. Your secret is safe with me." Bobbi said playfully.

Luckily, Mel chose that moment to reappear carrying a full tray of breakfast delights and coffee. I reached to assist, but Helen beat me to it and was now artfully distributing the plates around the table like a Vegas blackjack dealer. Sadly, no sooner had the tray been emptied than Mel left the room. I decided to distract myself with the 3-stack of honey colored Belgian waffles with melting white ice cream filling each depression.

"What did I tell you? Fucking delicious!" Lenahan stuffed a forkful of waffle into his mouth, then closed his eyes in a connoisseur's appreciation as he slowly chewed.

He was right, it was the best waffle I had ever tasted, and the home-made ice cream sealed the deal. Sorry Canada, but fuck maple syrup. All I could manage was a hybrid hum-moan in response. The ladies laughed.

I glanced over and was amazed that Lenahan had already cleared his plate. He reached over and grabbed the pot of coffee and topped off everyone's cup before refilling his own. Then he pushed his chair back and crossed his long lanky legs, gave his mouth a good wipe with his napkin, and addressed the table.

"Jimmy," he began. "I brought you here today for two reasons."

Bobbi continued eating her eggs benedict and held up three fingers. Lenahan shot her a confused expression but continued.

"The first, was to introduce you to this magnificent Belgian waffle!" he said, before taking a long pull from his coffee cup for dramatic effect. He then extended his open palm towards Helen, who was finishing her glass of iced tea.

"And the second was to introduce you to Helen, who you will come to appreciate is the person who knows everyone in Northern Colorado, and can hook you up with whoever you need to get whatever you need done."

Helen nodded in agreement. "It's true," she said, "I gotta a guy for everything."

"Well not quite everything," Bobbi countered with a wink. Helen blushed.

"Now-now, you two," Lenahan said paternally, "let's not embarrass our guest."

Bobbi giggled and squeezed Helen's hand. She then leaned into the table and assumed a more serious look.

"But third and most important," she began, "was to introduce you to me."

Helen and Lenahan both nodded in agreement.

"And why is that?" I asked, after washing down the last of the Belgian waffle with some coffee.

"Because, not only can I keep your secret safe," Bobbi answered, "but I can keep you safe from your secret."

CHAPTER TWELVE
GHOSTS & FAIRIES

No matter how far removed from the 'Old Sod,' or how many layers of applied formal education are donned, you don't have to dig very deep to find the strong vein of superstition that permeates the soul of any Celt. My maternal grandmother, Bridie Burke, who was the super of the apartment building we shared in the Highbridge section of the Bronx during my avian years, used to regale her grandchildren with stories of the "fey wee folk" who inhabited her home, outbuildings, farmland and woods, back in Tuam, Ireland.

'Nana Burke' was the Seanchai, the custodian of my mother's Clan's oral history, and on those nights we were lucky enough to have her as our babysitter, she would sit there with her Felix The Cat sized eyes—thanks to the coke-bottle glasses she wore—and tell us stories about how, as a child, during the twilight hour on warm summer nights, she used to sneak out into the woods and spy on the Daoine Sidhe, the last of the Tuatha De Danann, and watch as they danced and sang around their fairy mounds. She would describe each different type, look, and fairy personality in vivid detail. We gobbled it up.

Those fairies, we learned, were not to be fucked with, and to make her point, Nana once told us how one of her family's neighbors made the mistake of intentionally disturbing a fairy fort with a tractor on one of his back fields and ended up losing an arm in the thresher the very next day. I had no idea what a thresher was, but I wasn't about to lose an arm for any reason.

According to Nana, she knew more ghosts than people growing up, for she had 'an bronntanas,' what we 'narrowbacks' call 'the gift,' so the ghosts were always anxious for her to pass on a message or two to one of their loved ones in the neighboring farms or town. But her most frightening stories involved the banshees, and how their 'caoine' or cry inevitably foretold the death of a family member. She'd always let out a howl in her attempts to mimic the sound, and as frightening as it was, she swore it didn't do it justice. Nana would end each of her story nights with the line "So never forget, there is magic in this world, if you just know where to look for it."

I hadn't seen a lot of magic in the world since then, and I never had Nana's gift, so I couldn't help feeling uncomfortable that morning in Hygiene knowing that the stranger sitting across from me might have a free pass into my past, present or future. I had no problem with people like my Nana carrying secrets from the grave, but I didn't like the fatalistic concept that someone could peer into my future and tell me 'that's just how it's going to be.' I had too big an ego to believe that anyone but me could dictate the story of my life.

"And yet, here you are," Bobbi interrupted. "By the way, your Nana rocks."

I reflexively put on my best lawyer mask to cover my surprise, but if I had some tin foil on me, I would have quickly fashioned it into a hat.

Helen suddenly stood and said, "Lenny, why don't you follow me into the Kitchen. Eddie's been working on a new recipe I want to try out on you."

"Don't have to ask me twice," Lenahan said as he sprang up from his chair. "Go easy on him," he said to Bobbi. "He's obviously a virgin."

Helen found that particularly funny, and I could hear her still laughing after they exited the room.

Bobbi came around the table and took Lenahan's seat next to me.

"Who is Eddie?" I asked.

"My brother," Bobbi replied. "First, let me tell you how this works for me," she continued, "the women in my family have had these gifts going back generations. Some stronger than others, and me, stronger than most."

Over the years, I had learned to read the body language of my adversaries and witnesses, and right now Bobbi was oozing confidence.

"Simply put, I'm a medium and a psychic, so I can talk to the dead and sometimes see into the future."

"And just how does that work?" I asked, intrigued.

"I've found that the easiest analogy would be that our brains are like short-wave radios that can pick up different frequencies, depending on the location of the dial and the size of the antenna."

I wondered just how many people Bobbi's age knew what a short-wave radio was.

"I have a really big antenna, my hand firmly on the dial, and I know what channel handles what traffic," she continued. "I can do it all remotely, but it's always easier if I'm in your presence, and even better if I can touch you."

"But when you see something in the future, does that mean it is what it is, and I'm stuck with it?" I asked.

"No, what I'm seeing during any given reading is what will happen if you don't intentionally change your course," she said. "So, if I tell you I see you in a plane crashing in the ocean, I recommend boycotting all international flights. Ask any quantum physicist—the future is malleable, forewarned is forearmed."

I was surprised and impressed by her nod to science, and her answer gave my ego some comfort, but I fell back into lawyer mode and the questions kept coming.

"Can you read minds?" I asked, thinking back to my tinfoil hat.

"Not in the way you might think," she answered.

"Then how did you—"

"Well, it's not really reading—not word for word—it's my interpretation of a shorthand of words, images, colors, that I've refined over the years. I get the gist of it."

"Do you actually speak with the dead?" I asked.

"I can often see and hear them speak with me, but sometimes it's communication through my shorthand," she replied. "And on that note, I've got some male figures doing their best to get my attention," she laughed.

"Okay, there's three here," she continued. "They are lateral to you, meaning they are not above you, like a parent or grandparent."

She closed her eyes and focused. "And boy are they pissed," she said, "especially the Redhead... Not at you... They're telling me they're your brothers." She opened her eyes and stared past me. "They are standing right behind you."

The hair on my body suddenly galvanized and goose bumps formed on my legs and arms.

"No, I'm not going to tell him that," she said, shaking her head. "Wait, okay, the Redhead is telling me that they paid your debt."

I was suddenly overcome with the emotion I had been suppressing for the last six months. I hadn't cried publicly since I was late for my first day of kindergarten and was locked out my classroom. But it was like riding a bike, and I found myself sobbing out loud, tears flowing freely down my cheeks. Bobbi anxiously handed me one of the napkins from the table. I buried my face in it and just surrendered to the emotion—releasing the cry of the Banshee.

"Hey now, they're not blaming you," she said, gently rubbing my back. There was that warm comfort again. "They're just pissed that they let their guard down.... They just didn't see it coming that night."

"Tell them..." I sobbed, "Tell them I'm sorry." I fought to regain my composure. "I should have warned them."

"Red says, 'shit happens,'" Bobbi said. Then she stared at the ether behind me and started to laugh. "But he says that the good news is that he has a soul...and it's beautiful.... So, fuck you!"

The surprising laugh caught in my throat and was barely audible past my still trembling lips.

"Wait, the biggest one is saying that it's not over, and that you should watch your ass," she said, looking concerned. She held up her hand as if to stop someone else from talking, "now the youngest one is saying that they need you to get a message to their families to let them know they are all right."

I didn't know how I was going to pull that off, and automatically began to rack my brain for an answer, almost forgetting the surreal moment I was sharing.

"Red says, 'You'll figure it out. That's what you do,'" Bobbi said. "Now the oldest one is tapping his watch and they are all leaving. Wait, the younger one is coming back. He's telling me 'And find our sister.' Okay," Bobbi continued, then slumped back in her chair and took a deep breath. "They are gone now."

I needed a stiff drink but settled for the remaining coffee from the carafe on the table. The milk took the last of the warmth out of it, but I drank it anyway.

"About that warning," Bobbi said, "I'm not getting anything specific, but you can't drop your guard." She took out a small pad and purse and began scribbling. "Whatever it is, it hasn't happened yet," she continued to scribble. "I just can't get a fix on it."

Frustrated, Bobbi tossed the pen and pad onto the table.

"I'll pick it up again later," she said, "after I recharge my batteries."

At that moment Lenahan appeared through the doorway.

"Helen said she needs you in the kitchen, Bobbi. Your brother Eddie is giving her a hard time about that change you wanted in the weekend menu."

Bobbi looked apologetic, leaned in and whispered, "Eddie has PTSD and doesn't handle sudden change very well."

She patted my hand one more time before standing. "We'll talk again soon." She stopped to give Lenahan a quick hug and then headed out of the room. I wiped the last of my tears off my face and took a couple of deep breaths to regain my composure.

Lenahan politely ignored how I must have appeared and tossed forty dollars on the table. "C'mon, Jimmy, let's blow this joint. We need to go see a man about a gun."

CHAPTER THIRTEEN
IT'S NOT THE SIZE OF THE GUN

My emotional fog lifted about ten minutes after we left the restaurant. By then we were heading southwest on a two-way highway through the rolling foothills. Traffic in either direction was sparse, and the scenery was beautiful.

"Where are we going?" I asked, trying to distract myself from processing what had just happened at the restaurant.

"A piece of land I have stashed away in the mountains," Lenahan responded.

He suddenly reached into his center console and removed his handgun. Then, using just his right hand, he did something that made a metal piece drop from the bottom of the handle and back into the console. I could see that the falling metal contained a stack of brass colored bullets. He brought the gun over to his other hand, and while still holding onto the steering wheel, he rapidly rifled the top of the gun forward and back a few times. I saw a single bullet eject, bounce off the windshield and land down the center-side of his car seat. He then casually tossed the gun into my lap, never once taking his eyes off the road. I almost snapped the seatbelt jumping up. The gun bounced off my lap and landed in the front well.

"What the fuck!" I shouted.

"Easy big fella," Lenahan said with a laugh, "pick that up." He pointed to the gun.

I didn't move.

"C'mon now, pick it up. It ain't even loaded," he cajoled me. I still didn't move.

"I thought you knew how to handle a gun?" he asked.

"I lied."

"No shit," he said sarcastically. "Well, pick it up now and we'll change all that. I'm not going to be your babysitter forever you know."

His last line struck a nerve. I carefully lifted the gun from the well, keeping its business end pointed towards the floor.

"It's not a piece of dog shit!" Lenahan said, glancing over at me. "Hold it like your dick when you're about to jerk off, firmly but don't try to choke it," he laughed. "And keep your finger off the goddam trigger!"

Embarrassed on so many levels, I grabbed the handle firmly in my right hand and began to study the gun. It was colder and heavier than I expected. The Glock logo was imprinted on its dark grey, rectangular barrel just before the number 22 and the word Austria. There were seven uniform, straight ridges on either side of the rear part of the barrel, a triangular sight on the front and a notched sight on the rear end of the top of the barrel.

Lenahan glanced over at the gun in my hand.

"Just what I thought," he said. "That's too much fucking gun for your dainty little hand." He laughed as the insult registered on my face.

A muted "Fuck you" was all I could muster.

Like a magician, he then reached under his shirt and removed a smaller handgun from the right front inside of his belt and repeated the one-handed process of emptying it before flipping it, grabbing its barrel and offering it to me, handle first. The move took him all of ten seconds. Priding myself on my powers of observation, it shocked me I had never noticed the hidden weapon. I gently returned the first gun to its spot in the console before accepting its replacement.

"Now that's much better," Lenahan said, glancing over at the new gun in my hand.

I felt like a kid trying on his first Easter suit for his parents.

He was right, this gun was much more comfortable and lighter in my hand. The logo on the front left side of its barrel said, 'MP 9 Shield,' and on the opposite side 'Smith & Wesson, Springfield MA. USA.' The rectangular top of the barrel section was almost black, and its rear ridge work was wavy. The sights on this gun were much cooler looking than on the Glock, with bright iridescent green tubes that formed three bright dots when you looked down the top of the barrel. The bottom half of the gun was army green, hard polymer, and was much warmer to the touch than the barrel section. The handle had an inscribed pattern that made it more secure in my grip. The trigger was the same black polymer, and there were three black metal latches along the bottom of the left side of the barrel section, with a small black button where the trigger guard met the handle. It resembled the toy guns I used to play with as a kid.

"Now using your left hand," Lenahan said, "put the heel of your palm along those wavy ridges on the slide—the left rear of the gun—and curl your four fingers over the top and firmly grip the other wavy ridges on the opposite side."

I followed his instructions, my fear giving way to curiosity.

"Now using that left hand, slowly slide the top of the gun back towards your chest for about an inch or so," he continued.

This wasn't as easy as it sounded. The resistance was strong and the grip awkward, so it took a few tries before I could get it right.

"Now you see where that slot opens up on the top?" he asked.

I could see through the top of the opening down to the open end of the handle. I told him so.

"Good, now you're going to do that motion at least two times whenever you first pick up any handgun because that will ensure there are no rounds in the chamber," Lenahan continued. "And remember, your finger never goes near the trigger until you are aiming at something you want to destroy and are absolutely ready to fire the gun."

I wondered for a moment if I would ever be ready to "destroy" anything.

Lenahan now reached into the console and withdrew the metal piece he had just ejected, and using the nail of his thumb, proceeded to flip the bullets out of the magazine and into the console, like he was working a Pez dispenser. Once emptied, he offered it to me, all the while keeping his eyes on the road before him. I suddenly realized that we were driving on a steeper incline that wound deeper into the larger foothills. I experienced a touch of vertigo when I glanced beyond the low, roadside barriers, so I was happily distracted with the task in hand. I took the metal piece and double checked to make sure there were no bullets left in it.

"Make sure you have that magazine facing the right way," he said, pointing to the metal piece and continuing his traveling tutorial. "Then jam it in firmly until you feel it catch and lock. "

Again, this turned out to be harder than it appeared, but on my third attempt I nailed it. I held it out for his inspection. He glanced at it quickly, smiled and continued driving.

" Okay, now see that little button by the trigger guard?"

I pointed to it and he nodded. "Press it."

I did as instructed and watched as the magazine dropped to the floor of the passenger well. Finally, something easy.

I performed the task a few more times, finally catching the magazine mid-flight.

On the third catch, he said, "Okay, now give me the magazine." He reached into the console and fished out a single bullet. I handed it to him and watched as he now loaded the one bullet back into the magazine without looking, while still using just his one hand. He handed it back to me.

"Now load the magazine like you did before, but keep your finger off the trigger," his voice sounding more noticeably stern towards the end of that sentence.

I did, and luckily it caught on the first try.

"Now what did I tell you to do whenever you pick up a handgun?"

I thought for a second and then palmed the ridges at the back of the gun, pulled them back quickly two times and, viola, the shell ejected out of its top and struck me in the right eye.

"You've just learned why we wear safety glasses whenever we are handling guns," he said. "If that had been a freshly fired casing, you'd be a pirate tomorrow."

He continued to drive while I rubbed my eye.

"Now remember to do that a couple of more times anytime you eject a shell, to make sure there are no more in there."

I again did as instructed and luckily there were no more surprises.

Without warning, Lenahan made a sharp left turn into an unmarked road. It was unpaved, with two old ruts in the hardened muddy earth that seem to guide the car along like a drive-thru car wash. Ten yards in he stopped and got out to remove a thick, rusty chain connected to round wooden posts on either side of the road. He hopped back in and we continued for what seemed like a quarter mile where we reached a clearing in the woods.

At the far end of the clearing I could see a man-made grotto that included a makeshift wall of layers of plywood stretched across three tall, thick wooden posts. Behind the plywood rose a larger mound of stone and sand that extended a few yards on either side and peaked out from above the 8-foot wall. The mound extended solidly about six feet behind the plywood, followed immediately by some large, old fir trees. Hanging on the front of the plywood wall were several old frying pans, plastic jugs, and a few animal shaped metallic targets. They all showed their scars like a bad case of acne.

Lenahan grabbed his Glock from the console and slid it into his belt at the small of his back and then removed a couple of boxes of bullets from his glove compartment.

"Follow me, and bring the other handgun," he said.

He opened the tailgate and removed a box of equipment and walked to a point about thirty yards away from the grotto. I did as ordered.

He then handed me an old Broncos hat from the box, some large plastic ear coverings and finally a pair of clear protective glasses. He donned his own, nicer set of the same. His hat was black with a large silver circle enclosing a star, with "United States Marshal" lettering the circumference. His ear guards resembled wireless earphones you'd wear at the gym and his safety glasses were a pair of Givenchy aviators. He reminded me of a character from the movie Top Gun.

"Here put these on and give me that gun."

I handed him my weapon and watched as he quickly reloaded the magazine and reinserted it in the base of the gun handle. As he handed it back, I made a mental note that while he offered the handle to me, he made sure its barrel was always facing the ground.

"Keep that finger off the trigger," he kept repeating. I had to strain to hear him through the ear protection, which resembled giant yellow earmuffs from the 1950s.

Lenahan then moved forward so that he was standing about twenty-five yards away from the grotto, and in a direct line before the targets. He set his feet about shoulder length apart, bent his knees slightly, took a deep breath, and then in one smooth and continuous motion, reached behind him, drew his Glock and began to fire in rapid succession at the targets. The sound of the gun was much louder than expected, even with the ear covering, and I could feel the percussion. My body recoiled at each report and I prayed it wasn't noticeable. I watched as the various targets jumped when struck. He didn't miss. At last, the top of his gun slid back and froze, exposing the internal round barrel at the front of the gun that tilted upwards about ten-degrees, as the last trail of smoke slipped out. He ejected the magazine by the time he had returned to me and began to refill it from the boxes he had brought with him.

"Your turn," he said. "Line your sights up with the target then look to the target alone and let the sights become fuzzy. Don't touch the trigger until you are ready to fire. Take a deep breath, release it slowly and then gently squeeze the trigger in one slow and continuous movement."

I walked over to where he had stood, making sure to keep the barrel pointing towards the ground and my finger off the trigger. I tried to hide my anxiety and prayed that my hand wouldn't shake. I mimicked his stance and slowly brought the weapon up to my line of sight using both hands as he did. I cupped the bottom of the handle and trigger-guard with my left hand. Being right-handed, I tried to line up the three green dots on target with my right eye, but it wasn't working. So, I switched to my left eye, and then everything lined up perfectly. I focused on the twelve-inch frying pan in the middle of the grotto.

I took a deep breath and slowly released it. As the last of it passed my lips, I found and gently squeezed the trigger. Boom!

In that one moment I had an epiphany. I understood the irretrievable destruction I unleashed with the pull of the trigger. There were no mulligans, no do-overs, just one final decision made at the sound of the report. I was Zeus unleashing his thunderbolt, and God help anyone that got in its way.

I was astonished at how loud my small gun sounded, even with the ear protectors. The recoil seemed to pull the barrel down and to my left, and not kick back up in the air as I expected. The shell casing popped out of the gun and, in what seemed like slow motion, flew up in the air and landed on the top of my Broncos cap. I could feel its heat through the material.

Lenahan's hand firmly gripped my right shoulder, as he reached around and slowly lowered my gun towards the ground.

He lifted one side of my ear guards and whispered, "Take a second to savor this moment."

He walked around from behind me towards the targets and gestured for me to follow. When we reached the grotto, he took my hand and placed the tip of my index finger into the hole in the plywood just to the lower left of my target. I noticed for the first time that it was the only hole in the plywood. It was smooth and still warm to the touch.

"It's like the first time you have sex. Never pretty, explosive, and over in a moment," he said pensively. "But just like sex, you'll find your mark and get better with practice."

We returned to our firing spot. After Lenahan made a few minor adjustments in my stance and showed me how to compensate for the pull of the gun, I was pinging the pan consistently. It was an adrenaline rush, and I was disappointed when he finally tapped his watch and made a circle with his finger.

"Time to go," he said.

I popped the magazine out, rifled the barrel as instructed and recovered the ejected bullet from the ground, feeling like a kid who just rode his bike for the first time without his training wheels.

I offered Lenahan his gun, handle first, barrel pointing towards the ground. He held his hand up.

"You keep that one," he said, smiling. "She's yours now." He pulled a small leather holster from inside his belt and handed it to me. "But you better always treat her right because she's unforgiving if you don't."

We drove back to the house in silence and he dropped me off in the driveway. At the sound of his horn Maeve came barreling out of the front door and down the driveway. She replaced me at shotgun in the seat beside him.

"I've got some other matters to deal with coming up, so I won't be around for a few days," he said through the car window. "Remember everything I taught you today. And don't shoot your dick off trying any bullshit quick-draw moves with that holster."

I could have sworn Maeve laughed as Lenahan reversed the SUV and backed out of the driveway.

The strangest thing was that, for the first time since my arrest, I felt horny.

Gina met me at the door but before she could say anything, I kissed her hard and passionately, and she returned it in kind. When we broke, she stared deeply into my eyes, then grabbed my hand and led me up the stairs.

CHAPTER FOURTEEN
COSMIC NEIGHBORS

Pleasantly spent after christening the master bedroom and the hot tub, I intended to take a mental health day to sit back and contemplate my new life on Mars. But reality is reality, and Gina might have changed her last name, but not her personality.

"That front grass isn't going to cut itself," she said as she laced up her running shoes and headed out for a jog. The fact that she still looked great in Spandex running shorts didn't lessen the sting of her command or the inevitability of my compliance.

Gina had always been incredibly athletic, having completed four New York City Marathons before the turn of the century and having otherwise maintained an active lifestyle throughout our marriage. Her career as an RN for over twenty-five years required that she log many miles of hospital corridors in addition to her dedicated roadwork. She was built to last.

I had been far more inconsistent in this matter. I hated gyms and the people who inhabited them and always believed that my grandfather's farmer genes alone would carry me into blissful longevity without having really to work at it. For the longest time, that seemed to be the case, and despite having put on an extra twenty pounds over my fighting weight, I had avoided every malady that daytime television commercials regularly confirmed had consumed my entire generation. The fact that I never smoked, took drugs, and drank only in moderation, probably gave me some additional wiggle room.

Even after I started working for Valachi, I still performed any repairs or maintenance around my home, as the last vestiges of my blue-collar roots. I was hard-wired with the belief that you don't pay someone else to do what you can do for free, or at least for the cost of materials. Gina was right, I could still swing a hammer.

But as time went on and Valachi's money continued to roll in—in geometric progression—increasing the size of our home, property and bank accounts, I started to rationalize that the common good demanded that I redistribute some of my increasing wealth by delegating any and all manual labor, home improvements and upgrades to the hardworking tradesmen and women in my local community. The fact that I remained on call 24/7/365, to be ready to put out any 'family' brush fires, meant that any decent blocks of discretionary time I did manage to cobble together, was readily subjugated to the direction of my wife. Happy wife, busy life.

I stared out at the front property and saw just the summits of the various colored gnome hats peeking out of the undulating grass of my own private Serengeti. The overhead whirligigs were all slowly spinning in confirmation of the slight breeze blowing from the east. I could see Gina in the distance disappearing at a healthy pace around the next bend of the road, heading west towards the interior of our estate. I couldn't help but feel anxious about her going out on her own, but she wasn't one to be coddled, and this was the first real freedom she had tasted in quite a while. Anyway, as Lenahan said, the bad guys were going away for a long time on a planet far, far away. Just for good measure, I watched the road for another few minutes and took solace in the fact that no cars went past in either direction.

I knew I had better be at my chores before Gina returned from her run, so I found my oldest pair of shorts, T-shirt and my sneakers and got dressed. I had kept the old Broncos hat Lenahan had given me, to complete my Green Acres ensemble, and headed out to see just where the prior owners kept their outdoor equipment.

I hadn't had a chance to walk the back property, only observing it from my back deck during the twilight hours, so I had no real feel for what I would find. There was a decent-sized outbuilding to the far left of what, in the Bronx, we would have called the furthest corner of our 'back yard,' adjacent to the bordering fence separating us from the next property to the west on our street. There was another smaller shed-like structure a few yards from that. To the far right of our property, carved out from the remainder by a long, five-foot high, three-tier wooden post fence, lay a structure that resembled a miniature old barn with double Dutch doors half open on its southern facing front. In modern urban parlance, its color would have been described as 'distressed' natural wood.

Another three-tier wooden fence ran the entire distance between the western and eastern boundaries of my property, severing all three of these structures from the largest back section. In strategic points along each of the fences were wide corrugated-metal farm gates that allowed for passage between the contiguous divisions.

At the farthest and lowest point in the western corner of my back property lay a tiny pond. Lenahan had explained that it recently appeared from the spontaneous eruption of a freshwater spring due to the shifting water tables caused by the creation of a new reservoir in the local foothills. Local avian wildlife had quickly made their home there, including a massive colony of red-wing blackbirds in the surrounding high grass and a pair of Red Headed Pochards as the pond's anchor tenants. There was one final white structure, the size of a small cottage, situated in the far eastern corner of the back property. Lenahan had explained that it was an artist's studio. Directly beside its western facing door, was a tall whirligig with circulating industrial-sized metal funnels on four equidistant spokes.

Any one of these structures would have been right at home in an Andrew Wyatt painting.

Between these distant geographic markers and my house, lay a large open field, which could have easily entertained a Division I college soccer match, with fans. In the middle of this field I could see what appeared to be a burial mound, from which rose a tall wooden post approximately fifteen feet high. At its tip rested a large square black wooden structure. The entire field, and indeed, all other areas, were overgrown with the same waist-high grass that had commandeered the front property. It would have been a perfect place for an elaborate crop circle.

As a lawyer, I always found it easiest to begin daunting projects by starting small and then building up momentum to push forward to the larger, more complicated, or onerous issues. So, I opted today to proceed in size order, investigating the smallest structure—the shed—first, with hopes that I could quickly locate the tools that I needed and temporarily forego searching the larger structures. It turned out to be a mixed blessing.

The shed was a ten-foot square, white metal structure, with a slightly peaked roof and sliding pocket doors in the front. However, rust and time had frozen those doors and I could only manage to force them open about two inches. It was just wide enough to insert my arm and iPhone flashlight, which exposed some shovels, a pitchfork, scythe, a couple of five-gallon gas cans, and the largest hand-propelled, gas mower I had ever seen. Its four wheels had to be eighteen inches in diameter. It resembled the Mars Rover, down to a thick coating of reddish dust.

Like the wolf in The Three Little Pigs, I moved onto the next structure with the hope I could find something with which to pry open the doors of the shed. My luck appeared to be holding, as this larger structure, twice the size of the shed, was filled with all kinds of DeWalt hand and power tools, some scrap pieces of wood and MacGyver's best friend, a large can of 10W-40. Maybe life in the sticks won't be too bad.

I grabbed the oil spray and a three-foot scrap of two-by-four, and headed back to the shed, trying, for no real reason, to stay within the path I had already formed through the high grass. It took a few minutes for old reliable to loosen the doors, but with a little leverage from the wood, I opened it wide enough to shoulder it open the rest of the way, so I could step into the shed and remove the lawn mower.

In the sunlight I could see that this was a machine that had paid its dues, from the sun-bleached paint, rust spots and dents on its blade and canopy, to the jerry-rigged starter rope with a wooden handle that had replaced the original flexible metal cable. I checked its gas tank, which was dry, but its dipstick confirmed that it had oil. I retrieved one of the gas cans from the shed and was thrilled to see that there were a few gallons left, which I carefully poured into the gas tank, mourning the loss of every drop I spilled in the process.

I flipped the switch to choke and pulled hard on the starting cable. It smoked and sputtered, but never crossed the finish line. I repeated the process, but it still wouldn't turn over. On the third try it didn't even cough. In my youth, I could demo a room down to its studs, do the wiring, drywall, tape, sand, and paint, and hang the nicest fixtures you ever saw. But I didn't know shit about engines, and I wasn't about to learn now, especially when this was a machine that could remove body parts if I wasn't careful.

I returned to the shed and retrieved the scythe I saw lying in the corner. I checked its blade, which was sharp enough, and took a few practice swings at the grass in the yard. It seemed to do the trick.

I accompanied the scythe out to the front property, waded out to the front fence and, starting at my property line, went to work, old-school style. I began shearing a four-foot wide strip along the fence line and was finding a rhythm, for about ten yards, when I was forced to take a break. My shoulders were sore, and my body was overheating. The early sun was already searing in an otherwise cloudless, blue sky. The weird thing was that there was extraordinarily little sweat. The air was so arid that the perspiration never made it to your clothing. And I was parched. I went back inside to grab a bottle of water.

When I came back out, Gina was standing roadside at the fence looking at the relatively modest area I had cleared. I could tell she wasn't impressed.

She pointed at the scythe. "Lenahan told me there was a lawnmower," she said.

"There's a paper weight that looks like a lawn mower," I responded, with just a hint of testiness.

She surveyed the remaining front property and stared again at the small clearing, which seemed to be shrinking before my eyes.

"Well, I thought you'd be pretty much done by now, and was going to suggest a road trip to explore the local area," she said, "but I'd hate to interfere with you finishing up your chores."

I watched as she jogged over to our gate, down the driveway and into the house.

My resentment and injured pride fueled a second run at the lawn, which moved the markers another ten yards down-field. This time my lungs had joined the failing body chorus and were heaving to compensate for the diminished, mile-high, oxygen content. I leaned heavily on the front fence and cursed the lawnmower and its creator.

At that moment, a white Chevy Equinox with dark tinted windows slowed to a stop on the road in front of me. It must have come in from the main road. The passenger window gently lowered, and for a split second, I almost panicked. Pure exhaustion kept me from running back towards the house. I pulled my Broncos hat down low over my eyes, looked away from the car, and reached for the scythe.

"About time someone cut that lawn," said a man's voice.

"We thought it was one of those protected wild spaces," a woman's voice followed, with a slight giggle for emphasis.

Both voices sounded unusually chipper and friendly, which is a red flag for any New Yorker. I looked over at the car window and could see two smiling faces—a man wearing an off-white cowboy hat in the driver's seat and a woman wearing oversized sunglasses closer to me in the passenger window. She had thick blondish-grey hair tied up loosely by a yellow ribbon on top of her head, errant strands dancing as she talked. The effect was completed by two bright yellow earrings in the shape of stars dangling from her ears.

My face surely registered my confusion.

"I'm Michelle and this is my husband, Everett," the woman said, pointing for emphasis. "We live in the next house down, on the opposite side of the road. We heard someone bought this place, but this is the first time we saw you, so we figured we'd be neighborly and stop and say hello. Welcome to Berthoud!"

"Thanks," I responded more curtly than intended. I didn't want to get caught up in any long conversation. "Listen," I said, gesturing with scythe at the property, "I'd better get back to this."

"Don't you have a lawnmower?" the man said.

"I thought I did," I responded, "but it's on the fritz."

"Well let me take a look at it," the man said, throwing his car into park and hopping onto the roadway. "I'm really handy with machinery."

Before I could stop him, he had come around the car and had slid through the fence rails with the dexterity of a tag-team wrestler. He turned back to his wife.

"Honey, why don't you take the car home? I'll be over in a moment."

"Okay babe," she said with a smile. "Nice meeting you!" she called with a farewell wave as she slid over to the driver's seat. A moment later, the car pulled away.

"What did you say your name was?" Everett was now standing right beside me with his hand extended.

"Jimmy. Jimmy Moran," I said, shaking his hand. It was unusually cold and soft, but I attributed it to excellent air-conditioning in his vehicle. He was also shorter than I expected, no more than five foot six, and slightly built. I couldn't tell his age, his cowboy hat covered his hair, but his moustache had some grey in it. He didn't have the look of a man who was handy with machines.

"Well, Jimmy, let's go take a look at that lawn mower," he said, gesturing towards my house.

I led him back along the path through the high grass.

"You know, it's good you are taking this down," he said, studying the grass as he followed. "We've been known to have a rattlesnake or two around here, and they love the high grass."

I notably picked up my pace. As I reached the driveway, I saw Gina pulling out onto the road.

"Your wife?" Everett asked, as I gazed after her.

"Yeah, Gina," I said, "I'll have to introduce you next time." I turned and led him around the side of the house and down to the shed in the back yard.

Everett surveyed the lawn mower with unexpected interest.

"Oh, that's a beauty - a real classic," he said softly.

I reached down and pulled the starting cable, but it remained unresponsive. "It's got gas and oil, but it just won't kick over," I said, releasing the cord a bit too dramatically.

Everett squatted down next to the machine and looked up at me.

"Do you have an adjustable crescent wrench?" he asked, "and a Philips head screwdriver?"

I tried to remember the various tools I saw scattered around the tool shed.

"I think so, just give me a minute," I headed off towards the other building. When I reached its doorway, I took a quick glance back and was surprised to see Everett staring after me. I gave him an awkward wave and entered.

No sooner was I inside when I heard the lawnmower turn over, its engine purring solidly and smoothly. I found the closest window and saw Everett standing beside the machine, quickly slipping something silver, the size of butane lighter, into his pocket. I grabbed the wrench and screwdriver, exited the building, and raced back over to him.

"What the fu... the hell...," I stammered, as I watched him deftly maneuver the humming machine. For a little man, he seemed extraordinarily strong. Leveraging its handle, he raised the lawnmower on its back wheels and then lowered it onto the tall grass before him, taking it down to a more manageable height before finishing it off with another quick pass, repeating the process with a constant progression. I followed him around the side of the house as he skillfully carved a clean path to the side gate. He turned it off when we reached the driveway.

"There you go," he said, offering me the handle. "That shouldn't give you any more trouble."

"But how did you do that?" I asked, looking down at the pocket with the silver lighter.

"I just gave it a good shake," he said evasively. "It was probably just a stone jammed in the blade mechanism. I must have knocked it loose."

"Well, whatever you did, thanks," I said, studying the lawn mower.

"Okay, well I better head out," he said, starting down my driveway. "We'll have to have you and Gina over one of these nights for a welcome dinner," he called back over his shoulder.

The miracle mower started up on the first pull, and three hours later the front of my property was as nicely manicured as the other homes on the street. However, the gnomes suddenly looked very vulnerable standing exposed on their mound. There had to be a dozen of them, of all sizes and colors. I made a mental note to give them each a formal name.

At that moment, Gina pulled into the driveway.

She hopped out of the Toyota, carrying a pizza and a six pack.

"You finished! My hero!" she called. "Who fixed the mower?"

"Long story," I replied. "Tell you while we eat."

CHAPTER FIFTEEN
BACK IN THE SADDLE

Up again at four a.m., I left Gina snoring softly in our bed and made my way down to the kitchen where I surrendered to the coming day with a strong cup of coffee. Caffeine in hand, I sat in the dark on a barstool with my back to the kitchen bar counter, and rested my bare feet on a large windowsill. I proudly gazed out at the freshly mowed front property and wondered if my recurring back spasms and leg cramps were worth it. As with everything in my life once I passed fifty, my physical performance yesterday remained governed by the motto "I may not be as good as I once was, but I'm as good once as I ever was!" I made a mental note to speak to Helen about getting me a guy to handle the mowing in the future.

As my eyes adjusted to the ambient starlight transitioning to twilight, I noticed tiny creatures scurrying erratically across the open areas. Their rapid movements made me recall what one of Valachi's capos once told me: "Remember, if you are ever being shot at, run away in a zig-zag pattern, it makes you a harder target." Given that the purveyor of this survival advice was five-foot-five, about three hundred pounds, and a chain smoker, I was confident that his pearl of wisdom was gleaned from being a frustrated assailant, rather than a successful survivor.

Two of the smaller lawn creatures performed their version of a Jackie Chan kumite, with one leaping over its advancing opponent, when I heard a series of alternating, low-octave hoots. The louder set was coming from somewhere in the top of Jack, my guardian Spruce, and the other softer response echoed from one of the trees in the distance. They came in patterns of two quick hoots and then a short pause, followed by a slower, extended, exclamatory hoot.

The hooting sounds sent the creatures, which I could now see were actually rabbits of various sizes, into a frenzy, as they all darted at once for the vestiges of high grass I had left around the bases of the whirligigs and occasional tree that dotted my property. I could feel their collective, heightened anxiety, and found myself yearning for their safety. Suddenly, a large rabbit sprung from the high grass around Jack's base and raced across the now cleared property towards the remaining pastoral oasis along my front fence line. My eyes were focused on the rabbit, and the beauty of its powerful, elongated strides, and I rooted for its success as it reached the three-quarter's mark on its road to freedom. I didn't notice the large silent shape descend until it caught the rabbit in mid-stride and carried it off, its jerking body presenting no resistance to the grip of the now recognizable, horned owl's talons or the lift of its powerful wings as it headed off with its prize towards the last of the night in the western horizon. It was all over in an instant. I was horrified.

A chill ran half-way down my spine and hung there, as if the person stepping over my grave had paused mid-stride to enhance the effect. The sign from the universe was unmistakable and cruel. Death was out there, lurking in the shadows. I slid off my barstool and withdrew to the sanctuary of my living room, where I finished my coffee without glancing out any of the windows.

I heard Gina come down the stairs and go into the kitchen, and then the sound of the Keurig dolling out her caffeine fix. She appeared in the archway that separates the living room from the dining room, and stood studying me in silence, as I sat curled up in a fetal position on the couch, rocking ever so slightly.

"You look like you've seen a ghost," she said, crossing the room and sitting down beside me. She nuzzled in close and leaned her head on my shoulder.

"The mob has nothing on Nature when it comes to fucking cruelty," I whispered.

"You know," She whispered back, "you really need to get out a little more."

"What are you talking about?" I said defensively, turning my face towards hers. "I've been out every day since we got here."

"On your own," she said, giving my nose a gentle kiss. "You need to get out there beyond the fence line. You can't hide in here forever."

"Why not?" I whispered back. "I've got everything I need within these four walls."

Gina studied me for a moment, assessing my determination. As always, she rejected it.

"Come with me on my run this morning," she said, more animated. "It's beautiful back by the foothills. Nothing but farms and ranches."

"Not today," I said, hesitantly. "I've got to sort through all these new accounts, and I need to get an early jump on it."

Gina stood up and turned to me, her hands defiantly on her hips, arms akimbo.

"Tomorrow then," she said. "No excuses!"

She strode off towards the kitchen, and a moment later could be heard scampering up the steps towards the bedroom. I breathed a long sigh of relief. It was a short reprieve.

She was back within moments dressed in her running gear. She glanced at her running watch.

"Early start?" She gestured towards my still supine figure on the couch.

I stood up quickly.

"Now stop trying to delay me, woman!" I said with my deepest and most officious voice, suppressing a smile. "I've got to go make me millions!"

I brushed past her and gave her a tender slap on the spandex before heading upstairs to change.

I heard the front door close before I was out of my pajamas.

My office was located at the farthest part of the bottom floor, which I would have called the basement, if the house wasn't built into the side of a hill which left the first floor on ground level facing the front property, and the bottom floor on ground level facing the back property. If you had stripped the rest of the house away, the interior stairway would have appeared as a centralized fire escape running from the third-floor bedroom suite, to the lowest floor living area, with each set of stairs tucked ergonomically below the other. My office sat at the end of a long hallway and was brightly lit by the natural light entering from the two sliding bay windows on the eastern and southern walls. To the east, I could see the rising hill of the enclosed paddock area leading up to the end of the driveway. To the south, I could see the full expanse of my back property, the pond, and the foothills rising in the distance. My office had its own adjacent bathroom suite, complete with walk-in shower.

Lenahan had done a nice job furnishing my office. It had a beautiful, large walnut partner's desk with matching captain's chair, set facing the south window.

A similar colored, three drawer, long file cabinet under the east window, and a lawyer's bookcase, with over-head, pull-out glass panel doors for each shelf, completed the suite.

On the desk sat the latest version of the HP ENVY, curved screen, all-in-one, desktop computer with matching Officejet Pro printer off to one side, and a bronze-finished, swivel-armed, Bodhi Industrial Ribbed Task Lamp. A glowing Orbi Wireless router confirmed that despite the lack of perceivable wiring, the office was open for business.

There was a yellow sticker posted on the bottom of the computer screen, with the handwritten words "Wigner's Friend." I booted up the computer, and it welcomed me by name and asked for my password. I typed in Wigner's Friend and was pleasantly surprised how good it felt to be connected to the outside world, if only virtually.

There was a single file folder on screen entitled accounts. I clicked on it and it opened to a listing of all the fifty-odd brokerage cash accounts on the list Lenahan had provided me. They were spread across all the e-trading heavyweights—Schwab, E*TRADE and Ally—as well as some smaller, more independent start-ups. I opened each account and initiated small purchases of vanilla options — OEX, ETF, and S&P — across the various markets, just to get everything rolling. I created an indicators chart so I could track put/call ratios, money flow, open interest, relative strength, and Bollinger bands. I probably didn't give everything the attention it deserved, but I felt like the kid in the candy store and was so anxious to get my feet wet again that I was willing to risk it, knowing in the back of my mind that I still had a few extra million squirreled away in a number of overseas accounts.

Then I opened the forex account and took some long positions on Euros, Japanese Yen, British Pound and Danish Krone, setting up some cross-pairs among them. I created both candlestick and bar charts to follow their progress.

My Ring alarm on my iPhone chimed to let me know, with an accompanying pop-up video, that Gina had arrived back on our front porch and was now stretching against the railing. I was pleased to see that my security was working. I indulged my voyeurism for a few moments of appreciation and then said "nice ass" over the speaker. The surprise on Gina's face was worth the middle-finger salute that followed.

Once I had all of my new accounts up and running, with real-time notices synched to my iPhone, I was about to shut off the computer and hopefully surprise

Gina in the shower, when I remembered the mantra drilled into our heads during our transition training over the first few weeks in the WITSEC: Never go back. I accepted that command unconditionally for Jimmy McCarthy. But Jimmy Moran was a smart ass.

Mark Wallen was a childhood friend of mine. We had spent our formative teenage summers working as lifeguards in the local pools and tennis clubs. Lifeguarding was the best job you could have at that age. We would work the same shifts, ogle the same girls and dream of a day when we would be millionaires and have our own pools. Each spring during high school we would often get a jump on the competition by visiting possible employers and putting in our job applications as early as possible. Since this was before the genesis of the Internet, those applications had to be either mailed or hand-delivered. Sometimes, when conflicting schedules allowed only one of us to visit an employer, that person would fill out both applications, which required that we each memorize the other's social security number. Like your first phone number, it became indelibly etched in my mind.

Mark died in a motorcycle accident the summer before we entered college. I felt like I had lost my twin.

When I first started hiding my own Valachi money overseas, each of the accounts were set up in Mark's name and social security number in a way to ensure application of the strictest privacy rules. The lion's share of the money was in an offshore trust in his name as well. I knew he'd appreciate that he was finally a millionaire.

I accessed a few of his smaller overseas accounts, just to ensure I could, and that some foreign despot hadn't nationalized the banks and seized my money. Happily, Mark Wallen was still living the dream. Our collective nest eggs were safe and sound.

I used some of Mark's money in one account to retain a Jersey-based Solicitor to incorporate three cut-out, foreign shell companies through which I could launder Mark's money. When the time was right, I would create the fiction of providing consulting services to those companies at a comfortable annual retainer and have them deposit that fee into my forex accounts, where I would further run them through the laundry spin cycle. I would be sure to file and pay all the appropriate taxes and with any luck, no one would be the wiser.

My phone chimed again, and this time the video popped up just in time to show Lenahan and Maeve entering the house with his keys. I was surprised to see it was already mid-afternoon. I closed out the computer and headed upstairs.

As I reached the first-floor landing, I was almost knocked over by a lumbering Maeve, who was eager to pickup with the tongue bath from our last meeting. She only relented when she heard Gina's voice as she descended the stairs.

"Hello, Lenny," Gina called. "Where's my Maeve?"

The two females engaged in an emotional scrum at the foot of the stairs.

I greeted Lenahan in the foyer with a wave and led him into the Kitchen.

"Can I get you a coffee?" I asked.

"No, I really can't stay," he replied. "I only stopped by to give you this." He held out something the size of a driver's license.

I took it from him and read the words "Colorado Concealed Handgun Permit" superimposed over a stretch of the Rockies that included the Three Witches. It had the same sad photo on my driver's license and all the same identifying biographical and physical information.

"Is this legit?" I asked.

"Totally. I certified your training and pulled some strings at the Larimer County's Sheriff's Office," he said. "Now you can carry your new gun with you at all times. Just keep it tucked in your belt like I showed you."

"Thanks," I said, studying the license.

"But I'm not Santa so I'll need that other gun back," Lenahan said.

I nodded and retrieved the boxed gun set from upstairs.

"All right Maeve," Lenahan said, taking the box from me as he strolled past Gina to the front door. "Time to make a move."

Maeve gave Gina a farewell lick and headed through the door.

"I'll be in touch," Lenahan said, closing the door behind him. "Keep your finger off the trigger," he added with a laugh.

As we watched him pull out of the driveway, I showed Gina the permit.

"Does this mean you can carry your gun all the time?" She asked.

"Yeah," I said. "But I'll double check on-line just to be sure."

"Good," she said. "No more excuses. You can take it on your walk in the morning."

CHAPTER SIXTEEN
EE-I-EE-I-O

The next morning, I woke up and grabbed a cup of coffee, and then headed right down to my office. I checked on my existing portfolio, jotted down notes on some moves I wanted to make when the markets opened, and then executed a few trades on my 24/7 forex account, capitalizing on some currency fluctuations. I was glad to be back making money.

Just as the twilight brightened in the eastern sky, Gina appeared at my office door in her running gear, holding up a pair of my sneakers.

"Don't want to be late for your first day of school," she said.

"Yeah, about that–" I started to say.

"You got five minutes," she said, dropping the sneakers as she turned and left the room. She called out behind her, "your clothes are in the laundry room." I heard her run up the stairs and exit the front door. My phone chimed.

I walked to the laundry room and removed a pair of khaki shorts and a loose-fitting T-shirt from the dryer. Remembering the gun, I went up to my bedroom, and retrieved it from the back shelf of my walk-in closet. I selected my thickest leather belt and put it on.

I lay the gun on the bed and inserted the hard leather holster Lenahan had given me into the inside right of my waist, making sure that the metal clip caught firmly on the outside of my belt. I then stared for a moment at the gun lying on the bed. My confidence with the handgun had faded with the passing of the initial adrenaline rush from my outing with Lenahan, but I didn't want to be walking around outside unprotected. I also knew that Gina wasn't going to accept any excuses this time.

I decided that I would fake-it-till-I-make-it, grabbed the gun and ejected the magazine which fell onto the bed. Then I rifled the top slide twice as I was taught, and out popped a single bullet. I picked up the bullet and attempted to force it back into the magazine, but it refused to cooperate, no-matter how hard I pushed. I finally cracked my thumbnail before I surrendered and tossed the bullet in the drawer in the side table to my bed.

I carefully slid the now-loaded weapon into the holster which Lenahan had described as an 'appendix'. Given its occupant's destructive power, I figured the holster got its name from all the unexpected appendectomies it performed on every drunk male who thought it was a good idea to take his gun with him on the last beer run for the night. Lenahan's explanation—that it sits by that organ—was much more mundane.

I didn't like the fact that, when holstered, the gun's barrel pointed directly at my penis. Any accidental discharge while drawing it could open a whole new career singing falsetto as the oldest member of the Vienna Boys Choir. On the other hand, that same fear reinforced all the safety rules Lenahan had drilled into me. It was the Sword of Damocles over the Sword of Jimmy Moran.

I took one last look in the mirror to see if I could spot the imprint of the gun underneath my T-shirt, and, satisfied that it was safely camouflaged, headed out to meet Gina in front of the house.

Upon my arrival, Gina signaled that I shouldn't try to talk her out of this by vigorously jogging in place and shouting, "Let's go!"

I followed Gina out of the driveway at the fastest pace I could comfortably manage given the constant pressure of my deadly accessory and then headed westward on Beverly. She looped back to let me know with a look that I wasn't moving fast enough then transitioned into tour guide mode and began to lay out the course we would be following and the visual landmarks I should look for to bring me home.

With every stride westward, I was feeling more and more like one of those anxious rabbits in the field, and my concentration was on visually scanning my surroundings and listening for sounds beyond the drone of Gina's patter. My one solace was that there was so much open land on either side of the road that if something were coming, I would have plenty of heads up.

We came to the entrance to what must have been Everett and Michelle's property and as we drew alongside, I could see their house set back at the end of a long driveway. It was smaller than our house, but much better maintained. I could also see a second large structure set about a hundred yards behind their house. Their driveway extended past their attached garage and ended at a large industrial-sized metal door, large enough to drive a New York City bus through, in the side of that back structure. A long metal gate mounted on foot-high rubber wheels sealed the street end of their driveway. Matching solar panels with keypads and intercoms anchored either side of the sliding gate. I saw no other signs of life on their large flat property.

The next property on our side of the road was a large barn with a street side paddock containing four beautiful horses, each intently grazing on their own section of grass along the fence line. The owner's house was set off on the opposite side of a large driveway with a curbside, overhead, iron trellis bearing the sign 'Fronsdahl's Farm', situated a few hundred yards further down the lane. As we passed, each of the horses lifted their head seriatim, to steal a quick glance at our two-person parade. Having established that we were non-predatorial, each returned to their respective meals. The two larger horses, one black, one light brown, had similar, white facial markings. The oldest looking horse, a chestnut-colored mare with a slight dip in her back, stood next to the smallest horse, a beautiful reddish color with a long, dark brown mane. The oldest horse watched after us the longest until we had physically passed the area where the youngest horse was grazing.

Over the next quarter mile, we passed a few more entrances to properties on alternating spots along the road. On some I could see other horses grazing or cantering in their back pastures. The properties were all neatly maintained, if otherwise nondescript. Each had barn like structures set off in the distance and all of them had a Recreational Vehicle parked somewhere along their property line. On some point along each property's fence I would spot signage that would establish in no uncertain terms that the property was private and not to be trespassed. One in particular stands to memory:

NO TRESPASSING.
VIOLATORS WILL BE SHOT.
SURVIVORS WILL BE SHOT AGAIN.

I heard the sound of a vehicle slowly coming up the road behind us and shifted to the side on the closest property's setback to give it plenty of room to pass. As I turned toward the approaching Chevy Silverado, I noticed that driver waved at us. More surprisingly, I noticed that Gina waved back.

"Who is that?" I asked.

"Don't know," she responded, jogging in place.

"Then why the wave?" I asked.

"I noticed during my other runs that everyone you pass around here waves at you, so I wave back," she said, doing a loop of longer strides around the roadway. "I guess it's a thing!"

She checked her watch and I could see that she was anxious to continue.

"Why don't you go ahead?" I said.

"Are you sure?" she asked, her eyes hoping for only one answer.

"Sure." I lied.

She pointed down the road to where I could see a fork and jogged back beside me.

"Take that right," she said. "It's a five-mile loop back towards the foothills and returns on that road on the left fork. Stay on the main road, and don't take any of the side streets, I think they are all long dead ends."

"Got it," I said, not surprised at all that Gina had already figured it all out. "Just follow the yellow-brick road!"

"Exactly!" she shouted excitedly, "see you back at the house." She headed off westward at a steady clip with a final, no-look wave behind her.

I watched until she reached the right turn in the fork, where she looked back to make sure I didn't head back to the house. Resigned, I waved and started following down the road after her. After monitoring my progress for a few more moments, she disappeared.

Feeling very much abandoned, I picked up my pace knowing that the faster I walked, the quicker I would be back home, safe within my fortress. I tapped the hidden gun for courage with every other step.

I followed Gina's instructions and made the right at the fork. Before me lay an endless road running northwest, with rolling hills and properties spread out along its route towards the foothills.

The closest property looked quite different from those I had passed. There was an old white farmhouse that sat at the end of a hard clay road. It had a small, weather-beaten barn at the far corner of a flat open field, which was enclosed by a similarly worn, continuous three wire fence anchored with flat metal postings along its perimeter. The fence itself was tilted outward along the front property line where time and weather had bent some metal posts. Farm machinery in various states of disrepair littered the property. Given the height of the grass that surrounded each piece, they hadn't been moved in some time.

Off in the distance by the barn, stood a horse-like creature. It was only as tall as the smallest horse I had seen on the other properties and was stockier. It was a uniform chestnut color and its coat was duller, coarser, and less groomed than those of the other horses. And where the other horses all appeared to have a self-assured, almost cockiness about them, this animal seemed a bit forlorn. It stood perfectly still, with its head no higher than its shoulders and its long ears tucked back along its neckline. Its long tail hung perfectly still behind it. It appeared to be staring in my direction. I felt compelled by pity to acknowledge the animal with a quick wave before I continued along my way.

Down the road was another farmhouse with a huge barn set back on its property. An endless number of steel framed pens of various sizes were ergonomically situated between the house and the barn. These pens were all busy with activity and seemed to include every animal from Old MacDonald's Farm, with the unexpected addition of a tall, cream-colored Llama for good measure. There were a couple of horses in a separate corral at the farthest end of the property who were busy removing hay from a large metal container that resembled an oversized v-shaped dish rack. Interspersed among the animal pens were the first children I had seen in the area.

I counted about a half dozen kids, three of each sex, ranging from early teens to about six years old. Each was working at their capacity to distribute various forms of feed to their animals, with the youngest, a small boy, struggling to throw an armful of hay over one of the rails into a pen of impatient miniature goats. One of the children, a blonde preteen girl who was herding sheep from one pen to another, spotted me walking by and tentatively waved. I smiled and waved back and continued along my way.

I was more comfortable around this property. It seemed more working-class, where the horse ranches all seemed more indulgent, like an expensive hobby.

At this point, I spotted the occasional vehicle heading in my direction and out towards the main road. Most bore signage that advertised their owners' respective trades in landscaping, construction, and the horse industry. Given the early hour, I assumed it was the locals going off to work.

Gina was right, each of the drivers slowed down as they passed me and gave me a wave, but I could tell by their looks that they were not sure about who I was or what I was doing walking their road. Overall, they each looked pleasant enough, and, most importantly, none resembled a mafia hitman.

I heeded Gina's warning to avoid the side roads that assuredly led to other unseen homes, properties and who knows what. Beyond here lies dragons.

The next property was a compound, with its street-side perimeter protected by a five-foot-high picket-fence. The house, or what I could see of it, was set back on the property and mostly hidden behind a high, man-made berm consisting of compacted earth and boulders. There were various forms of earth-moving machinery and a flatbed truck that could transport them. Out in its back field sat a contiguous set of ten-foot square solar panels, all facing south-east with a thick cable leading to the house. There were no animals or people in sight. Or so I thought. The only thing missing was an obvious set of security cameras.

When I reached about mid-point along the front of the property, the first of three large dogs appeared at the top of the berm, scanning the perimeter until it spotted me walking by. It let off a howl, heralding the arrival of its two obvious littermates, a large shepherd mix. All three then raced down the face of the berm and across the front of the property, barking ferociously.

I strategically crossed to the opposite side of the road, kept my eyes focused forward and, overcoming my inclination to run, maintained a quick and steady pace, as the dogs leaped against the picket fence and escorted me until I was clear of their property line. I wondered how Gina had managed when she passed this property. Poor dogs probably didn't know what hit them.

As I continued my journey, the properties got larger. They looked more like professional farms and ranches whose products sustained the local communities and beyond. When I finally reached the road that bordered the actual foothills, it was a half-mile of completely unpaved dirt. It was enclosed on both sides by barbed wire fencing that defended open pastures that had to be at least fifty-acres in size. I assumed that the appurtenant property owners lived in dwellings out of sight on the far side of the closest foothills. I finally passed an adjoining dirt road that carved its way through a pass into the foothills. A set of worn mailboxes by the gate were the only acknowledgment to human existence beyond that point.

I thought of Gina jogging along this isolated stretch, tapped on my gun and made a mental note to ask Helen if she could get Gina a stun gun to carry with her, if only to provide me with peace of mind.

The return loop of my route offered more of the same, with small herds of horses happily inhabiting manicured properties with lived-in homes and cars, trucks and RVs in their driveways. The strange thing was that the further along the route I went, the less anxious I was about being alone. It was almost as if the presence of all the animals had a calming effect. Other than the drivers in their passing cars, and the children at that farm, I hadn't interacted with any humans at all.

During the last quarter mile before the end of the loop, I passed a fenced-off field with five young looking alpacas. They were standing close together in one corner of their field. They looked surprised to see me, and suddenly moved *en masse* towards the fence at the front of the property, as if to get a closer look. They each began to mimic the whistling and kissing sounds once prevalently suffered by women passing Manhattan construction sites. This was the first time I was on the receiving end of the experience. When I turned to face them down, they eyeballed me like a bunch of brazen teenagers. I had to laugh out loud, which sent them all scurrying towards the back of their field.

The final property I passed before ending the loop was probably the nicest I had seen. Its four-acres of golf-course-quality grass rose steadily upwards and back from its white picket fence line to a beautiful small house and barn on the top of the hill. In a separately fenced off paddock by the barn, stood a magnificent horse. Its shiny light red coat was accessorized by a flowing thick tan mane and long, matching tail. Both danced as the horse gently trotted in circles around a petite, grey haired woman, dressed in a collared white shirt, blue jeans, and cowboy boots, standing in the center of the paddock. I could see that the woman was talking lovingly to the horse as it trotted around her, although I could not make out what she was saying. Then the woman gave a signal with her hand, and the horse brought the circle closer until it finally came to a stop and began to nuzzle the woman. The woman removed something from her pocket and slipped it to the horse, while gently stroking her muzzle and whispering in its ear. Neither woman nor horse seemed to notice me as I passed, and I was fine with that. I didn't want to intrude.

When I finally walked through the door of my house, I felt the calmest I had in years. I spotted Gina standing in the kitchen, having coffee. She was already showered and changed.

As I was about to tell her about my walk, she said, "Michelle from across the way just stopped by and invited us to dinner."

CHAPTER SEVENTEEN
MASTER OF MY DOMAIN

"Michelle's very nice!" Gina declared. She was in the kitchen preparing two bowls of fruit and yogurt.

"Too fuckin' nice!" I countered in my best Bronx accent.

"Look, her husband did us a solid fixing the lawn mower," she continued, defensively shifting into offensive mode, "otherwise you would have ended up killing yourself."

"Yeah, and I still haven't figured out that bit of alchemy," I said, recalling the shiny slight-of-hand. "I may not be mechanically inclined, but that mower was definitely DOA."

"Well, then," she replied, "you can name it Lazarus."

"I'm telling you," I said, "My gut is telling me there is something off about them."

"It's good you started exercising then," Gina said. Sliding my breakfast bowl across the counter like a pro, "that gut is getting way too big for its britches."

"Why don't we reschedule for another time?" I pleaded.

"I told her we'd be there," she said, softly but firmly, "so put on your big-boy pants and man the fuck up."

Gina's fortitude was a blessing and a curse. She had handled this whole arrest and WITSEC mess like a trooper, when a weaker spouse might have had a nervous breakdown, or worse, headed right out the door to the nearest divorce attorney.

On top of that she carried my weight when I was ready to crack. I'm sure I would never had made it through the trial without her.

If I could have stomped my feet without making an absolute ass of myself, I would have. But instead I gave her my best stink-eye, grabbed my coffee and breakfast, and retreated downstairs to my office, where I sought solace in generating a little more income trading on the back of the most recent Middle East volatility.

A half hour later, Gina appeared in my doorway jangling the car keys. She held up her debit card.

"I gotta do some shopping, and I need to pick up some wine to bring tonight, so I want to make sure there's enough money in our checking account," she said.

As modern a woman as Gina was, in every sense of the term, for some reason she left all the financial dealings to me. I used to tell her she needed to get more involved in that end, and she would always snap back, "That's why I married a lawyer."

Funny how my reason for marrying a nurse never had to do with money.

I pulled up the appropriate screen and showed her the balance. She smiled.

"Maybe I'll do a lot of shopping then," she said, giving me a wink and kiss and heading out the door. "See you later."

"Wait," I called after her, "where are you going to do this shopping?"

"Longmont. Call me if you need anything!" She called back to me before I heard her trotting up the stairs and out through the interior garage door.

She might as well have told me Timbuktu.

As much as I admired Gina's independence, I was a bit concerned over her nonchalance when it came to venturing out on her own, especially since I had been reduced to the level of paranoia. But I had learned early on in our relationship that Gina bridled at the first inkling, real or imagined, that I or anyone else was trying to control her, so I wasn't going to start now. Given how controlled both our lives had been over the past six months, it was no wonder that she was grabbing independence firmly with both hands. I had to keep reminding myself that the bad guys were far, far away.

I finished up with my work and decided to venture out exploring the rest of my property. I stopped by the shed and grabbed the scythe, not to do any more work with it, but to have it just in case I came across any of those rattlers Everett had mentioned. I waded through the high grass down the centerline of the back property then drifted to the left as I approached the pond.

It was an irregular oval, about twenty-five yards long and fifteen yards wide from the solid edges of the pond on my property, to the wall of marsh grass and cattails that rose along my partially submerged fence line on my westward neighbor's border. It continued for as far as I could see along the northern edge of his property. A slight current parted a spot in the cattails and continued towards the center of the pond which told me that the spring that fed my pond flowed from my neighbor's property as well.

The marsh grass and cattails were alive with the movements of hundreds of small black birds, all brandishing a bright red stripe on their wings. They appeared to come and go about their work independently, but every once in a while, something would happen which would cause them to rise as a dark cloud above the vegetation like a swarm of locust, where they would perform an elaborate synchronized circle of my neighbor's property and then all at once dive back into their marshy thicket.

I could see one of the redheaded ducks sitting on a small nest just inside my neighbor's property line while the other spent its time on my pond drifting along and occasionally dipping below the water's surface to retrieve some unseen morsel.

I was glad that the pond was there. It brought life to my property, and its fresh water would continue to feed my soil.

I continued to the northern fence line and saw that beyond it was a deep gulley that divided my property from the neighbor's to the north, whose own fence line started on its opposite side, twenty yards away. I could see that the gulley ran east-west and continued beyond my sight line in both directions.

I continued east along the northern boundary until I reached the large white cottage-like structure on its northeastern corner, and the tall whirligig that stood guard before its entryway. Up close I could see the mechanical intricacies that went into the whirligig's creation and watched as the gentle breeze caused the tin industrial-sized funnels to chase each other silently, counter-clockwise around the tall metal pole. I realized then that this whirligig, and all the others dotting my property, was its creator's way of engaging and interacting with nature. Constant movement signaled life.

The door to the structure was unlocked, but its resistance to my entrance gave testimony to the fact that it hadn't been opened in some time. Natural light flowed through its southern windows, cutting through the shadows and causing the dust motes to dance on the breeze from the open doorway. I tried the light switch to the left of the door, and the room flickered into clear white view, care of the line of hanging fluorescent lights that ran along the peak at the center of its ceiling.

The interior floor was glass-smooth, poured concrete which gave off an unnatural coolness against the warm air of the summer morning. Kitty-cornered to the entrance way sat a large gun-metal stove, set on a firebrick foundation, and whose piping exited into the wall directly behind it. The forty-pound canvas sack sitting to its right in a large metal basket had the words "wood pellets" stenciled on it.

A two-inch, lacquered, oak-top workbench mounted on a beautifully detailed set of storage cabinets with small printer's drawers started about five feet away from the stove and continued fifteen feet along the remaining base of the back wall. Three articulated magnifying lamps sat equidistant along the work bench with their corresponding bar stools marking time on the floor directly before them. I could see from the parts that littered the workbench, including a couple of butane soldering torches still attached to their tanks, that this is where the weathervane Geppetto built the whirligigs.

An original, brown maple, Amish Mission Farmer's Roll-Top desk with a beautifully detailed matching maple chair anchored the front wall of the room, immediately to the left of the doorway. Everything in the room, including the dance hall sized floor, had a fine patina of reddish dust.

I walked over to the desk and raised the roll-top cover, and there, spread out among the desktop, were draftsman drawings of the various whirligigs that littered my property, along with drawings for a number of other Rube-Goldberg type creations, that either hadn't been built, or that I had obviously overlooked. I made a mental note to seek them out and gently closed the roll-top with a new appreciation for the creative sanctity that filled this room. Its energy told me that this was a place to be earned, not purchased. I took one final look around the room, before shutting the light and gently pulling the door tightly closed behind me.

I headed back towards the burial mound at the center of the soccer field and examined the large black rectangle mounted on the top of the tall wooden post. I could see that the black box was mounted from behind to a crossbar at the top of the post, invoking Golgotha from this southern facing vantage point.

As I circled around to the front, I could see that there was an opening in its bottom, and thought I spotted something moving deep within the shadows in each of the three compartments of its recessed interior. A drop of guano fell from the darkness, just missing my upturned face, which was enough of a warning from the denizens within to overcome my natural curiosity and send me packing.

I reached the large metal swinging gate that led from the back property into the bottom of the side paddock, and after my attempts to open it were stymied by the thick tall grass that abutted it on both sides, I decided to hop the fence instead. When I say "hop" I meant to climb carefully up and down both sides of the fence's ladder-like structure.

There lay the final outdoor building on my property, a small weather-beaten barn, whose thirty-foot back wall sat about four feet off the gated fence line I had just scaled, leaving a shadowed corridor leading to the western corner of the paddock.

Inside, the barn was divided into three sections, a rectangular open area running along the front of the structure, a stall area further into the right of its entrance, and a smaller storage area recessed in the back-left corner. The floor throughout was hardened clay and a tall center post obviously carried the weight of its sloping, Spanish-tiled rooftop. Rivulets of light peeked through the shadows from the holes in the ceiling. Along the walls of the stall area were high set hooks and a basket which contained various grooming brushes. The interior of the barn was about ten degrees cooler than outside.

A tattered trail of dry hay led from the stall to the door of the storage area. Inside its entryway, loose hay about a foot deep covered the floor. Along the back wall was a stack of four-foot bales, bursting at their straps. The loud creak of the scrap-wood door and the sunlight that crept in behind it, must have disturbed this area's occupants, because I could see numerous furrows rising along its top layer as the surprised mice within raced for sanctuary beneath the hay bales.

I ran through my memory of the horses I had seen during my walk and tried to imagine what manner of beast had occupied this building at one time. I tried the light switch stationed along the corner between the stall and storage areas, but either the overhead yellow bulb was dead, or the electricity was off.

I entered a note to check on this lighting on my growing mental list of things to do, headed up the paddock to the gate along its western fence line that accessed my back-yard area, and returned to the house.

As soon as I got inside, I looked up the number for The Oracle in Hygiene. The soft Latina voice that answered caused me to salivate. I quickly asked for Helen.

A few moments later, Helen's husky voice came online. I explained my need for someone who could mow the back property for me.

"I gotta guy who can do that for sure," she said, "but I gotta another guy who is selling his John Deere rider-mower for a really decent price. More expensive up front, but big savings over time."

I took the number of the John Deere guy, thanked her and went to end the call.

"Hold on," Helen said, "Bobbi wants to talk to you."

Before I could say anything, Bobbi picked up.

"Jimmy," she said excitedly, "your brothers were just here. The youngest one said that three old dudes in black robes are stepping on your Karma."

"What the fuck does that mean?" I asked, far more curtly than I intended, as the fight-or-flight adrenaline flooded my veins.

"That's all I got for now," she said. "Stay tuned!"

CHAPTER EIGHTEEN
MORE IN HEAVEN AND EARTH

I phoned Lenahan as soon as I hung up with Bobbi and was about to repeat what she said when he cut me off.

"Bobbi already told me. I just got off the phone with D.C.," he said. "Seems like your friends have been granted an emergency appeal before the Second Circuit based on the trial court's failure to grant a mistrial."

"Fuck me," I murmured, cursing my courtroom impulsiveness. I just had to open my mouth. I knew I would never had done that in my role as a lawyer.

"Seems their lawyers have filed a second motion seeking their temporary release on bail pending the outcome of the appeal," he added.

I now cursed Meloni—for being way too good at his job.

"I've got a call into that Lafayette fellow in New York to find out the actual timing on both motions," Lenahan said.

I ran both motion scenarios in my head and tried to gage the possible timelines on each, based upon my professional experience. I guessed no more than a month at the outside, but I'd seen courts go forward as quickly as ten days if the facts or equities warranted. I was banking on the lack of any compelling sympathy by a court in a civilized society.

"Don't worry about shit you can't control," Lenahan offered, "right now the bad guys are still safe and sound in the Metropolitan Detention Center in Brooklyn."

"Okay," I responded, unconvinced. "Thanks for the update. Keep me posted."

"If anything changes, I'll tell you in person," Lenahan added. "But just to be sure, don't go anywhere without your gun."

I hung up the phone and retrieved my gun from the closet. I left it holstered in the middle of my dining room table so I wouldn't forget to take it with me.

I was still sitting there, going over the possible legal scenarios an hour later, when I heard someone pull up on the gravel in our driveway. Before I could see who it was, I heard the garage door opening. Just as I reached the interior garage door, it flew open and huge black shape sprung through it and slammed into my chest, knocking me down the hallway and over the arm of the couch in the living room.

"Blue!" I heard Gina shout assertively from the garage door, "Get off Daddy!"

I stared up at a set of onyx colored eyes and felt the blast of hot breath on my face. Using my chest as a springboard, the shape leapt off me and bounded back towards Gina, where it rolled around her feet excitedly, and then popped up and raced through the house as it performed its grand tour. I heard it hurl itself up the stairs of the Tower.

"Isn't she beautiful," Gina declared as she passed through the living room towards the kitchen carrying pet paraphernalia. "There're some groceries in the back of the car. Bring the bag with the dog food first."

By the time I arrived in the kitchen with the grocery bags, Gina had already set up a doggy bed, bowls and doggy toys in the sunroom, off the dining room. Blue, who I could now see was a muscular black pit bull, was in the sunroom slurping from a freshly filled water bowl, her tail flailing happily like a whip.

"When did this happen?" I asked, apprehensively.

"I stopped by the Longmont Humane Society," she said in that tone that let me know up front that it wasn't going to be a real discussion. "She had just been dropped off yesterday morning by a couple who were moving to Denver, which for some stupid reason doesn't allow pit bulls. They had just finished her temperament tests, which she passed with flying colors. When I said I was interested in adopting her, their vet gave her the required shots right there and then, and here we are!"

Blue raced past me and began rubbing up against Gina's legs as she circled her. Gina responded by squatting down and scratching her enthusiastically. I thought for sure Gina was going to draw blood or break a nail. Blue looked up at

Gina in ecstasy before rising to her feet, racing over and executing a few excited rotations around my legs. She then headed off to the sunroom and leapt into her new bed, now warmed by the afternoon sunlight, and rolled on her back and wiggled her hips, while her large pink tongue lolled alternately out both sides of her gaping mouth. I watched that tongue dance around four large, thick canines.

"How old do you think she is?" I asked.

"Still a juvenile. Not even a year," Gina replied, as she removed a can of dog food and placed its contents in a bowl which she then left in the sunroom. Blue polished it off before I had placed the can into the recycling container.

"You got your gun," Gina said, "I have my dog. And, I can take her running with me in the mornings."

I was fine with the dog and thrilled that Gina would have its company on her morning treks. I suddenly realized an unexpected benefit to our newest acquisition.

"Well, I guess we'll have to cancel tonight then," I said, trying to sound totally understanding.

"Nice try," Gina replied. "They told me Blue is completely house trained and does not suffer separation anxiety."

I looked over at the beast, now snoring peacefully in her new bed. Oh well, can't blame a guy for trying.

I spent the rest of the afternoon hanging out with Blue in the back property. She loved racing through the high grass and leaping in and out of the pond, disturbing the ducks and the blackbirds along the way. She was also a big fan of fetching the equally black Kong Ball Gina had brought home with her, although she had far more energy and enthusiasm than I had rotations in my arm. In short order I went from hurling the ball into the high grass thirty yards downfield on the first toss, to underhand flips that Blue caught in mid-air ten feet away.

Gina called to us from the back deck and tapped her watch. Blue gave me an apologetic glance and then took off towards our master. She cleared the backyard fence effortlessly and was inside the house before I reached the burial mound.

Gina and I arrived at Everett and Michelle's driveway gate at six-o'clock sharp. I was carrying a Josh Cabernet Sauvignon and Yellow-Tail Chardonnay. Gina had also brought along a tiramisu for dessert. Given my earlier conversations with Bobbi and Lenahan, I also had my gun tucked safely in my belt. I hadn't told Gina the latest news because I didn't want to worry her. And when Gina suggested I should leave it behind, I told her I wanted it in case we ran across an unexpected critter in the dark on our way home.

We rang the intercom at the gate and it slowly rolled open wide enough to allow us entry. By the time we reached the front door, Michelle was there to greet us in the open doorway.

"Welcome to Casa Corfee!" She said, cheerily, as she gave us both a warm hug and led us inside to where Everett stood waiting.

"Glad you could make it," he said, taking the wine bottles from my outstretched hands and escorting them into the kitchen, which was to the right at the end of the entrance hallway. I noticed that both our hosts were barefoot.

"Do you want us to take off our shoes?" I asked, thinking that this was some weird Colorado custom.

"Only if you feel the need," he responded with a grin. "Michelle and I just like to walk barefoot on the cool tile floor."

I looked at both sets of their feet and was surprised to see that they appeared to be identical in size and shape. I could have sworn they even shared the same clear nail polish.

"Ooohhhh, that looks delicious," Michelle said, coming up from behind and removing the tiramisu from Gina's hands before placing it carefully in the refrigerator.

"I'm going to love having a big slice of that after dinner," Everett said, appreciatively.

"We have a real sweet tooth," Michelle said, "especially because we're such pot heads!" she added laughing. She then assumed an earnest posture and said, "We smoke pot.... A lot! I hope you don't mind."

Gina burst into laughter. "Of course not girl. Whatever floats your boat."

Michelle looked relieved and gave Gina a hug.

Everett looked at me. "Do you guys partake?"

It was my turn to laugh. "Nah, for untold generations my family has been cursed by drink," I said in my best imitation of Spaghetti's Northern Ireland brogue, "if it ain't broke, why fix it."

"Well let me give you guys the tour," Michelle said. Everett has been doing some remodeling on house, and I've been dying to show it off."

We followed her into their living room, which was designed, like the rest of the house, in a Southwestern motif. Luckily, Gina was happy to accompany Michelle along on her Better Homes and Gardens tour. Everett caught my eye from behind Michelle and gave me a knowing nod to follow him. He led me out to the back-deck area that opened onto an enclosed back yard. He sidled over to where a variety of chicken, burgers and sausages were sputtering on the low open gas flame of a top-of-the-line 'Broil King' Imperial grill. A platter of mixed vegetables was roasting on a side burner.

He reached into a nearby metal cooler and handed me a 'Coors Light', opened another for himself and held it forward in a toast. "Welcome to Berthoud."

I clinked bottle necks and took a long sip of the ice-cold beer. I had been a fan of Coors since B.J. Delaney, a legend from the old neighborhood, gave me a can from the case he brought back from a road trip to Colorado in the seventies. That was before Coors itself had become a ubiquitous staple of Bronx Bodegas. I spilled a little from the bottle I was holding into the Colorado grass in B.J.'s memory.

I surveyed the backyard layout while Everett continued to work his magic at the grill with the confidence and dexterity of a short-order cook.

It amazed me how thick and green their lawn was. Golf-course and barefoot worthy, it extended throughout the yard from the edge of house as far back as the large back structure I had observed during my earlier walk. The grass on the rest of the front property that you could see from the street, and the grass on the back property I could now see in the distance beyond the fencing, looked more like the hard scrabble grass that had survived and thrived in Colorado's dense clay soil, including on my property. I noticed that the five-foot high wooden fencing that enclosed this area did not run in straight lines between the two structures but bowed outward in a curve like two separated halves of an octagon. Along the eastern fence were two apple trees and a pear tree. Off to the western side was a subsection staked out by a series of garden boxes, each surrounded by patterned paving stones. They filled each box with a bounty of vegetables that would have made Whole Foods jealous, including tomatoes, eggplant, peppers and squash, with a separate box containing a variety of common herbs. On the far side of the vegetable garden, tucked right against the fence line, sat a small open patio with an outdoor table and chairs, and a large metallic fire pit in its core. The center of the green was large enough to host a six-player volleyball game. None of this was visible from the street view.

I was surprised that the back building had an oversized front door, given that Everett and Michelle could have been comfortably accommodated in a hobbit hotel.

"What do you have back there?" I asked, gesturing towards the building.

"Oh, that's his man cave!" Michelle said, leading Gina from the kitchen to the deck, both with re-filled wine glasses in hand.

"I have my music studio back there," Everett confirmed, "along with some other toys."

"He'll give you a tour later," Michelle said, "but first, we eat."

"Their house is beautiful," Gina whispered to me with a hint of jealousy. "They brought a lot of their stuff with them from New Mexico."

Everett led our procession across the lush lawn through the vegetable garden to the patio while carrying the caramelized food. The rest of us followed with the plates, cutlery and glasses, along with our drinks and the bottle of chardonnay.

"Smell those herbs," Gina noted as she passed. "If I wasn't hungry before, I am now."

The delicious meal that followed was further pleasantly seasoned over the next hour by polite conversation as Everett and Michelle regaled us with their in-depth knowledge of the history of Berthoud and the surrounding area. They told us stories about the silver-mines, the sugar beet farms, and the railroads. I felt like I had squandered a large part of my life, having spent sixty-years in the Bronx, and knew nothing about its history beyond its riots and murder rate.

The strange thing was that neither Everett nor Michelle volunteered any information about their own past, other than that they were both retirees, and thankfully never asked us about ours. I returned the favor by not inquiring.

As I finished up, I complemented the meal, especially the roasted vegetables, which had no runts in the litter.

"All picked from our garden," Michelle said proudly with a wave towards the nearby vegetable beds.

"Those vegetables are amazing," Gina gushed, following Michelle's gesture. "Their colors are so vibrant, how do you do it?"

"We're pretty proud of our green thumbs," Michelle said with a giggle, the wine obviously taking effect. "Aren't we Babe?"

The sky had started to darken, and the air began to get cooler. Everett pressed a button underneath the table and the fire pit roared to life, throwing off dancing shadows and warmth. Michelle started to clear the table and Gina stood up to assist her.

"Jimmy, grab some of those plates," Gina instructed.

"No, Jimmy. Sit, sit! We got this," Michelle said dismissively. "Everett, why don't you show Jimmy your man-cave, while we take care of the dessert and coffee?"

"Would you like to hear me play guitar?" Everett asked, with the excitement of a young child.

"Absolutely," I said. "Lead on Macduff."

The doorway to the back structure had a keypad lock, which Everett deftly addressed, leading the door to open with a "swish" sound as cool air escaped what must be a hermetically sealed interior.

Inside there were the usual accoutrements to any self-respecting man cave. Soft leather couches and recliners, a bar in the corner with a discrete line of expensive whiskies and single malt scotch on the shelf behind it. There was a fully stocked, bar-sized fridge and off in the other corner, a small half bathroom.

Along the floor of one wall were guitars of different sizes and shapes, each one resting in its own velvet covered stand. Names like Gibson, Fender, Martin, Roland, and Epiphone were etched on their face plates. "What would you like me to play?" Everett called from behind me, concluding my inventory.

"What can you play?" I asked, hoping to narrow it down. Then, just to be a Bronx prick, I quickly added, "how about Hendrix?"

Everett smiled, put down the acoustic guitar he was tuning and selected a Fender Stratocaster electric from his stable. He glided over and plugged it into a large amplifier, and a moment later, was effortlessly performing a medley of selections from Voodoo Child, Watchtower, and finally the Star Spangle Banner. He was as lost in the performance as I was transfixed by his playing, his fingers a dancing blur across the strings. Jimi would have been proud. I gave him the well-deserved, slow clap at its conclusion.

"That was fucking awesome," I said, emphasizing every syllable.

He bowed slightly, endearingly embarrassed.

"I really prefer Grateful Dead," he said softly, it's more suited to my voice.

As he was returning the Fender to its stand, I looked up above him and noticed a series of metallic objects of various sizes and colors, each in a separate resin container, all recessed mounted on a large dark wooden plaque. Below each piece of encased metal was a corresponding engraved metal tab. I stood below them and started reading the tabs to myself: Skylab—1979; Envisat—2002; Cosmos 2251—2009; Kepler-2013; Hubble—2018.

"I see you've spotted Everett's mementos," Michelle said from behind me as she entered the room, Gina in tow, both with half-filled wine glasses at the ready.

"What are they?" I asked, intrigued.

"Just pieces of space junk," Everett said dismissively, returning to tuning another one of his acoustic guitars.

"Was that you playing just now?" Gina asked.

He nodded.

"Impressive," Gina cooed.

"Everett used to work for NASA," Michelle continued, proudly. "Top government security clearance."

"Really?" I said, a whole new level of impressed.

"A long time ago," Everett answered.

That's when I noticed a small model of what resembled a stripped-down version of the 'Millennium Falcon' from Star Wars, resting in its own recessed cubby built into the wall a few feet away from the space junk collection. It was small enough to fit in the palm of my hand, and as detailed as any full-sized model. It was shiny, almost translucent. I couldn't take my eyes off it. My childlike curiosity got the better of me and I started to reach for it.

"Don't touch that!" Everett barked, loud enough to get my attention, just short of rude.

My hand recoiled as if bitten. I felt instantly embarrassed.

"It's just... er... very delicate," he stammered, apologetically.

"Why don't we have some of that delicious tiramisu?" Michelle chimed in, instantly alleviating the awkwardness that had filled the room.

"Sounds great." I said, recovering.

We finished dessert and coffee at their kitchen table in relative silence. I missed the tiramisu from 'Angelo's' in Little Italy.

Michelle stood and started clearing our plates and cups.

"Well," Gina said. "We've really had a wonderful time tonight. But Jimmy gets up early for work, so we'd better be going."

I was up on my feet and heading for the door.

"We must do this again," Michelle called after me.

"Sure thing," I called back over my shoulder. "Thanks for dinner."

I almost shit when Everett met me on the front steps as I was exiting the front door. I did a double take and looked back to see how he could have passed me.

"I'm sorry about shouting before," he said, softly, offering his hand.

"No worries," I said, taking his hand and giving it a gentle shake. It was still colder than mine.

"Good," he said, smiling appreciatively. Gina gave Michelle a hug and followed down the steps behind me and we left our hosts standing there, watching after us.

As we approached the front gate it rolled opened wide enough for us to exit and then immediately closed behind us. Neither one of us looked back until we were half-way home.

"Everett sure was possessive about his toys," Gina said, and we both laughed nervously.

I thought about the tiny spaceship and the collection of space debris. Something was off and my lawyer Spidey-sense was tingling. But I was tired, and I would have to leave it for another day.

I opened our front door, having completely forgotten about our fur baby, and proceeded to trip over the solid black road bump laying silently across my foyer. As I lay on the floor cursing, Gina flipped on the light, and I could see she was fighting to keep from laughing.

"Are you all right, sweetie?" She asked.

"What do you think?!" I stammered, rubbing a very sore shoulder.

"I was talking to Blue," Gina said, chuckling as she stepped over me and passed into the kitchen, her black Amazon dog, happily following directly on her heels.

CHAPTER NINETEEN
A HORSE, OF COURSE

I sat in my office, sipping my coffee at four a.m., while balancing on the tightrope between hedging and speculation with some option trades in my forex accounts. My mind kept going back to those tiny pieces of metal in Everett's man-cave. Obsessively distracted, I closed the accounts and started to plug in some names.

I recalled the Skylab falling to earth in the late seventies, the year after Gina and I were married. We used to kid each other that we better cram in all the sex we could muster, in case it landed on our apartment building. When it finally did land in the western part of Australia, all U.S. citizens breathed a collective sigh of relief. The Aussies, on the other hand, were not happy that they were stuck taking out our garbage. Or so we thought at the time, until one smart Aussie couple, Nigel and Sarah Moss, in the purest capitalist sense, figured out that one man's garbage soon becomes another man's treasures, and they began to sell the Skylab wreckage back to the gullible Americans one tiny piece at a time, at an astronomical profit.

I did an internet search and saw that a bit of the wreckage had recently been sold at auction for over thirty thousand dollars. NASA must have a hell of a retirement package for Everett to be splashing that kind of cash around.

But when I started searching some of the other names in Everett's collection, it surprised me to find that while each of the satellites had gone out of commission at some point in time, they were still floating aimlessly somewhere out in space. Something was not adding up.

I heard the front door slam, and my Ring alarm chimed. The automatic video popped up showing the last of Gina and Blue turning the corner of the end of my driveway. They were both moving at a healthy clip.

I knew that I had better get a move on if I wanted to get past the fork in the road without meeting and being shamed by the returning physical goddesses, so I shut down the computer and headed upstairs to change.

Before I left, I grabbed a handful of the dog scoobies that Gina had brought home for Blue and tucked them in my pocket. My time with Valachi had taught me that if you can't win the opposition over with the righteousness of your cause, a well-placed bribe wouldn't go amiss. I wondered how Blue would handle the Cerberus triplets along the route, but now I was prepared for them.

When I reached the fork in the road, I saw the youngest boy from that farm further down the road standing there looking equal parts helpless and anxious. He spotted me, waved me on and disappeared around the bend. Fearing something terrible had happened to one of the other children, I broke into my fastest jog and by the time I had rounded the first bend, my lungs were heaving as they burned through the thin oxygen. Clutching the ends of my shorts to gather my breath, I could see a small bicycle on its side in front of the first property on the left. The little boy appeared on the road and motioned me onward, then disappeared onto the property. As I reached the front, I could see the boy standing along the fence-line, before the sad horse-like creature I had spotted yesterday. It seemed to be struggling, and the boy stood directly before it with his hands raised above his head, trying to calm it.

As I approached, I could see that the horse had somehow gotten its front legs entangled in the three descending wires where some front fence posts had been bent forward. Like Chinese handcuffs, the more it struggled to extricate itself the tighter the wires were closing on its legs.

Now that I was right before the creature, I could see that it was larger than I had thought, and as it desperately tried to rear up on its hind legs, I realized that it could do some serious damage to itself and me if I wasn't careful. The little boy, on the other hand, seemed oblivious to his own personal safety as he tried to calm the animal. I grabbed him on his shoulder and told him to run up to the old farmhouse and find the owner. He said he had tried, but no one answered the door.

With no clue what to do next, I mimicked the boy and raised my hands over my head and slowly approached the struggling animal, talking in as soothing a voice as I could muster at the moment, given that I could feel my heart pounding in my chest and hear the sound of the blood rushing past my ears. Surprisingly, the animal calmed down and stopped struggling against the wires.

I got close enough where I could squat down and examine the creature's legs. While the wires were tightly pressed into its fur, I couldn't see any blood. I slowly reached for the highest two wires and tried to pull them apart with just my arm strength, but I couldn't find the leverage I needed. So, taking a deep breath, I carefully leaned my body forward so that my head and shoulders were now underneath the horse's chest and between its trapped front legs. Pulling the top two wires apart in front of my chest like an original Bowflex, I leaned my two-hundred-pound body onto the spreading wires and forced them flat to the ground.

My full weight rested heavily on the gun and holster and I prayed that it wouldn't accidently discharge. Then I looked at the large legs on either side of my supine body and prayed that neither of them would crush my head like a cantaloupe.

A rock and a hard place moment.

"Move, goddam it!" I whispered, as my arms struggled to maintain control of the wires.

I watched as first one, and then the other leg slowly backed away, free from the flattened wires and my exposed cranium. When I saw that the legs were completely clear, I released the wires and relaxed on top of them for a moment to recover, absorbing their continued vibration.

"Thank you," I heard a woman's voice say from somewhere above me. It was a smoky, whiskey, growling kind of voice that went out of style in the 1940s.

"You're welcome," I said reflexively as I hopped up from the ground and looked around, expecting to see the horse's owner. Finding no one, I turned to the little boy.

"Was that you?" I asked, frightened that he may say yes.

He looked a little spooked. He shook his head slowly and pointed tentatively towards the horse, then ran over to his bike and quickly rode off towards home. I watched until he was out of sight.

When I turned back to the creature, it was standing there, its neck and head extended over the fence, and its eyes at my level, staring directly at mine. It had soft brown eyes and the longest black lashes I had ever seen. The forelock of its mane was caked with mud and twisted into tiny dreadlocks on its forehead. Its ears were long with thick beige fur on their interior, and the tip of its right ear was permanently bent back like a dog-eared page in a book. The ears twitched and turned independently like separate radar receivers before both falling into line and facing forward, giving me their full attention.

I could see now that this creature wasn't a horse, and I suddenly remembered the old Junkie's mule from my childhood.

"You're a lot smarter than you look, Jimmy," the woman's voice I had heard before returned, but this time it was clearly coming from the mule.

For the very first time in my life, I was dumbfounded.

"There you are!" I heard Gina call from the distance. "I've been looking all over for you."

I continued to stare at the mule, who nodded then turned away and headed back towards its barn.

I turned quickly and spotted Gina and Blue jogging towards me.

"Honey, come here, quick," I said excitedly.

"We ran the opposite way from the fork this morning to see if we could meet up with you," Gina started to explain breathlessly. "But we thought you'd be further along"

"This fucking mule can talk!" I blurted, ignoring her.

Gina smiled in her patronizing way. Blue did her best to do the same.

"No really. I swear on my testicles," I practically shouted. "She told me I am smarter than I look!"

"Well then she's a terrible judge of intellect," Gina said, giggling. "C'mon Blue. We'll see your crazy Daddy at home, after he finishes his conversation!"

She took one last inquisitive look at me before shaking her head and jogging off. I watched her disappear around the corner then turned back towards the mule.

The creature had stopped about half-way to the barn and now turned its head back to me and stared for a moment before calling out, "See you tomorrow, Jimmy. And thanks again for the help."

Then she turned and walked the remaining distance to the barn without looking back and disappeared inside.

I must have stood there for another twenty minutes staring at the open barn door. Then finally I shook my head to try to clear the fog. I knew I couldn't have just seen and heard what I had just seen and heard. I ran my hands over my head again to see if I had been accidently kicked when I had freed the mule, but it all seemed to be in one piece, at least on the outside.

I know I finished walking the circuit that morning, but I'll be damned if I could say another word about it. I'm not even sure if the Cerberus dogs came out to greet me.

When I reached home, I passed Gina and Blue pulling out of the driveway in the car. Blue looked right at home riding shotgun, with a 'snooze you lose' stare as they slowly passed me. Gina rolled down the passenger window and called out, "we're heading to Home Depot to look at some paint colors for the bedrooms. I've got my phone. See you later. Love ya."

"But what about the talking mule?" I shouted.

"I don't care if she can sing like Pavarotti. She still doesn't get a vote on the paint colors," Gina said and laughed as she closed the window and pulled away.

I stood in the shower for almost an hour, letting the steam from the hot water envelope me as I repeatedly replayed what had happened in my mind, trying to find a rational explanation. If I hadn't been kicked, then maybe I was suffering from a brain tumor or nervous breakdown from the stress. The only positive that came out of it was that it distracted me from worrying about Valachi.

Gina obviously thought I was pulling her leg, and I didn't know who else I could talk to about it. For the first time since my arrest, I really felt alone.

As I was toweling off, I heard my cell-phone ring. The number appeared as "Oracle."

I answered and heard Bobbi's excited voice.

"Your brothers say to buy the mule!"

CHAPTER TWENTY
PICKING THE BONES

"I swear to you, this is no joke. I'm not making this up." I reached across the table and gently stroked the back of Gina's free hand, as she lifted the last piece of filet off her plate with her fork and placed it in her mouth.

I had been unsuccessfully trying to convince her since she returned home late that afternoon that what I said was gospel. I think it might have freaked her out to see her husband acting so strangely, and I'm sure the nurse in her was wondering if I was having a mini stroke that was impacting my mental capacity. But I kept at it little by little while I helped her prep the dinner and continued through the meal itself. Gina in turn, did her best to ignore me, until now.

"Let me get this straight," she finally said after swallowing, while waving her fork around for effect, "you're honestly telling me that—no bullshit—this horse—"

"This mule," I corrected her for the umpteenth time.

"—this mule," she repeated, "not only thanked you for helping her get free of the fence, but she actually called you by your first name?"

I nodded.

"And now this psychic, this Bobbi-person, is telling you that your dead brothers want you to buy this mule?" She stood up from the table to clear her dish.

"In a nutshell," I said, trying to look as sane as possible while rotating in my seat to follow her path to the kitchen sink.

She stood quietly while she rinsed her plate and placed it in the dishwasher, then returned to the table, sat down, and gathered her thoughts for a moment.

"Okay," she finally said, looking me in the eyes. "I gotta tell you that this whole thing sounds fucking insane."

Fearing the worst, I buried my face into my hands, my elbows propped up on the table, as if awaiting a final blow.

"But, in forty years, you have never lied to me, even about your work," she continued, "so if you're telling me this mule can talk, then as crazy as that sounds, I believe you. Of course, you should buy her."

I'm sure I looked as shocked as I felt. I stood up, reached across the table, lifted Gina to her feet and gave her a passionate kiss. I realized at that moment that as long as she believed in me, I didn't care if I was crazy or not.

"In for a dime, in for a dollar," she said, smiling, "so how are you going to buy this mule?"

Up until that moment, I had been too distracted by the insanity of the event itself to even consider how I would pull that off. I knew I had enough fenced in property for the mule, given that most of my neighbors kept three or four horses on the same amount of land. I also had the little barn in the side paddock, which, with a little TLC could serve as a nice enough place to house it. But I really didn't know how to approach the owner.

At that moment the front doorbell rang. Blue raced over and took a defensive position in the foyer and I waited while my Ring doorbell chimed, and its video popped up on my iPhone. Gina chose the more expedient, old-fashioned, look-out-the-kitchen-window move, and before the image on my phone finally came into focus, she confirmed.

"It's Everett!"

"Blue, get outta there," I commanded. The dog ignored me and looked over at Gina, who walked by it and headed up the stairs. "C'mon Blue." The animal raced up behind her and I heard the bedroom door close before I opened the front door.

"Heyyyyy, Everett," I said as I slid through the front door and pulled it closed hard behind me. Everett looked past me at the closed door.

"I'd ask you in, but the place is still a bit of a shambles," I said, apologetically.

"No worries," he replied. "I would have called first, but I forgot to get your number last night."

"Oh, here ya go," I said, pulling out my phone and showing him my number on the screen. He took his phone out and, without me seeing his thumbs move, entered it into his contacts. As he checked his entry, his eyes lit up.

"Oh, and I wanted to invite you to join the Nextdoor group," he said. "It's an invitation only, online group that services our local community."

"Not sure I want to be joining any on-line groups," I said as politely as I could. "I'm a bit of a commitment-phobe."

"Oh no, it's not like that," Everett continued. "It's just a network that posts local events you might be interested in, and it also provides a neighborhood watch for the homeowners in the area. No obligation."

"Still not feeling it," I said.

Everett ignored me and worked his phone. "Look," he said, showing me the screen. "For example, one of the neighbors posted this photo of a stranger walking through the area the other morning."

I looked at the grainy still photo that was downloaded from a security video-stream. It was obviously taken from a distance from a high vantage point. Luckily, the camera's focus was on the back of the head and ears of a large dog in the immediate foreground, which left the distant figure in the street undistinguishable, other than being a white male about my height and weight wearing an old, Denver Broncos sports cap. I wondered if I showed up on anyone else's cameras.

I decided at that moment that it might be better for me to stay informed by joining the group and gave Everett my most recently acquired "mountainmoran@aol.com" email address. As he entered it into his phone, he pulled up and showed me another posting for a local estate sale. The address sounded familiar and when I looked at the accompanying photo, I saw that it was for the property where the mule lived.

"What the fuck is this?" I asked, a little more desperately than I intended.

"Oh, yeah. That's the Reynolds' place. The old widow recently died, leaving only some niece in Wyoming to cash in," Everett said. "They're selling off everything on sight this Saturday. Tomorrow, actually. Then the house will be put on the market for a quick sale."

That explained why no one was answering that door this morning.

"Isn't that the place with the mule?" I asked.

He thought about it and then nodded. "Yeah, I think she had an old mule."

"What's going to happen to it?" I asked.

"Probably auction it off with everything else," he replied.

"You gotta take me to that estate sale," I said.

"Sure thing," he said, looking delighted. "I'll pick you up first thing tomorrow and we'll go in my truck. Just bring some cash with you," Everett added. "Some of these estate brokers don't accept plastic."

"Thanks. I'll see you in the morning," I said.

He watched, amused, as I carefully slid backwards through the smallest opening in the front door I could get through, before turning and heading back out the driveway. I could have sworn I saw him leap up and kick his heels together, but it was a blur between his regular stride, so I just shook it off.

Gina appeared at the top landing and Blue raced past her down the stairs and stood growling at the closed door.

"C'mon," I said. "We have to go hit as many ATM's as we can find."

"Why do I have to go?" she asked.

"Because I haven't a fucking clue where to find them," I replied, grabbing the car keys from the hook by the door and heading towards the garage.

CHAPTER TWENTY-ONE
AN OFFER YOU CAN'T REFUSE

I didn't sleep at all that night.

Gina had driven me through three separate towns as we maxed out the withdrawals permitted in each ATM we could locate. Thank God for gas stations and liquor stores, the country could not run without them. We ended up with just over three thousand in cash. I had no idea how much that mule was going to go for but come hell or high water, I was determined to buy her, if only to prove to myself that I wasn't crazy.

Gina and I skipped our morning routines, and instead sat through twilight sipping our coffee in silence, waiting for the day to begin.

Everett's large black Durango pulled into the driveway at seven a.m. I made a mental note that since every family's second car out here was a pick-up truck, I needed to invest in four wheels of testosterone.

Gina handed me the envelope with the money, gave me a peck and said "Go!"

I was out on the driveway before Everett's text of arrival reached my phone. As I struggled to climb up into the passenger side of the cab, I wondered how Everett managed to access it and pictured one of those portable steel stairways that they roll up to jets on a tarmac.

The interior of the cab was beautifully accessorized, with leather everything and real wood paneling on the dash and consol. The largest center screen I had ever seen short of a man-cave, displayed images and information not found on your average GPS or sound system.

"I brought a little extra cash with me," he said, "just in case you need it."

"Thanks," I said. "But I think I'm good."

Given the proximity, the ride there was quick. However, the parking was another story.

We started seeing trucks and cars being parked along both sides of the street before we reached the end of Beverly, over a quarter mile before we reached the property, and from the looks of things, a quarter mile past it. I had not seen this many people in one location, truthfully, not even in the aggregate, since my arrival in Colorado. I was wondering why I had not seen any of the cars go by the house that morning and Everett suddenly mentioned that they probably all came in over the foothills from the North on County Road 6. I was about to comment on the synchronicity of his statement, but our arrival at the farm cut me short. Everett dropped me at the front of the property and went to find parking.

There was a weathered old horse trailer parked in its driveway. It was hooked to a large and equally old pickup truck facing the road. I saw the little boy from down the way standing by the far end of the horse trailer.

When the boy spotted me, he rushed over, grabbed my hand and pulled me along to where he had been standing. He pointed at the back door.

I couldn't see anything from that vantage point, so I climbed up on the back rim and peaked through the small cut-out opening at the top of the door.

"Hello, Jimmy," came that sultry voice from the shadows inside. "Glad you could make it."

I jumped down from the trailer. My heart was racing.

"What's going on?" I asked the boy.

"Some man came and bought the mule as soon as they opened for business," he said.

"Where is this man now?" I asked.

"I saw him go back to the barn," the boy answered, pointing in that direction.

"Take me there," I said.

The boy led me through the crowd of locals of various ages and appearances, as they milled around the property, stopping on occasion to look at several bits of tools and farm equipment with well-positioned price tags. The majority was moving in and out of the buildings on the property, with those exiting invariably carrying some small piece of the dead woman's life in their hands. It had the festive feeling of a country fair. It reminded me of that scene in Charles Dickens' *A*

Christmas Carol when the Scrooge is shown how the street denizens went through his belongings after he died.

The boy led me into the small barn where the mule had disappeared into the day before. The place was surprisingly crowded, and the boy had difficulty seeing through the crowd.

I leaned down to him. "What's your name?" I asked.

"John Lucian, but they just call me Lucian," he replied softly.

"Well, I'm Jimmy," I said to him. "Is it all right for me to lift you up to see better?"

"Sure," he said. Reflexively raising his arms to make it easier.

I hoisted him up under his arms and lifted him above the crowd, rotating him until his arm shot out like a pointer.

"There he is!"

I followed his line of sight until I spotted a large middle-aged man holding a rope halter. He was dressed in coveralls and had a sweaty bandana tied around his head. He was examining the price ticket on a large metal vise.

"Listen," I said to Lucian as I opened my iPhone to the camera app and handed it to him, "do you know how to work this camera?"

I showed him the red button on the screen. He nodded.

"I need you to go back out to the trailer and truck and snap a photo of its license plate. Can you do that for me?" I asked. He nodded again.

"And whatever you do," I said, "don't let anyone move that truck until you hear from me."

Lucian nodded a third time and then disappeared through the crowd.

I located the man Lucian had pointed out and made my way over to him. I stood next to him and politely waited to gain his intention. After a few moments, he looked up from some tools he was scrutinizing and seemed surprised to catch me staring at him. I reached out my hand.

"My name is Jimmy Moran," I said, grasping his right hand and giving it a firm shake. I made sure not to let it go. "I understand that you bought Mrs. Reynolds' mule this morning."

"Yeah, I did," he said impatiently, shaking off my grip, "what's it to you?"

"Well," I replied, "this is kind of embarrassing, but I promised my little grandson that I would buy that mule for him as a birthday gift. So, if you tell me how much you paid for it, I'd like to buy it from you. I'll even add ten percent on top for your trouble."

The man looked at me like I was soft in the head.

"A birthday gift!" he said, contemptuously. "That's not some puppy, mister. That's livestock. And I need it to help me haul some logs off the mountain before winter. Then, when I'm done with her, I'll auction her off to whatever slaughterhouse will give me the five hundred dollars I paid for her."

Every Bronx bone in me wanted to smack this prick, just for fouling the same air I was breathing. He reminded me of every rat-bastard-scumbag I crossed paths with back in New York, just without the shiny suit. I could not remember feeling that angry since I learned of my brothers' murders.

I may have been a back-room boy in Valachi's office, but I had been a part of enough of illegal deals to understand how to close this one. I removed the envelope of money from my pocket and leaned in close to the man, staring directly into his eyes.

"Forgive me mister, I'm not from around here," I whispered in my thickest Bronx accent with as much menace in my voice that my shared brothers' gene pool would allow, "but where I come from, back east, family trumps tree stumps. So, here's three grand, cash," I said, as I gently removed the rope halter from his grip and handed him the envelope. "The mule's coming home with me."

The man was just bright enough to be frightened, and he said nothing as he stared down at the envelope in his hand. I leaned back in and whispered.

"A friend of mine is taking photographs of your license plate as we speak, so in ten minutes I'm going to know everything about you and your family I need to know, in case you have any second thoughts."

He slid the envelope into his pocket.

"It's been a pleasure doing business with you," I said, before turning and walking through the crowd. *Never look back.*

When I arrived back at the trailer, Lucian was standing there, talking with Everett. Lucian showed me that he had gotten photos of the license plates and I slipped the phone in my pocket. Then he pointed to the ground by the truck and the trailer. Every single tire had been deflated. I looked at Everett.

"It wasn't me," he said, laughing.

I pointed to Lucian and raised my eyebrows inquisitively. He smiled and nodded.

"Everett," I said. "Can you lend me twenty?"

Everett fished out a large wad of bills from his pocket and peeled off a twenty-dollar bill. I took it from him and handed it to Lucian, showing him the halter.

"Now do you know how to put one of these on the mule?" I asked.

He took the halter and jumped up on the trailer, flipped open its latch and entered the shadows. A moment later he returned leading the mule and handed me the lead rope, then gently talked her down from the back of the trailer.

"Her name is Claire," Lucian whispered to me. I looked at the mule and she nodded. He took the lead from me and led her around the back of the trailer and out to the street. Then he handed it back to me. He looked sad.

"Listen," I said. "I only live down the road a bit." I pointed in the general direction.

"If I'm going to be honest. I don't know anything about taking care of a mule." I squatted down, so I was closer to his size. "And I could really use the help of someone that knew his way around farm animals."

His eyes lit up.

"Tell your folks I'll stop by soon and introduce myself," I leaned in and whispered, "but let's keep Claire's little trick our secret, okay?

Lucian nodded and then ran over to his bike. A few seconds later was peddling furiously in direction of home.

Everett looked at the mule and scratched his head.

"How are we going to get her home?" he asked.

"It's just a short stretch of the legs," I answered. "See you back at the ranch."

CHAPTER TWENTY-TWO
A LITTLE LIGHT CONVERSATION

I knew from the moment I took the lead and started in the direction of home that I was in way over my head. My life had just crossed over into the Twilight Zone, and I was afraid there was no going back.

Claire and I walked in silence past the line of parked cars and occasional pedestrians. While I may have been holding the lead, I didn't for one moment believe I was in control of this situation. I could hear Claire's hooves clopping behind my right shoulder and could feel the ebb and flow of her energy from the tugging of the rope in my hand with each of those steps.

"Pretty gangster move back there," came that sultry voice from behind me.

Panicked, I looked around to see if anyone was in ear shot. Claire just stared back at me. I turned back and continued to walk towards home.

"I meant the kid and the tires," Claire said, "although your Goodfellas move was a nice touch."

This time I spun completely around to respond but held off because I could see Everett pulling up on the road behind us. He gave a short toot on the horn, which caused Claire to canter around to the front of me whispering "asshole" as she passed. I felt a slight rope burn as the lead pulled through my fingers and I had to jog and tug it hard to the left to get her to go to that side of the road.

"I'll meet you back at the house," Everett called as he carefully made his way past, then accelerated down the road.

"There's way more to him than meets the eye," Claire said once Everett had left us behind.

I suddenly stopped short and turned to her.

"How is this possible?" I whispered with a hint of psychological desperation in my voice. "How do you know what you know? Goodfellas for God's sake! And how am I standing here having a conversation with a horse?"

"That's mule!" Claire responded, indignantly.

I shook my head and laughed. Now I knew how Gina felt.

"You humans love your gangster movies," she added. "Explains a lot."

"I'm fucking insane, aren't I?" I said to her.

"Would it really make you feel any better if I told you you're not?" Claire answered. "C'mon, let's get moving. You really don't want any of these nosey neighbors seeing us having this conversation. They're all suspicious enough of you already."

She started forward, and I fell in step beside her and we walked the rest of the way home in silence. I distracted myself by cataloguing the numerous scars I could see on Claire's coat, including several slashes along the top of her rear legs. I noticed for the first time that she had a large cross of dark tufted fur running down the centerline of her back from her mane to her tail and across her shoulder line. She needed a good brushing.

Gina, Everett and Michelle were waiting at the end of the driveway. Given their comparable stature, they resembled the welcoming committee from munchkin land. Everett's facial hair made him the Mayor. I could hear Blue barking from inside the house.

Claire turned her head and whispered to me, "you can let Blue out, she'll be fine."

I shouted that to Gina, and a moment later Blue came flying out the driveway and began to circle Claire and me as we ambled down the driveway. By the time we reached the others, Blue had calmed down and was walking alongside us. Claire leaned down and nuzzled her back.

"Everyone," I said in my best sell-it-to-the-Jurors' voice, "Meet Claire!"

Gina walked up and gently touched Claire's face. Claire reciprocated by nuzzling Gina's shoulder. I could see that Everett and Michelle were a little nervous and gave Claire lots of space.

"She is sooooo sweet!" Gina cooed as she continued to stroke her face and neck. "C'mon. Let's show you your new home."

Gina walked to the large gate and dragged it open, displaying the rich green property and pond beyond it from a perfect viewpoint.

Claire nodded to me. I clumsily removed her harness. She entered the gate and began to descend the long hill towards the tiny barn. She picked up momentum as she went, and by the time she had reached the bottom of the hill she went cantering past the barn and through the next gate to the back property. Blue suddenly took off after her and began to run beside her. When the two hit the large soccer field Claire broke into a full gallop and proceeded to circle the property, with Blue racing dangerously close to her legs, the two of them leaving rivulets in the high grass as they ran. Claire looked every bit a horse.

"She's magnificent," Michelle said.

"She's big," Everett added.

After a few rotations, Claire slowed to a canter and began to kick-up her back legs every few strides, like a bucking bronco. You could see the striations of the muscles on Claire's body with each extension. Without looking up at her, Blue gave Claire plenty of space and managed to anticipate her moves, occasionally crossing sides between Claire's powerful legs with the agile timing of a double-dutch champion. At one point near the pond, Claire reared up on her hind legs and flailed her front hooves in the air, like a boxer working a speed bag. She seemed to be a completely different animal from the one I first saw the day before.

"I wouldn't want to be on the receiving end of that!" Everett said.

Michelle then abruptly tapped Everett on the shoulder.

"We have to go, Babe," she said, pointing to her watch. Everett nodded.

"Oh," Gina said, sounding disappointed. "I was hoping you could come in for a cup of coffee?"

"Another time, sweetie!" Michelle said, giving Gina a hug. "It's the weekend delivery and we have to make it to the Dispensary before the youngsters Bogart the best selections." She giggled.

Everett helped me close the gate and turned to join Michelle.

"Wait, I owe you twenty," I said. I started to turn to Gina to ask her for it.

"Forget it," Everett said, waving me off. "It was worth the price of admission just to watch that kid vandalize the truck," he laughed.

I watched the two of them walk side-by-side out the driveway. Halfway out, Michelle reached beside her without looking or breaking stride and took Everett's hand. From my vantage point, they resembled a couple of preschoolers on a hallmark card.

Gina then took my hand and started to drag me down the hill toward the barn.

"C'mon," she said excitedly. "I want to show you something."

When we reached the barn, Gina raised both arms outstretched and entered it with the slow spin of a game-show hostess displaying the prize I just won. I followed and, as my eyes acclimated to the shadows, I could see that she had transformed it into a working barn with all the accoutrements, including a new metal hayrack on the wall, filled with hay, and a large water trough tucked against another wall. Directly opposite hung a set of inverted rakes, which Gina proclaimed to be horse pooper scoopers. There was a large plastic storage container that she told me contained something called "Sweet Mix," and there were a couple of fresh bales of hay tucked into the storage area. Gina even had a few Great-Dane sized food bowls scattered strategically around the floor. Some power drills and screw drivers sat abandoned right inside to the left of the doorway.

"How?" I stuttered.

Michelle came by this morning right after you left with Everett and took me to Murdoch's in Longmont," she said. "It's got everything a cowboy could want," she added, giggling. "I was even able to pick up this beautiful pair of boots!" She proudly raised her leg to show me.

"But how did you get this all together so quickly?" I asked.

"That Michelle was amazing!" Gina replied. "It was like watching a video in fast motion. Every time I turned my back it seemed she had the next thing mounted, and the tools hung. And she carried that water trough and the hay bales down from the driveway all by herself."

I knew how physically strong Gina was. She had been a gymnast through college, and when I met her, she could crush my hands in the traditional, macho, two-handed test of strength. Forty years later, she still maintained a relative strength that freed me from any chauvinistic tendencies of offering to do things for her, unless instructed. I walked over and lifted one of the hay bales a few inches and was surprised at just how heavy it was. I just couldn't imagine the tiny Michelle out-muscling Gina.

"I love what you've done with the place," came Claire's sultry voice from behind us, "although it could still use a coat of paint. Something off-white perhaps."

We both spun on our heels and faced to doorway. Claire stood there, Blue by her side, studying the interior. The sunlight streaming in behind her gave her a halo effect.

"Holy Shit!" Gina screamed. "You really can talk!"

Claire ambled in past us, walked over to the hay rack, pulled out a mouthful of hay from between the bars and started to chew.

Gina turned to me. "I'm sorry honey, I really thought you were crazy." She laughed. "Whhheew, what a relief!"

"You know... this ain't bad," Claire said as she chewed another mouthful. The crunching sound and image brought back memories of my mother, who was notorious for chewing with her mouth open while fully engaged in dinner conversation. Sorry mom.

"Next time maybe you could change it up with some alfalfa hay, it's a bit richer," Claire continued. She spotted and followed one of the rivulets of light to the ceiling and gestured with her nose. "Need to take care of that before the next rain, Jimmy. Mules' coats aren't waterproof like our mother's."

Gina gave me a crushing hug, then released me and repeated the move with Claire's neck. Blue stood directly underneath Claire's body and started to lick the inside of Claire's knees. All I needed was a dwarf and this would have been the closing scene from a Fellini movie.

"Easy does it Wonder Woman!" Claire whispered to Gina. "I can't swallow my cud."

Gina released her and took a few steps back. "Sorry," she said, giddily. "I just can't believe what is happening!"

"Yeah, I'm getting that," Claire said, giving her head a quick shake to get the blood flowing back through her neck muscles. "I guess I do owe you guys an explanation."

CHAPTER TWENTY-THREE
CLAIRE'S STORY-PART ONE

"I was born in October 2002 on a ranch in Northern Wyoming, along the foothills of the Eastern Rocky Mountains," Claire began. She looked at us for a moment before proceeding. "You may want to sit down for this, it's a bit of a tale."

I grabbed a couple of five-gallon buckets stacked in the corner and inverted them, giving Gina her choice of stools. Once we were seated, Claire continued.

"It seems that my mother, an Arabian mare named Juno, was owned and raised by a wealthy rancher. He was hands-on and hardworking, but his word was final. He used to ride my mother around his five-thousand-acre ranch to check on the sheep, cattle, and other horses he bred that were grazing in different locations. The rancher had a young wife and two beautiful girls, whose names were Scarlett and Savanna. Scarlett, the oldest daughter, was five years old, with fair skin and beautiful blond hair like her mother. She often accompanied her father on his rides, with Scarlett sitting on the saddle before him, wrapped tightly in his left arm, while he held my mother's reins with his right. Scarlett loved her daddy.

"Savanna was just a toddler and used to follow her big sister around the house and barn areas whenever she could. Scarlett was a brilliant little girl and loved to read books to her baby sister.

"Scarlett used to come into the barn and help her daddy groom my mother. Her daddy used to tell Scarlett that he would give her my mother for her seventh birthday. On most days, if the weather was nice, the rancher used to let my mother run free in the fifty-acre field that ran along the border of the neighboring ranch.

"One day, our neighbor's mammoth Jack Donkey, named Zeus, managed to clear our border fence while Juno was out in the field. Eleven months later, I was foaled.

"The rancher was so angry that my mother had gotten pregnant by a donkey that he threatened Zeus' owner that he would kill it if it ever crossed onto his property again.

"For the first four months of my life, my mother and I were inseparable. She would nurse me, groom me tenderly and never strayed more than a few yards from my side. She would whinny to me to make sure I stayed close by and I would try to do the same, although my voice was never as sweet as hers. I never knew that I was any different from her and couldn't wait to grow up beautiful like my mother.

"When I reached the age of four months, things changed. The rancher took me from my mother and placed me in a small pen in a separate barn. I never saw my mother again.

"For the first few days I cried uncontrollably. I missed my mother so much I couldn't eat or sleep. I just laid around the pen, sobbing to myself.

"Then one day, Scarlett led Savana into my barn. Scarlett was carrying what I would later learn were books under her arm. She led Savanna over to the pen where I lay sobbing and sat themselves both down on a small bale of hay right next to the gate.

"Scarlett told me 'Claire, that's your name little horsey, I'm sorry you are so sad. When I'm sad, my mommy reads to me, so since your mommy's not here, I'm going to read to you. And I'm going to come back here and read every day until you are not sad anymore.'

"Scarlett then opened the first book and began to read out loud. Her voice was soft and sweet and while, at first, I didn't really know what she was saying, its melodic sound and her presence on the haystack next to me, made me feel a little better. Scarlett continued to read for hours until she had read every book she had brought with her. By then, poor little Savanna had fallen asleep in Scarlett's lap.

"Scarlett then stood up and reached through the gate and rubbed my ears. She was so gentle that I nuzzled her hand like it was my mother. She blew me a kiss, and then gathered her books and woke her little sister, who after rubbing the sleep from her eyes, gave me a tiny wave. Scarlett said to me, 'See you tomorrow, Claire.', and the two of them left the barn.

"That was the first night I had slept soundly since I was separated from my mother.

"Scarlett kept her promise and came back the next day, and the next day after that, and then every day after that for what seemed like forever in my short lifetime, but which were probably only months. Sometimes she was alone and sometimes accompanied by Savanna. During that time, I continued to eat, sleep and grow strong. I would stay fit by running in circles around my pen and kicking up my hooves.

"I also found that as Scarlett continued to read to me, little by little, I began to understand what she was saying. More than that, I found that I could hear what she was saying before she said it. The same was true with Savanna, and I loved listening to both their thoughts, even if they weren't in the barn with me.

"The more I could hear their thoughts, the more I tried to vocalize what I was hearing. I would lay in my pen at night, trying to mimic the sounds of the words as they appeared to me. At first, it sounded like gurgling brays, but as I continued to watch Scarlett's mouth each time she read to me, over time I found I was able to shape my lips the way she did.

Claire demonstrated the dexterity of her lips by forming them into all kinds of shapes. It reminded me of a chimpanzee making fun of the passing humans in the Bronx zoo. Claire then continued.

"Scarlett loved her 'mummy' and thoughts of her mother were constantly on her mind. Indeed, I could feel that Scarlett had the same love for her mummy as I had for mine. I drew comfort in the warmth of Scarlett's thoughts.

"Because I heard it so much in her thoughts, I found that 'mummy' was the easiest word for me to vocalize. I practiced and practiced each night, getting better and better at it until one day, when Scarlett came in to read to me without Savanna, I blurted out 'mummy' as soon as she sat down on the hay bale.

"She had the same look of amazement as you just did Gina," Claire said. "Anyway, I digress.

"After Scarlett heard me speak that first time, she became quite the little teacher. She would hold my face in her little hands and then slowly say other simple words to me, always exaggerating her mouth when she did so, and then ask me to repeat them. She was so patient. Whenever I would get one right, Scarlett would squeal with delight and dance around the barn and I would hop up and down and spin in circles in my pen. The more words I learned, the faster I learned the next word.

"I would never speak around anyone except Scarlett, not even around Savanna.

"Whenever their father came in to clean my stall or leave me fresh hay or water, he would never speak or even look at me, so I stood silently in the far corner of the pen, with my back to him, waiting for him to leave. Then one day, I heard his thoughts.

"He had come into the pen, and I took my position at the opposite end, with my back to him, my tail swishing wildly. I could feel him staring at me. Then I saw an image of my mother in his thoughts. And I saw her being taken away in a trailer, and I could hear her pitiful whinnying as she went. And I could feel how much he hated me just for being born.

"Then I could see Scarlett crying uncontrollably on her bed as he stood over her. He was speaking very sternly to her, and then I saw the anger-filled images in his head of another ugly young horse in the same pen as mine, and I realized he was thinking of me.

"He was visualizing placing me in a trailer like the one that took my mother, and then I saw an image of another man handing him money before driving away with me.

"And now, for the first time, I understood what hatred was.

"I really don't remember how it happened, but I must have turned and crossed the pen and before I could stop myself, I spun around and kicked the rancher hard in the side with my back legs, sending him flying against the wall of the pen. As he sank to the ground, I turned on him and reared up on my hind legs and was just about to stomp him with my front hooves, when I heard Scarlett from behind me shouting 'Claire no! Don't hurt my daddy!' At the sound of her voice, the blood left my eyes, and I dropped down and returned to my far corner.

"Scarlett ran into the pen and helped her father to his feet. Luckily, I was still a young foal, so the first kick didn't do any lasting damage. She led him away, came back and closed the pen, and the two left the barn.

"That night my mind was full of images of the father loading his gun, and Scarlett pleading with him, and sobbing in her mother's arms while Savanna cried pitifully beside them. I saw images of Scarlett's mummy shouting at her husband and taking the gun away from him.

"The next morning, two strange men entered the barn carrying ropes. One tossed a rope around my neck and pulled me to the fence while the other man entered the pen and slipped a harness around my head. The harness had two large nots on the top rope, that rested and pressed against my nostrils, and so I couldn't breathe if I tried to pull against the harness.

"Using this harness and the rope, the men led me out of the barn and into a trailer with only a small window at the very top of its rear door. As they slammed the door shut behind me, and began to pull away, I could hear Scarlett and Savanna crying, and I could see a water blurred image of the trailer disappearing along a dusty road in the distance."

Claire let that last image hang in the air.

"That's the first time I've ever told anyone that story," Claire said to no one in particular. "Boy, now that I've said that out loud, that really did suck."

CHAPTER TWENTY-FOUR
CLAIRE'S STORY-PART TWO

Gina was sobbing at this point. I was fighting back tears.

Claire came over and nuzzled Gina.

"C'mon," Claire said softly. "It was a long time ago. Look we all made it here. We're okay now."

Gina's sobbing slowly subsided.

"Atta girl." Claire said, before walking over and taking a long pull of water from the trough. She raised her head up and faced us. "Now, where was I?" She stared at Gina and before Gina could say anything, Claire continued.

"That's right Gina, I had just left my birth home," Claire continued, reading her thoughts. "Nicely put!"

"So, we must have driven a long time that day because it was dark by the time we had arrived at our destination. What little I could pick up from the two men's thoughts as they drove revolved around what I later came to learn was food, drink, and women. I have since heard more evolved thoughts coming from fish. And they call us animals.

"When the trailer finally came to a stop, the two men came around to the back, threw open its door and roughly dragged me out by the harness and ropes. They led me into an outdoor pen beside a large barn. In the pen were other animals like me. I could hear one of the men think the words 'goddam mules' as they wrestled me into the pen with the others and slammed the gate. I finally knew what I was.

"The other mules were of various sexes, sizes and ages and they all looked worn out. The herd, another new word the men shared, looked up at me all at once as the men stormed back to their truck. While I was comforted to be finally among my own—it had been forever since I had seen anything but humans—I was immediately aware of the consistent feeling of unhappiness they all shared. I could hear each of their thoughts as they sized me up while I carefully walked among them, searching for a friendly face. I could tell from what I was hearing that they each could hear my thoughts as well. This wasn't a happy bunch. And while I hate to say this about my own, they weren't very bright, either.

"Finally, a large male mule approached me. I could tell by the way that the others all quickly moved out of his way, that he was the leader of this group.

"'Welcome to Steamboat,' the big mule said, (and when I say 'said' I mean 'thought' Claire added as an aside). 'My name is Samson. The humans here want me to make sure I keep the rest of the herd in order,' he said.

"I wasn't about to tip my hand as to my newfound ability, so I thought right back at him, 'And what is it we mules do here in Steamboat?'

"'Lots of things,' Samson replied. 'Sometimes we take humans on trail-rides. Sometimes we haul the human's food and tents and things to and from their campsites in the mountains, and—'

"Samson took a moment here to collect his thoughts, searching for the right mental images to display to me. I scanned his mind for the rest of it and saw images of other enormous animals being shot by humans and dying on the mountain tops. It horrified me.

"'We carry back the dead from the mountains,' Samson completed his thought. 'Just keep your head down,' Samson continued, 'and you'll be fine.'

"With that Samson turned and headed back through the herd. I could hear them all whispering thoughts as he passed.

"Now I will not burden you two with my first ten years on the mountains in Steamboat. Suffice it to say that it was as boring, exhausting and painful as Samson's thoughts had promised. I owe the loss of the tip of my ear to the frostbite from one bitterly icy winter on those mountains.

At this point Claire wiggled the afflicted ear for effect, then brought it forward so she could examine the damaged tip. Her eyes squinted in anger, but she whiffled it off, returned her ear to its place beside the other one, and then took another long draught of water. She expressed an extended yawn, before continuing.

"The best thing about this time is that I got to be among my own. They were all nice enough, but most of them were timid and simple. I could see how confused they were whenever they read my thoughts. And it bored me reading theirs. All but one of them. A handsome, grey Jack named Mr. Rogers.

Claire walked over to the doorway and stared up into sky. A passing wind blew her mane back off her face and neckline and she closed her eyes, lost in memories.

"Tell us about Mr. Rogers," Gina said.

"Another time, perhaps," Claire whispered as she returned to her spot before us.

"During my Steamboat years I grew larger and stronger, and I got to listen in on the minds of some of the most successful and powerful humans in the world, who all wanted to come to Steamboat to embrace mother nature and prove to themselves that they were more than tiny little beings who liked to dominate every other creature on this planet. Most of the time I didn't understand what they were thinking about, but I could hear their thoughts loud and clear in my mind. It helped to develop my vocabulary, including their curse words.

"That's where I learned about movies. You'd be surprised how many of them replayed movie scenes in their head, like their actual lives weren't good enough for them. I first thought they were just random memories, but when different men kept playing the same movie scenes, I finally figured it out. I'm sure I managed to visualize the Godfather and Goodfellas a hundred times over the years. Humans always idolize what they cannot be.

"And at times over the years, when I was alone in the middle of the night, at the edge of some campsite in the mountains, tied up to some tree, I would call out my word of the day. Just to see the lights come on in all the tents and force the frightened men and their camping guides to have to search the perimeter to make sure they were safe from imagined marauders. In no time the rumor had spread among the humans that the mountain was haunted."

At this point Claire made a sound that reminded me of the laugh of the character Lurch from the Addams' Family television show from the sixties. Both Gina and I joined in her laughter. When we finally regained our composure, Claire continued.

"I never minded the hard work, or even carrying the obese humans who needed one of my cousins just to carry their food, but I hated carrying all those dead animals, ruthlessly slaughtered by these weak humans just because they felt like it.

"The breaking point came five years ago, when I drew the short straw among the herd and had to accompany a group of humans on an elk hunt in the mountains. It was a young investment banker from a land called 'Wall Street.' He paid my owners a lot of money so that he could bring home the head of a large elk to hang in his 'man-cave,' which from his thoughts didn't look like a cave at all. So, they took him up in the mountains and stuck him and his big gun in a heated box that was hidden among the shrubs. Then they baited the trail a few yards away that they knew the elks would cross, so these unsuspecting innocents would stop and lick these blocks of salt, just long enough to die.

"They kept me tied up at camp a quarter mile away, while the humans hiked off for the slaughter. After a while, I heard the blast of the rifle echoing in the distance, and then another, and then a third, and then one of the guides came running back into camp and led me to the body.

"The investment banker was standing over the elk, holding his head up by his large horns. This human was so weak, he needed both hands to do so. His gun was leaning on his shoulder, while one of the guides snapped and showed the man lots of photographs until he saw one that finally satisfied his ego. Then the investment banker carelessly dropped the elk's head and strutted proudly back towards the campsite with the lead guide. The other guides then used rope pulleys tied off to a nearby tree branch to hoist this massive animal into the air before they positioned me under it and lowered the body onto my back.

"As they went to tie the animal down, I suddenly visualized the most intense pain I could ever imagine, heard again the sound of the three shots, and saw images of a young doe and two yearlings looking back at me, terrified, before leaping through the brush.

"Then I heard it in my mind as clear as if you said it to me right now. 'Help me.'

"I looked back at the face of the elk, dangling close to my withers, and could see that there was still life in his eyes. I heard his mouth suck in a last breath of air.

"I took off with the elk only partially tied to my back and hurled down the path with his body bouncing loose from its binds while his antlers tore into the flesh of my hindquarters with each stride. Ahead of me I spotted the investment banker and the lead guide walking side-by-side, each smoking a large cigar, but I didn't slow down. I watched their terrified faces as they leapt off opposite sides of the path and felt the now dead elk being thrown free off my back. It flew towards the investment banker as he scrambled through the brush to avoid being crushed. I didn't wait to see the impact, but I felt the little man's fear, and the excruciating pain he suffered as the elk rolled over his leg, and that was enough. I ran all the way down the mountain back to the ranch.

"That night another trailer came for me. This time it took me to a 'slaughter auction.'"

Gina gasped. Okay, I'm lying, I gasped.

Claire looked at us both for a moment, gauging our response, then shook her head and continued.

"I won't bore you with the gruesome details of the horrors that awaited the less fortunate animals that were sharing the ring with me that night. Suffice it to say, that if it wasn't for sweet Mrs. Reynolds buying me based upon the poundage of my gross weight, I would have joined them all at an *abattoire* in Canada and ended up in pieces in some exotic butcher shop in Saskatoon."

"Thank God for old Mrs. Reynolds!" Gina said.

"But how did you know I would even come back for you this morning?" I asked.

"How do I explain this?" Claire said. "All animals share their thoughts with their own kind freely, which is why you see a herd of animals all break into a run simultaneously at the first sign of danger, or see a school of fish suddenly all change direction at once while swimming. Otherwise, most animals keep their thoughts to themselves—except dogs, who are an open book and will pretty much communicate with anything that will listen. No offense, Blue," Claire said, looking down where she lay by Gina's feet. Blue wagged her tail in response.

"If I focus hard enough, I can pick up on pretty much anything's thoughts. So since I have been standing mostly alone in Mrs. Reynolds farm for about five years now, and really alone for the past year since she fell and broke her hip, I spent most of that time scanning the airwaves to see what I could pick up, just to keep the boredom from killing me. As I said, most animals like to keep to themselves, but humans are worse than dogs. Their minds are always on, even when they're sleeping."

Claire took a break to grab another mouthful of hay and washed it down with another long draw of water from the trough. Then she walked over and stood right before me.

"Your mind, Jimmy, is the busiest mind I have ever encountered. It's like the noisiest neighbor in an apartment complex. Oh yes, I learned about them from a group of hunters from Los Angeles. Anyway, I heard your thoughts from the moment you arrived in Colorado. And thanks to Gina thinking about how she was going to get you healthy as she ran past me the first couple of days, I knew it was just a matter of time before you crossed my path.

"Mrs. Reynolds' passing just accelerated my need to make it all happen. But she gave me enough of a heads-up beforehand to allow me to figure out my next move. She also made sure that one of the neighbors she was friends with, Pam Ervin, would come by each day and take care of me until the niece closed up shop.

Claire took another moment to gather her thoughts.

"I've been listening in on little Lucian—that boy down the road—since he was a yearling. What a character, letting the air out of those tires." Claire made that funny laughing sound again.

"He's been coming by every morning to talk with me since he learned how to ride his two-wheeler. But I never showed my hand because I didn't want to frighten him, so I just stood there and listened to his little kid problems—being the youngest, living on hand-me-downs, you know what I mean.

"The first day you walked the circuit Jimmy, I could see that you were able to release all the mental crap that had landed you here—talk about Goodfellas—and for the first day in a very long time you felt relaxed. I could see in your mind that you felt good, and that you planned to be back again the next day. I just needed to get myself all tangled up in that fence the next morning. When I saw the image of Lucian riding my way and the image of you leaving the house the next morning, I made my move, and the rest, as you humans like to say, is history."

I was impressed with this wise ass, but not totally convinced.

"What if I couldn't get that redneck to make a deal?" I asked her. "What would you have done then?"

Claire thought a moment before responding, "I would have waited for the right moment up on that next mountain and crushed that—is 'fat bastard' the right term—under a log." She stood there a moment more to let the thought sink in. "I'm no killer, but I ain't ever going back to the slaughterhouse."

Claire walked past us to the doorway of the barn and then turned back to us.

"Listen, if you don't mind, I'd like to go mark my new territory." As she walked out of view, around the bend towards the back gate, she called out behind her, "if I need anything else, I'll come knocking."

Blue looked up at Gina and then ran out after Claire. Gina took a long, deep breath and then slowly released it through her clenched teeth with a slight whooshing sound. She stood up and shook out her arms and legs as if dispelling the horror of the story we had just heard.

"I'm going for a run," she said. "Have a strong cup of coffee waiting for me, will ya?"

CHAPTER TWENTY-FIVE
A PENNY FOR YOUR NUMBERS

I was sitting in my living room, thinking about Claire's story while I waited for Gina to return from her run with Blue. I understood what it was like to be ripped away from those you love, but with me it was my own fault, so I had it coming. And when it was all said and done, I always had Gina by my side, even in my darkest moments, so I was never alone. Claire had been through hell, from a very tender age. Up until now, the only humans who had ever shown her any love were two little girls and a dead old lady. I wondered where those two not-so-little girls were now.

I thought about the redneck I had dealt with whom looked upon Claire as just some object to be tossed upon the butcher block when all other uses for her had been spent. Then I thought about all the other animals I had had contact with during my life, those I loved as pets, and those I had seen since I had arrived in Colorado. I realized that each of them, from the largest to the smallest, were sentient beings on this earth, and that their lives deserved the same respect and protection as any human did. I thought about all of those animals that give birth to their young, which they love as dearly as any human parent can love its child, solely for the inevitable experience of a frightening death at the end of a chute in a slaughterhouse. And why? So that mankind can continue to enjoy the taste of their flesh, or organs, or to wear their skins, or feathers, or fur as an accessory. The worst thing for me was my knowledge that I was a lifetime offender. I vowed to change that.

At that moment I heard pounding, like a sledgehammer on concrete. It seemed to be coming from below me. I grabbed my gun and quietly descended the stairs. When I reached the bottom landing, the pounding started again. As I cautiously peaked around the corner of the landing, I saw Claire standing at the large glass sliding doors, the steam from her nostrils causing the glass to fog around her face. Then I heard the sound again and looked down and saw that she was pounding the cement pad directly outside the doorway with her front right hoof. I was happy she hadn't tried knocking on the glass door.

I put the gun down on the closest counter. As I approached the door, I could see that Claire was studying herself in the outside reflection of the tempered glass. She let out a loud whinny and stepped back a few steps when I quickly slid the glass door open.

"Oh good," she said, regaining her composure when she saw me. "I wasn't sure if you heard me knocking."

She spun her body in a circle and then returned to the doorway.

"Listen," she continued, "two things. If you are going to throw the bolts on any of the gates, you need to tie a piece of rope on them so I can grab at them with my teeth, or I won't be able to open them. The one going from here directly into the back is closed."

I walked past her and out into the yard and over to the offending gate. I noticed that the earth muffled the sounds of her hoofs as she walked behind me. I wedged the gate open on the high grass. I stood at its opening and gazed out onto the back property; I saw that Claire had already eaten a small section of the grass around the other back gate.

"I was going to trim that all down for you," I said, pointing towards the back.

"Don't bother," Claire said. "No use eating dried hay when I can get it fresh every morning. That will do me until the fall."

"What about the snakes?" I said.

"They know to stay clear of these hooves," Claire said, lifting her right one and stomping down hard for emphasis. While it didn't have the same auditory effect as knocking on concrete, I could still feel its power on the earth beside me.

"Okay," I said, suddenly realizing just how weirdly comfortable my conversation with this mule was now feeling. I also realized how isolated my life had become, having gone from decades of a New York reality wherein I was compelled to interact with hundreds of people a day, good, bad, or indifferent, to a life on Mars. Here, any extended conversations were limited to those with my one-and-only, when she wasn't out exploring, and now with the occasional exchange with my new mission control consisting of an eccentric circle of Lenahan, Helen and Bobbi, and even Everett and Michelle. Oddly, I preferred my present, boiled-down version of society.

However, with Claire in the mix, I had really crossed the rainbow.

"Now pay attention, Jimmy. So you see where that dip in the locking bolt you just slid on the gate," Claire said pointing with her nose, "just tie a piece of rope there, just a few inches long, and put a good knot in it so I can grab it with my teeth." She leaned in closer and mimed the movement to show me how she would do it.

"Mrs. Reynolds taught me," Claire said proudly, "so she didn't have to worry about getting up every morning to let me out of my stall. Or in case there was an emergency during the night."

"Did she know about?" I asked, tapping my lips with my index finger.

"Oh yeah," Claire said. "After all, she saved my life."

"And she never told anyone else?" I continued.

"Her mind was an open book," Claire said. "I could see that she wasn't a fan of most people and kept to herself. She once told me that she never met an animal that disappointed her, but with people it was a fifty-fifty crapshoot. So no, she never told anyone."

"Not even the niece that just sold off her place?" I asked.

"Funny thing that," Claire responded. "I listened in on her thoughts every day for five years and never once did this 'niece' cross her mind."

Claire stopped and studied me for a second.

"That's a good one!" Claire said suddenly. "A laughing heir."

I smiled. It was a term we lawyers used to describe the lowest form of descendants that come crawling out of the woodwork when an old, distant relative dies, looking to cash in on their estate and laughing all the way to the bank with money they didn't deserve. Mrs. Reynolds' niece was a classic example.

"So how deep can you get into my head?" I asked her.

"If it's in your memory, I can get to it," Claire answered. "But first it has to surface in a present thought, so I can follow it down the rabbit hole."

"Take Gina, for instance," Claire continued. "That lady lives every day in the moment. She deals with today's problems and moves on. She never carries any baggage or worries about what could have been. No regrets. So, I couldn't even tell you her mother's name."

"Delores," I answered. I hadn't thought about her since she had passed thirty years ago, and with good reason.

"Oh, there she is," Claire said. "Not a big fan of yours, I see."

I laughed.

"Now you, on the other hand," Claire said, "that mind of yours is an absolute warren. Everything you do in life is connected to your past. Absolutely everything. You don't take one step forward without looking two steps backward. So, there's nothing I can't get to. I can tell you where both sets of your grandparents were born in Ireland. But that would be showing off."

I suddenly thought about my life with Valachi. Claire's nose wrinkled up like she had just smelled shit.

"Go easy on yourself. Nobody's perfect," Claire said solemnly, "especially you. You've made a lot of mistakes, but you've never intentionally hurt anyone. From where I'm standing, you are better than most. Trust me, I've seen the worst of them. Let it go."

That tiny bit of equine absolution was more comforting than anything I had ever gotten in a Catholic confessional.

"Weren't you ever afraid someone would let it slip?" I asked.

"And what? Sound like a crazy person?" Claire responded. "No one can make me speak unless I want to."

I thought about that for a moment and realized she was right. Then I remembered something from before.

"Two things," I said. "When you came to the door, you said you had two things to tell me."

Claire must have been replaying my memory.

"Now that's embarrassing," she said. "Didn't realize you could see me through the doorway. I thought it was a mirror." She did that funny laughing sound.

"But you did say two things," I said.

"That's right," Claire said, back in the moment. "The second thing was about those friends of yours, Everett and Michelle."

"What about them?" I asked, suddenly concerned.

"When I listen to their minds, all I get is numbers. Not one word. So, I can't understand what they're saying," Claire said. "And," she added, "they can communicate with each other with just their minds, like the animals."

CHAPTER TWENTY-SIX
GREEKS BEARING GIFTS

Just then Blue came running out to greet us and I turned and saw Gina on the back deck, stretching on its railing. I returned Gina's wave before turning back to Claire. I was about to say something when she cut me off.

"Yeah, then there's the silver pocket thingy, space junk collection and model spaceship. Not sure what any of those things are but I see you're wondering about them," Claire said. "I'll keep tabs on those two and I'll let you know if I get anything more."

Claire turned and headed down the hill towards the back-soccer field picking up speed until she was cantering. Blue took off after her. I watched them enjoying their race through the high grass for a moment before turning back to the house.

By the time I got inside Gina was already in the shower. I was about to mention my latest conversation about Everett and Michelle, when my Ring chime went off, followed by the sound of the front doorbell. I waited a moment for the image to come up on my phone.

"Somebody's at the front door!" Gina screamed over the running water, not knowing I was right outside the bathroom door.

As the image cleared, I saw Helen standing on my porch waiting patiently. She turned and stared at Jack the Spruce, then looked down at the base of the tree-trunk. She was carrying two insulated bags that were filled to the top.

"I'll be right there," I called out through the intercom.

I quickly descended the stairs and opened the door.

"Here, take these," she said, handing the bags to me. "I've got another one in the car."

She turned and headed back out to the driveway. There sat a beautiful candy apple red, vintage Mercedes Benz 300 SL roadster. Its white rag top canopy was down, and I could see its white leather seats. Helen went around to the trunk and removed another insulated bag and a moment later passed me and entered the house as I stood holding the door. The bags all smelled delicious.

"Nice place," she said as she entered the kitchen area. "Love that tree out there, and the fairy door at its base."

My face disclosed that I didn't know what she was talking about, so she led me to the front window and pointed to the base of the tree. Sure enough, there was a small, ceramic door embedded in Jack's base. I guess I was so engaged by the face on the tree, I never looked down at its base. A common male mistake. I made a mental note to check it out later.

Helen was back in the kitchen unpacking her three bags. Each new item carried its own vibrant aroma. Before I could say anything, Helen looked past me and said, "Hi, I'm Helen!"

Gina walked past me, her hair in a towel, and went over to Helen and gave her a hug.

"Hi Helen, I'm Gina. Jimmy's told me all about The Oracle," Gina picked up a couple of the food containers. "What have you brought us; it smells delicious."

"Well, Bobbi wanted to come and meet the mule," Helen said. "And today The Oracle is closed. So, I just packed up a light lunch and figured we'd stop by."

"We?" I said, looking around.

"Oh yeah," Helen said. "Bobbi and Eddie went straight to your back area. Hope you don't mind, but Bobbi can be insistent that way."

I walked out the back deck and spotted Bobbi and her brother standing out in the back field with Claire and Blue. Bobbi, dressed in a blue-jeans' ensemble, was standing in front of Claire stroking her muzzle and talking to her. Her brother, Eddie, was brushing Claire.

Eddie wasn't much taller than Bobbi. He was also outfitted in a worn blue-jeans outfit with a faded 80s band T-shirt. He was slim and wiry looking and wore his long grey hair tied in a ponytail. He had a wispy, almost Asian, grey beard that extended to the middle of his chest. I wondered how he dealt with the beard when he was cooking over the hot stove at The Oracle.

I left Helen and Gina to work out the dining arrangements and headed out back. When I got within fifteen feet of the group, Bobbi and Claire both looked over at me and said simultaneously:

"She's great!"

I wanted to shout, "Jinx, you owe me a coke," but then Bobbi turned back to Claire and shrieked.

"Holy shit! You can talk too?!"

Bobbi turned back to me. "Your brothers didn't mention this!" Then back to Claire. "Ms. Claire Voyyyy-Aauunttttt! You are utterly amazing!"

"Why thank you, Ms. Bobbi Angelini," Claire replied in equally dramatic fashion.

"Amazing is the understatement of the century!" Eddie added. "And this is coming from a guy who grew up around the definition of 'amazing,'" he nodded towards Bobbi.

I almost had forgotten he was there. I extended my hand.

"I'm sorry. We didn't get to meet at The Oracle. I'm Jimmy."

Eddie took it and gave it a firm shake. I noticed an intricate military tattoo with the word 'Ranger' at the top on his forearm.

"Eddie Allison," he replied. "Bobbi's older brother. Angelini is her stage name."

He went back to carefully grooming Claire.

"I hope you don't mind," he added. "I grabbed a brush out of the barn. I just love being around horses."

"That's mule, Eddie," Claire added.

I waved her off. "Not a problem."

"Why am I the only one excited by all of this?!" Bobbi shouted.

"In all fairness, Jimmy has already had a few days to get used to it," Claire responded. "But Eddie here is a bit of a surprise. Oh wait, I get it now," Claire added, tuning in, "if half the images of growing up with Bobbi in Eddie's head are true, a talking mule is just another day at the office."

Claire looked at Bobbi. "So, you can talk to the dead!"

Bobbi nodded.

"Animals too?" Claire asked.

Bobbi again nodded.

"Girl, we gotta talk," Claire said, "but first, Gina's telling me that lunch is served."

I looked up at the house and, right on cue, Gina appeared on the deck, waving us in.

"I'm going to stay out here with Claire, if you don't mind," Eddie said. "I was picking the whole time I was preparing that meal."

Bobbi and I returned to the house, leaving Eddie, Blue and Claire grooming away in the soccer field. As we walked along, I asked her, "Was that true about the animals?"

"Absolutely," Bobbi replied. "Sometimes when I'm reading someone, a pet will come through and I won't even realize it's a pet until the client tells me after the reading is over."

"So was Claire communicating with you in your shorthand?"

"No, it was a clear conversation," she said. "Pure, straight up, telepathy. I've only had that happen once or twice before, and that was only with other psychics in my family."

"I could see she's a lot smarter than most people I deal with," Bobbi laughed. "And once she let me into her mind, I was seeing the images all replaying through her eyes," Bobbi added, pensively. "Such pain."

"Yeah," I responded, "she shared a little of it with me and Gina. But we did it the old-fashioned way, assuming you consider talking to a mule the old-fashioned way."

We both laughed at that.

"Welcome to the new normal," Bobbi said with a wink as we reached the house.

Inside, Helen and Gina had laid out the spread on our dining room table. The center piece was a large salad.

"What's all this?" I asked.

"Bobbi told me your brothers said you were, as they put it, 'turning into a pussy vegetarian,'" Helen said.

Bobbi confirmed it with a nod. "So, I had Eddie make you some of our best Greek vegetarian dishes."

"This is Horiatiki," Helen said, pointing to the salad. "Tomatoes, olives, cucumbers, onions and some feta cheese. A little salt, oregano, olive oil, vinegar and a dash of lemon juice and viola."

"Bring on the Briam!" Bobbi said, grabbing a plate and ladling a serving of a chunky vegetable dish, "and the Spanakopita!" She placed what resembled an egg roll on her plate.

"And don't forget to try the Dolmades!" Helen added. She grabbed a plate and started adding servings from every platter, then handed it to me. "Fage!"

I picked up the little bag of rice wrapped in a leaf and popped it in my mouth. It was delicious.

There is nothing that enhances the flavor of a meal more than sharing it with friends in your home. As good as the Belgian waffles were at The Oracle, everything Helen served us was even better. After all the crap she had been through on my account, it was fun to see Gina talking and laughing with Helen and Bobbi throughout dinner like best friends.

Eddie arrived just as we were clearing off the table. He grabbed one of the empty containers from the recycle bin and began filling it with some leftovers.

Helen said, apologetically, "Eddie, they told me you weren't hungry!"

"I'm not," he said, "but when Claire got a peak at what I prepared today, she sent me inside to get her some." He laughed.

"Don't worry," he added. "I'll be right back for some coffee and Diples."

As we sat around devouring the last of the Baklava, I asked Helen how she ended up in Hygiene.

"Same way you ended up in Berthoud," she replied.

"Lenny?" Gina asked.

"I used to work for my Uncle Gus at a jewelry store just outside Las Vegas," Helen began. "Gus, God bless his soul, was the only one in my family who accepted me for who I am. The rest of them, the restaurateurs, all turned their back on me."

"Gus still comes through for her in every reading!" Bobbi added. "As a matter of fact, that's how we met."

"Anyway," Helen said patiently, "One day, just before closing, these two young Latinos came in with shotguns. They had gang tattoos on their faces. They didn't give a shit; they blew the buzzer lock right off the door and walked in like they owned the place. Gus told them to take what they wanted from the display cases and go. But they also wanted what was in the safe, and when Gus didn't move fast enough, one of them shot him. And then the other one shot me."

"But they didn't know what a tough son-of-a-bitch my Helen is!" Bobbi added proudly.

Helen pulled the opening at the top of her shirt over just far enough to show us the dimpled circular scar right above her heart.

"The gunshot nicked my aorta and I died on the table," Helen continued. "Uncle Gus met me on the other side and told me I had to go back and nail those two pricks for him."

"He's since evolved," Bobbi added with a wink.

"When I finally recovered, I picked the two assholes out from the LVPD catalogue of known MS-13 gang members," Helen said. "The cops called them boomerangs. Seems they had both been deported back to El Salvador multiple times but kept coming back. This last time they settled in Las Vegas."

"The cops told me that I could put them away for good if I testified at trial, but that the gang had already posted a bounty on my head," Helen said. "When I told them I would do it anyway, they offered me WITSEC. I had nothing left holding me in Las Vegas, so I figured why not?"

"They both got life without parole!" Bobbi said.

"Five years ago, Lenny met me at the airport and here we are," Helen said.

"Gus' insurance money paid for The Oracle!" Bobbi added. "Of course, the government laundered it for her."

"God bless you Gus," Helen said, raising her coffee cup in a toast. We all did the same.

"And then Helen came for a reading in the Mystical Shop I worked at on Pearl Street in Boulder, and before I knew what hit me, I was shacking-up in Hygiene," Bobbi said with a laugh, "later on, Eddie joined us."

"Helen taught me my way around the kitchen," Eddie said. "Never had bad food at a Greek diner. Now I know why."

"So, what do you know about Lenahan?" Gina asked. "He seems a little sad."

"He told me he came here from D.C., after his wife divorced him," I mentioned.

"That's only half the story," Bobbi said in her best gossipy tone, leaning in conspiratorially.

"Bobbi," Helen said, "that was never proven."

"Doesn't need to be," Bobbi said, "I got it from the guy he killed."

"He killed a guy?" Gina asked, her jaw dropping open.

"Yes," Bobbi continued. "He was working a detail back in D.C. protecting a wealthy pedophile who used to take all his high powered pedo-friends on trips on his private jet to his private island somewhere off South America, where they would get up to all kinds of bad shit with kids. I needed a hot shower after that visitation."

Helen turned to Bobbi and said sternly, "I warned you not to go digging into Lenny's shit."

"Why protect a pedophile?" I asked, trying to diffuse the situation.

"Because somehow the witness got nailed in a government sting, so he immediately flipped on some of his most powerful clients," Bobbi responded. "The night after the pedo testified against his pedo-friends, Lenny got assigned the midnight detail to keep him alive until he could be fully processed through WITSEC," Bobbi continued. "He was still facing some jail time, but it was in protective custody in club fed, and nothing like what faced him if he didn't flip."

"They were staying in a top floor suite in one of those posh hotels in D.C. when the witness took a header out of the thirtieth-story window," Helen said. "Lenny said he jumped."

"Well the dead guy told me he got a ten finger lift off from Lenny." Bobbi added. "Though to give the shit his due, he knew he had it coming."

"Either way, the Washington elite were quite happy with the outcome, given the rumors that more names were dropping, so there was no real investigation," Helen said. "But the bosses at the U.S. Marshall's office needed to make an example out of Lenny, so they offered him the option—Northern Colorado or termination."

"Poor bastard. When he got the push, his wife left him," Bobbi said, then added, resignedly, "she was bitch anyway. Karma took care of her."

"She died of cancer two years ago," Helen said. "Lenny tried not to show it, but I could tell he was devastated."

Bobbi suddenly stood up.

"Holy shit?" Bobbi said, her face showing her amazement. "Claire just asked me if we have any more of those Diples Eddie was raving about. And she is showing me that she's standing outside the back door."

I heard the pounding of hoof on cement, grabbed the last Diples from the plate and headed downstairs.

CHAPTER TWENTY-SEVEN
SECRETS SHARED

Processing my 'New Normal,' as Bobbi put it, had turned my already busy mind into modern day Manhattan—the subway kept running from end to end and all points in between, 24/7, and the lights never went out. Real sleep became a steadily diminishing luxury.

When I awoke that morning, July's full moon had not yet reached its apex. I left Gina sharing her softly snoring sonata with Blue in our king-sized bed and slipped down to the kitchen to surrender any chance of sleep to a strong cup of coffee and that last piece of Baklava. The touch of the cool evening air on my skin as I ventured out onto my back deck drove the last vestiges of sleep from my eyes.

The moonlight bathed my property in a luminescent pale glimmer. I scanned the area, sighting seriatim each of its landmarks. The pond was an irregular silver mirror, defiantly reflecting the moonlight back at its source. Its resident ducks were nowhere to be seen—tucked away sleeping safely somewhere in the marsh grass on my neighbor's property. At its farthest end I could see a young fox, its normally vibrant red coat muted in the moonlight, slipping silently through the fence-line to sip from the pond's revitalizing waters, before disappearing back into the high grass from whence it came.

Over in the center of the back property, at the black box rising on its post from the burial mound, tiny black forms dropped in free-fall like lemming base-jumpers until their wing suits opened a few feet from the ground. They then ascended skyward in erratic patterns, before heading out over my neighbor's marshland to feast on the summer fattened mosquitos. Others returned to the roost, landing awkwardly at its base and scurrying up the post into its darkness. I could barely make out their high-pitched call to arms. Blood in, blood out.

Geppetto's studio stood quietly like a ghost in its far-off corner, its whirligig standing guard with a slow and deliberate rotation in the soft night breeze.

Finally, I gazed over at the small barn in the side paddock and saw no sign of movement. The angle of the moonlight offered no incursion to the pitch-black interior of the barn, except for a tiny beam of moonlight that passed through the hole in the roof, and I could discern no sounds coming from within. For a moment, I wondered if I had dreamt the existence of everything related to Claire.

I exited the deck from the western side of the house directly onto the highest point of the property then descended and crossed the backyard area eastward towards Claire's side paddock. Rather than disturb the silence by the clang of the sliding metal bolt to open the gate, I climbed over the fence and into the paddock. I could see no sign of Claire.

I circled behind the barn to see if she was there, but only found piles of mule dung, and laughed to myself at the thought that she had selected this location because it offered her some semblance of privacy, like a bathroom stall. As I came back around to the front of the barn and approached the door, Claire came flying out from the shadows within and would have trampled me had she not nimbly veered to my right at the last second. I never heard her coming.

"Jesus Fucking Christ!" I shouted in full Bronx mode, not caring if my words would be carried by the soft but steady wind along the valley floor through my nearest neighbors' open windows.

"Sorry about that Jimmy," Claire responded as she looped around in a circle and returned to where I was standing, frozen in place. "I was woken out of a dead sleep in the back corner of the stall when I heard something moving outside my crib. I didn't have time to scan to see who it was and just reacted."

"I almost reacted in my pants!" I responded, fighting to regain my composure.

Claire stood there for a moment watching me, gathering the image I had formed in my head, and then she began that strange laughing sound.

"Very funny, very funny," I said, surrendering a smile.

"You should have seen your face," Claire said between laughs. "You humans really have such expressive faces, and yours was priceless!"

"Okay, okay, I'm glad I amuse you," I said.

Claire suddenly stopped laughing. Her withers stiffened and her chest jutted out. Her ears began adjusting their positions independently like an Eagle Scout performing semaphore.

"I'm picking up Everett and Michelle," Claire said. "Their minds are chatting away to each other in that numerical code."

Claire slowly rotated a full 360 degrees, her ears twitching away.

"They're watching us," she said, suddenly breaking at full gallop towards Geppetto's Studio. "There they go!" she shouted behind her.

I knew that if that were Michelle and Everett back there, they would have to circle around at least a half mile to reach their property without crossing back across mine. I turned and ran in the opposite direction towards the front road that connected our two driveways, hoping to head them off. By the time I reached the back end of my driveway by the side of my house, I saw two small blurred figures racing past my property down the road towards Everett and Michelle's. They were traveling so fast I couldn't make out any individual characteristics, or even the sex of the figures, just two continuous blurs silently fleeing faster than a crotch-rocket motorcycle. Before I had passed through my side gate, they were gone.

A month ago, I would have freaked out at what I had just witnessed, but my time in Berthoud had desensitized me to the blurring of the lines between reality and the realm of the remarkable. I went into lawyer mode.

I may not have been able to pick them out of a line-up, but there was enough circumstantial evidence for me to believe that it was Everett and Michelle that just broke the human land-speed record. I ran through every interaction I had with them, what Gina had described about Michelle, and then what Claire had described about their thought process. There was nothing human about them.

Claire had come up to the front gate and met me as I returned.

"I didn't get a clear look at them either," Claire said, reading my thoughts. "They disappeared down the back gulley and headed east towards the county road before I got back there."

Claire turned and walked beside me down the hill.

"But given everything you know," Claire said, "and I recognized the chatter. Zeros and Ones. It was them."

"Do you think they saw us talking?" I asked.

"Don't know," Claire said. "Maybe. But they have to know that we saw them."

I'd been around enough guilty people in my life to know how dangerous they can become once they think they've been found out. I also knew that I had too many secrets to continue to ignore this risk to my and Gina's safety. And Claire's secret was for her to share, not anyone's to take.

I went inside and got my gun.

Five minutes later, I climbed over Everett and Michelle's fence and crossed the grass, staying close to the trees to avoid being spotted from inside their house. The moonlight wasn't helping, but you play the cards you are dealt and hope for the best.

I circled around to a spot on the west side of the house where I knew from my last visit, I could find a window that would let me see into their living room and kitchen. A faint glow, a night light perhaps, could be seen coming from inside. As I peeked over the sill, I could see the forms of Everett and Michelle sitting motionless in their recliners in the far corner of the living room. I couldn't tell if they were speaking with each other, or even if they were awake. But I was sure that they certainly weren't where the rest of the locals were at this hour. In bed.

The brilliant flash from inside instantly blinded me, and I dropped to the ground struggling to regain my sight. When I had recovered enough to get my bearings, my fight-or-flight reflex kicked in and I turned back in the direction of the road, where Everett and Michelle were standing, blocking my path. Everett was holding that shiny little gadget in his hand, and it was pointed in my direction.

"I think you need to come inside," Everett said.

I reached for my gun but only found an empty holster. I was never going to be a gunslinger.

Michelle held up my gun. She removed the magazine and with one hand flipped out the shells with a dexterity that would have shamed Lenahan. Then she nimbly reinserted the magazine and tossed me the gun. I holstered the now useless paperweight.

"Please," Everett said, gesturing towards the back building. "We really need to talk."

We walked in silence through their oasis, Everett leading the way and Michelle walking behind me. I thought for a New York second about making a run for it, but then recalled the blur. I hoped that Claire was getting all of this. As we entered Everett's man-cave, Michelle gestured to a chair and I sat down. Everett walked over to the bar area and poured a couple of tumblers of single malt, neat. He also poured a Bordeaux glass of Cabernet Sauvignon. He handed me one of the tumblers and Michelle the wine. Then he lifted his own tumbler for a toast.

"To secrets shared!" Everett said.

CHAPTER TWENTY-EIGHT
MY FAVORITE MARTIANS

"Let us first apologize," Everett began. "We didn't mean to spy like that. It's just that we thought you and Gina were interesting enough, given your colorful backgrounds, but we were fascinated by Claire."

"You see," Michelle added, after sipping some wine, "we've been around a long time, and this was the first equine we've come across that could actually speak."

"I first caught wind of it when I arrived that morning at the Reynolds' farm," Everett continued. "I overheard little Lucian talking to her through the back door of the trailer."

He laughed. "It was actually Claire that told Lucian to let the air out of the tires."

Michelle removed a Rasta-sized blunt from her pocket and fired it up. She held that first toke for a couple of seconds before slowly releasing the sweet-scented smoke into the room.

"You see, I insisted that we sneak around your place to see if we could catch her in the act tonight," Michelle said, the remnants of smoke trailing from her nostrils. "Once we spotted you walking towards her barn, we snuck up as close as we could in the grass to see what would happen."

Michelle took another hit on the joint.

"You should have seen your face when she leapt out at you!" Michelle said, breaking into a stoner's laugh. "It took all we had not to laugh. Who could have guessed that she could also scan our minds?"

"We really never expected to get caught out like that," Everett added, walking over and taking the joint from Michelle.

"Don't take this personally," Michelle continued, "but we were surprised you were smart enough to try to cut us off at the pass like that." She laughed, the weed having the appropriate effect.

"That's when we realized that you were going to force us to deal with this sooner rather than later," Everett said. "So, sooner it is."

I hadn't escaped all the bullshit back east just to be taken out but a couple of weird stoner hobbits in the middle of no-where. I went to reach for the closest lamp but before my free hand moved an inch, Michelle had crossed the room and grabbed my wrist with the force of a man far stronger than me. I almost dropped my scotch.

"Relax, Jimmy," she said softly, "we're not going to hurt you."

I winced and stared at my wrist.

"Well," she laughed, as she gently released her grip. "Not intentionally."

I consumed the scotch in one gulp and placed the empty glass on a side table, using my now free hand to rub the now freed wrist.

Everett walked over by the seventy-inch flat screen by the wall and started to rummage through some drawers in the countertop below it. Michelle watched him fumbling for a few more moments and then crossed the room in one quick leap, opened a separate drawer, withdrew the coolest looking remote I ever saw and handed it to him. Then she snatched the blunt from his lips and was back beside me, sitting on the arm of my chair. I don't think there was time for the weed to leave a smoke trail. She offered me a hit, but I waved her off. The scotch was beginning to take effect.

Everett pressed a few buttons and the screen came alive with three-dimensional images of star formations.

"Centaurus," I said, the scotch loosening my lips as I pointed to the screen, "Chiron the Centaur."

"Very good, Jimmy," Everett said in his best Mr. Chips impersonation. "Now can you tell me the names of these stars in that formation?"

Unfortunately, I had just shot my load when it came to astronomy. I knew the names of most of the formations because of my childhood love of the legends of the Greek gods. But there were just too many fucking stars in each of those formations for me to want to spend that much time trying to memorize them.

"That was really great scotch," I said, waving the empty glass. I didn't even feel it leave my hand before I realized that it was replaced half full. Nor did I see Michelle refill it. I took another large sip. Single malt really was smoother. It even took the edge off the supernatural.

The images on the screen changed and there was a vibrant, close image of a sun.

"I've watched every Cosmos show from Carl Sagan to Neil deGrasse Tyson, and I've never seen any images as clear as this one."

"That's because you don't have direct access to the Hubble telescope," Everett said, gesturing to the screen with his fancy remote.

I looked over at Everett's space junk collection and focused on the piece marked Hubble.

"And that's not your sun," Michelle added. "It's ours."

"You're looking at what your scientists call 'Proxima Centauri.'" Everett said.

"Our planet circles that star," Michelle said, a touch of melancholy in her voice. "You can't even see it from Colorado."

Your scientists call it 'Proxima Centauri b,'" Everett said.

I gulped the rest of my second scotch.

"I'm going to really need another one of these," I said, my speech slurring just a touch.

Just like before, it reappeared refilled.

"It's a lot like here," Everett said. "A bit larger, and it only takes us about a dozen days to circle our sun."

"It's beautiful," Michelle said, in full buzz mode. "I miss it."

"Why did you come here then?" I asked her.

"We had to babysit you guys," she said, and started to giggle. She removed a second blunt from her pocket and ignited it, the first flame dancing inches above its tip.

"We were part of an expedition sent here in the 1940s," Everett said. "Right after you went nuclear."

It might have been the scotch, but this was getting interesting.

"You're not trying to take over the world, are you?" I asked, this time seriously.

Everett and Michelle laughed in unison.

"No, we're just trying to keep you from blowing it up." Michelle laughed. "And once you got into space, to keep from ever blowing us up."

"It was my job to make sure your satellites and telescopes didn't see or hear anything we didn't want them to," Everett added. "In each case I replaced just enough of each one's technology to accomplish that." Then pointing to his wall, "or if I couldn't, I just rendered it completely useless. However, as I just showed you, I kept Hubble on-line for my own use."

"Those are some of his mementos," Michelle said, nodding towards the wall.

"You didn't crash the space station, did you?" I said, pointing to the first one.

"No," Everett said, laughing. "That went down all on its own. It surprised me it stayed up for as long as it did. I just grabbed a piece of it before it crashed."

"But how did you do all of that?" I asked.

"Wormholes," Everett said.

"In that!" Michelle pointed at the model ship.

"The model?" I asked.

"That is our ship!" Michelle said.

I had instant images of Wonderland, with Everett and Michelle eating Alice's magic mushrooms to shrink down to the size of their ship. I started doing that finger thumb measurement thing before my eye, going back and forth between Everett to the spaceship, adjusting the space each time. Boy that scotch was good.

Everett took the silver thing out of his pocket, placed the spaceship on the floor and then zapped it for a second with a green light from the silver thing. The ship instantly grew to the size of a football. Its details became much clearer. Everett then zapped the ship with a red light, and it returned to its tiny scale size and carefully returned it to its spot on the wall.

"At its full operational size, it's about as large as a luxury RV," Everett said. I finished the last of my scotch. My head was really beginning to spin.

"Does that little silver thing work on everything?" I asked, giggling. "Because I always wanted to be seven feet tall."

"Theoretically, it's possible, but I've only used mine to shrink things down and return them to their original size," Everett said. "Although the laws of biomechanics and gravity would probably create serious problems if you were expanded beyond the size your earth's physics has dictated for you. The bone density of your body's skeleton most likely couldn't handle the load. You'd be crippled in a week."

I was never much of a science-guy, and I was hitting the limit on what I could wrap my head around, even without the heavenly scotch actively destroying my brain cells.

"Anyone else out there we need to worry about?" I asked. "Or is it just you guys?"

Everett thought about it for a moment. "Actually, one of your scientists, a radio astronomer named Frank Drake got it right back in 1961."

"His equation was pretty awesome," Michelle added, "especially for a human!" She took another big hit on her blunt. "Gave the rest of us hope."

"Drake figured that there are about fifty-thousand civilizations just in this galaxy alone," Everett continued. "He was right on the money."

"Yeah," Michelle chimed in as she released a cloud of smoke into the air, "but only a few of them have bothered with this planet."

"We were the closest to mankind in appearance and sensibility, and had been coming here for centuries, so the—shit, how do I phrase this—the galactic federation decided that we should take the lead in bringing you guys along until you were ready to join with the rest of the galaxy," Everett said.

"There's a Galactic Federation?" I mumbled, "like in Doctor Who?"

"You guys kill me," Everett said. "Every analogy is to film or television."

"Well if we must go down that path, then it's more like the one in Star Wars," Michelle added.

I looked out the window and saw the night sky shifting into twilight. My mind was becoming truly overwhelmed at all that I was hearing, and the last semblance of functioning lawyer in me wanted to nail down the more pressing issues that brought me here. I downed the last of my scotch and made my move.

"So here we are, me with my secret talking mule and you a couple of secret extraterrestrial babysitters," I said, more slurred than I would have liked. "Where does that leave us?"

"Oh, you have far more to hide than just Claire," Michelle replied. "We also enjoyed your colorful 'family' background, Mr. McCarthy."

The sound of my real name struck me like a hammer.

"How the fuck—"

"We just showed you how we can manipulate physics," Michelle cut me off. "And you're surprised we can hack into your government files?"

I've handled enough negotiations to know when to stop talking, shake hands and make a deal. It was time to close this mother of all deals. I raised my hands in defeat.

"You got me between the rock and the hard place. My lips are sealed."

"Go home and get some sleep, Jimmy," Michelle said, lighting up another blunt.

"You too," I said reflexively.

She laughed, then said matter-of-factly, "We don't sleep, Jimmy. Getting high is as close as we come."

Everett opened the door and led me back out through the oasis and around to their front gate, which opened as we approached.

"Relax, Jimmy," Everett said. "Just like your gnomes over in front of your house. We know how to keep secrets. We've been doing it for a long time," he winked. "Talk again soon."

CHAPTER TWENTY-NINE
THE PENNY DROPS

I really don't remember the actual walk home that night, only that the first yellow rays of our sun were peeking over the eastern horizon when I reached my side gate, where Claire waited patiently.

"I knew it!" she declared, as I fumbled with the slide lock. She finally grabbed the rope on it with her teeth and slid it open.

"You are one hot mess!" Claire said as she nosed the gate closed and slid the bolt back into place. "Here, lean on me."

I threw my arm around her neck and leaned most of my weight on her as she effortlessly half-dragged-half-carried me down the hill and around to our back door. I could feel the strength in her muscles as she walked. I guess that after a thousand-pound elk, I was child's play.

I got the back door open and made it as far as the basement couch. Then blackness.

"Jimmy!"

"Jimmy!"

"Jimmy, wake up!"

As I slowly regained consciousness, I literally heard my blood pumping hard through my badly dehydrated blood vessels, each beat a large fist landing between my temples. My tongue felt like a lint filter from the dryer in an Alphabet City laundromat. I didn't remember the last time I had gotten drunk, but the last time

I felt this hung over was the day after my bachelor party, over forty years before. Hangovers were the true Irish curse.

"Gina said to wake you before she gets back!" Claire said.

I gingerly pulled myself into a sitting position. My head objected passionately.

"You need some strong coffee. And to hydrate!" I heard Claire saying as my eyes slowly adjusted to the late morning light flooding through the sliding glass doors.

Claire's silhouette filled the open gap in the back door, and I could just make out that she had extended her head in though the open doorway. The aura from the surrounding light made her look angelic.

"Gina's almost back!" Claire said. "She left that bottle of water on the counter and primed the Keurig for you before she left on her run."

I rose to my feet and slowly hobbled over to the kitchen counter. I twisted the cap off the Arrowhead water bottle with the same determination my Nana used to ring the neck of a chicken, then carefully guzzled its contents down in one, long pull. I could feel its immediate effects on the dulling of my headache. Luckily, the true benefit of drinking fine, single-malt scotch is that no matter how hung over you are, your body refuses to throw it up the next morning. It's just that good. I tapped the blinking button on my Keurig and awaited its magic.

"So, what exactly is a 'fucking alien?'" Claire asked.

"Wait?" I said groggily. "Weren't you listening in last night?"

"It was radio silence the moment you entered the man-cave," Claire said.

Given what I experienced last night, I wouldn't put it past them to have some sort of jammer in place.

"And by the time you made it home your thoughts were a tossed salad," Claire continued. "Your mind kept repeating 'ET phone home!'"

Steaming coffee finally in hand, I shuffled out onto the back patio, took a seat in a deck chair by a glass-top wicker table and proceeded to recount the events of the night before. Thought by thought, without saying a word, I went into what I remembered chronologically and what I surmised after the fact. The only sound I made was the slurping of my coffee.

"Holy shit!" Claire finally declared in what was beginning sound like a Bronx accent. "You can't make this stuff up."

I would have burst out laughing at the absurdity of the moment where my talking mule was having a hard time wrapping her head around the existence of extra-terrestrial life, but I knew the truce I was forging with my headache was too fragile to chance it.

Just then Blue came flying around the back side of the house. A moment later Maeve appeared in hot pursuit and the two tumbled frantically in the high grass where Blue chose to take a stand. The resulting melee sounded like the diabolic desert dog-fight scene during the first ten minutes of the movie *The Exorcist*. Before I could leap out of my chair, Claire stopped me.

"Relax," she said, "they're playing."

A moment later, Maeve sprung out of the scrum and headed off through the closest gate into the high weeds of the back property, Blue now in chase, two porpoises undulating over the top of the straw ocean as they circled the burial mound and headed off towards Geppetto's workshop. I was exhausted just watching them.

"I thought I'd find you here," I heard Gina say as she rounded the corner with Lenahan in tow. "Look what the cat dragged in?" she said, shooting a warning glance at Claire. Claire nodded and ambled off towards the side paddock.

For the first time since I met him, Lenahan seemed distracted.

"I could really use some of that coffee," he said, gesturing towards my cup.

"Why don't I brew a full pot and bring it down here?" Gina said. "It's nice and cool here under the shade of the back deck."

"That would be great," Lenahan replied, forcing a smile.

As soon as Gina left, I said, "Okay, what's up?"

"Remember that I told you I would only give you bad news face-to-face," he began, hesitantly. "The lawyers for those friends of yours just got the Second Circuit to reverse the trial court."

My head was still too foggy to process what he was saying.

"They got a new trial, scheduled for the fall," Lenahan said, "but they are out on bail until then."

My stomach, on the other hand, got it in one, and a moment later I was vomiting all that good caffeinated scotch into the nearby weeds. I could hear Claire braying in the distance.

When I returned to the table, Gina appeared with a tray of fresh coffee and croissants.

"You look terrible," she said to me as she played mother and laid out the service. "That's what you get for sneaking out and drinking moonshine with the neighbors," she added, laughing.

"Sit down, sweetie," Lenahan said, his serious tone quelling her merriment.

Gina complied, and Lenahan went into a more detailed explanation of what had been reported to him from the higher ups in D.C. It turned out that my final 'fuck you soliloquy' at trial was considered so prejudicial by the liberal Second Circuit panel that they declared a mistrial, vacated the jury verdict and sent the case back down to the trial court for a new trial. Evidently, Meloni's impassioned argument that Valachi was a senior citizen who, along with his caretaker 'nephew,' had already unjustly served too much time behind bars based on the frivolous conspiracy charges, hit its mark, because the panel also ordered Valachi and Pearsall released on two-million dollars bail each, conditioned on the surrender of their passports.

"At least they kept the actual hitmen remanded through trial," Lenahan offered.

"What does that mean for us?" Gina asked, a hint of worry in her voice.

"Business as usual," Lenahan replied, "with just a heightened degree of vigilance."

Lenahan then explained how WITSEC handled problems like this all the time and that there's no way Valachi would find out where we were located. Unfortunately, he sounded like he was trying to convince himself more than us.

He concluded with, "I have never lost a client I didn't intend to. I'm not about to let that happen now."

Gina looked over at me seeking reassurance and I gave her my most convincing smile.

"Okay," she said, hesitantly. She stood up and started to the clear the table.

Lenahan put his hand on her arm and guided her back into her chair.

"Let Jimmy take care of that," he said, removing a small handgun from the pocket of his shorts and gently placing it on the table before her. It made my gun look like a cannon.

"Just in case," he continued. "I think it's time you knew your way around this little purse gun."

She stared at the gun for a moment, then reached out and carefully slid it back to him. She looked Lenahan squarely in the eye.

"You either teach me how to shoot with Jimmy's gun," she said with a smile, "or you can go to hell!"

CHAPTER THIRTY
THE LULL BEFORE-PART ONE

Gina took to shooting the same way she took to everything in her life, like a natural. Some people just have that knack. And it was all a matter of fact. You showed her something once, she watched, she did it perfectly. No arrogance. If I didn't love her, I'd hate her out of pure jealousy.

Two days after taking us back to his private shooting range, Lenahan returned to our home with a newly minted, concealed carry permit in Gina's name and a brand new, gun-metal grey, Smith & Wesson MP Shield 2.0, with a fancy after-market grip and a laser site. When I looked at my gun, I felt like Arnold Schwarzenegger in Terminator 2, still macho enough, but a bit behind the times. Lenahan also brought her a lightweight, rayon shoulder holster so she could carry it with her on her runs. And she did.

Shortly afterwards, she came home to tell me that she had signed us up for a family membership in the Liberty Firearms Institute, which turned out to be this beautiful new complex in the neighboring Johnstown, Colorado. It was the size of a New York City block and was where like-minded Second Amendment supporters regularly congregated to express their faith. Once a week, we both bent our knee, and fired two hundred rounds at targets that resembled Osama Bin Laden. While I was consistently able to strike some part of his paper anatomy at twenty-five yards, soon she was shooting in clusters.

After a few hours researching on YouTube, and a delivery of a cleaning kit from Amazon, Gina was able to take both our guns apart and clean them. After watching her a couple of times, I was able to do so as well, but she did a better job.

Gina insisted that we continue to embrace our new lives without fear of what we couldn't control, which meant she returned to her morning runs, Blue and gun in tow, and her afternoons exploring Northern Colorado's ubiquitous antique shops and the mega malls that line I-25. I was back to walking my morning circuit each day with my own gun secured in its holster, followed by a couple of hours of day-trading to fund Gina's new hobbies. I tried to convince her that I was burning enough calories just having to follow Claire around our property every day and scooping up her shit, which, by the way, was prodigious, and then building, maintaining and dispensing compost piles, but she said I still needed the cardio from a brisk, five-mile walk. Resistance is futile.

It turned out that these walks became very therapeutic for me. It was like mobile meditation. I was rarely interrupted by the incursion of a passing human being, and I began to become familiar with all the animals I would meet along the way. The perpetually observant Claire would always debrief me on my return and give me the skinny about the personalities and interrelationships among each group of animals. They didn't all come to greet me at their fences. Some were just naturally disinterested, Claire said, so I shouldn't take it personally.

Soon I was addressing all the animals along my route by name, as I stopped to meet them at the edge of their respective properties. For example, the four horses of the apocalypse, as Claire like to call them, that were just down my road were Molly, Dolly, Trouble and Francis. Three more horses further down the road were Apollo, Dusty and Butterscotch. The three heads of Cerberus were Harley, Quinn and Beaker and they learned that stifling their barking meant a tasty game of 'catch the Scooby' over their front fence. The more friendly canines included April, a charming collie with one eye, and her two feisty neighboring mutts, Wayland and Sadie. The exotic members of the collective included two Nigerian dwarf goats, Stella and Rosie, that spent their time trying to secure the best fence position by butting each other off their high ground perch. Finally, five alpacas, all named Chico, distinguished themselves by adding a color suffix, so it was Chico white, red, grey, brown and tan.

Claire told me that the animals all found me to be a curiosity, since my only purpose in our interactions was pure socialization, not dominance. She said they all appreciated the personal attention I shared with each of them, and the gentle touch I delivered. She suggested that I carry a bag of chopped carrots and a larger stash of doggy treats to share along the way. Gina found a decent sized canvas 'Brooks Brothers' bag covering a pair of Golden Fleece penny loafers I no longer wore, which was perfect to sling over my shoulder during my daily rounds. She said it would have the same effect of walking with a weighted vest. She was right, I soon noticed that my weight was dropping.

After a week of dispensing those goodies, Claire told me that the animals were now calling me "Carrot Claus."

The last stop on my daily tour was reserved for a beautiful Arabian named Mystique, who I had seen that first morning running circles and sharing secrets with the petite but classy white-haired woman. "Tique" as she called herself, was the beautiful prom queen, and I was the nerd who always did her homework, bringing her a separate stash of chopped apples—she didn't like carrots—just to share a few moments each morning in the high school cafeteria. Having now had the chance to study several horses along my route, I could see that Tique was flawless. No sooner were the apples gone, than she would be off galloping magnificently around her paddock, and I was dismissed. Claire liked to call Tique, "That Hussy."

Most of the disinterested animals, except the cattle and sheep, soon changed their ways as word along the route spread. They now also lined up during the Blue Hour each morning, like devout Catholic communicants, to receive their daily handfuls of tasty orange hosts. By the end of the second week, I was starting out on my rounds each morning with thirty pounds of carrots.

I asked Claire about the cattle and sheep. She told me that they had no use for humans because they all knew that the humans controlled the 'Process' so until their time came to be 'processed,' they would just as soon suck what little joy they could from their daily lives and keep to themselves. I would never eat meat again.

That was easier said than done. First off, I couldn't go vegan because I just couldn't give up milk in my coffee, or cheese, or ice cream, so I rationalized an exception to dairy by convincing myself that taking the milk didn't kill the animal. Then there was a painful period of the trial and error of finding a meat substitute that didn't chew like Styrofoam and taste like shit. I had resigned myself to a life of eating cheese-covered, vegetable-sides, but Gina never gave up searching and finally discovered Beyond Meat, a vegetable-based product which would have fooled the most notorious carnivore. I had found my True Blood.

It was now late summer. The days were getting shorter and the nights cooler. I decided I would fix up what Gina and I had taken to calling 'Claire's Lair' before the real cool weather set in. I patched the roof and installed hanging heaters and an upgraded lighting and outlet system. Then I reinforced the interior frame of the building and slapped on three coats of exterior 'Barn White' paint. Working again with my hands proved to be a wonderful distraction from the worries imposed by the outside world.

On that end, Lenahan checked in regularly to keep us updated with news from the East Coast. It seemed that Valachi and Pearsall spent most of their time meeting with their lawyers and preparing for their new trial, which was now scheduled to begin in October. Lenahan said that I would again have to testify, but that it would all be arranged last minute because they didn't want to chance a leak as to my whereabouts.

Helen and Bobbi spent August in Greece. Bobbi promised before she left that if she got any messages, she would call right away, so I took her constant radio silence to be good news.

The Friday evening of the Labor Day weekend found Gina and I enjoying the hot tub, sky clad, while Blue and Claire were off in the distance—the mule grazing a section by the pond, with the Pit, ever vigilant, at her heels. The soft summer breeze was hypnotically spinning the whirligig by Geppetto's studio. Our bliss was unexpectedly interrupted by the pinging of our front doorbell, followed by the video on my iPhone of Everett and Michelle, Everett holding a bottle of Macallan, Michelle holding up a piece of paper with the words 'Earthlings, We Come In Peace!' written in magic marker. I wondered if aliens did stand-up comedy where they come from.

"Better answer that before they walk around the back," Gina said as she exited the hot tub and slipped her still fit body into a terrycloth bathrobe.

I had shared with Gina the highlights of my foggy memory from my last night with Everett and Michelle as soon as my corresponding hangover had allowed. She, like me, had been down so many rabbit holes over the past three months that we were both approaching a Bronx 'no kidding' response to just about everything. She, of course, had mentally leapt right over the insanity of my story, and immediately went to the cooler questions that I was probably too much in shock (or too drunk) to ask.

I could tell by her look that she was going to get those answers tonight.

CHAPTER THIRTY-ONE
THE LULL BEFORE-PART TWO

I called over the intercom to give us a minute while I struggled to pull dry clothes over a wet body. By the time I reached the front door, Everett and Michelle had turned and sat down next to each other on the front steps of the porch. Their heads leaned together, barely touching, as Michelle silently pointed to Jack the Spruce and the fairy door, a perfect cover for the Saturday Evening Post magazine.

Before my door was open, without discernible movement, they were both on their feet and facing me. Everett held out the bottle.

"No fucking way!" I said, refusing to take it from him.

"I told you he's a lightweight," Michelle said as she breezed by me into the house. "You smell like chlorine."

Everett shrugged his shoulders and followed her in.

"That's actually Bromine!" he said, sniffing me as he passed.

For some reason I stood for a moment scanning the front of my property, fighting a feeling of uneasiness, before following them in and double bolting the door behind me.

Gina had come down the stairs by then, Blue in tow, and was administering hugs all around when I entered the kitchen. Blue watched them carefully, to make sure Gina remained safe while in their embrace.

After completing the circuit, Gina stopped in her tracks and put her hand to her mouth in mock horror. "I hope hugging isn't considered inappropriate on PCb. I don't want to start an intergalactic incident."

Everett and Michelle stood quietly for a moment, but I could see they were communicating. They both looked uncomfortable. Their silence became awkward. Gina started to panic.

"Oh my God, oh my God, I'm sorry. It is taboo! Oh my God, I'm sorry!" Gina blurted out.

Michelle and Everett burst into laughter.

"You're way too easy, girl," Michelle said.

"Now if you French-kissed me that would be inappropriate!" Everett added with a wink.

"Or maybe not!" Michelle added, smiling.

"Now c'mon Jimmy, it's the Labor Day weekend," Everett added excitedly, brandishing his bottle. "You humans love your holidays. Break out some glasses and let's crack this baby."

I defensively removed a couple of bottles of Chardonnay from the fridge.

"Why don't we start with these instead and see where that takes us," I said, my recent hangover all too clear in my memory.

Gina grabbed some wine glasses from the cupboard and passed them around while I pulled the corks and started doling out the contents of the first bottle equally among the four glasses.

Michelle raised her glass in a toast. "Okay, what shall we toast to?"

"To no more bullshit!" Gina answered, tapping her glass with the rest of ours, seriatim.

"That'll work," Michelle said, as she took a large sip from her glass.

"Let's take this party out on the back deck," I said, ushering them out through the side door in the dining area. "It's going to be a beautiful evening, so let's enjoy it."

Gina hung back with Blue and quickly prepared some cheese, crackers, pretzels, chips and dip, which she then placed strategically between the tables and chairs on the deck. Having vetted the visitors, Blue remained in the house and emptied her bowl of some tasty kibbles Gina had left for her.

No sooner were we seated, all facing out towards the foothills and mountains in the distance, when Gina started in.

"Do you guys have religion where you come from?" she asked.

"And my money was on 'Are you guys anatomically correct?'" Everett said.

I guffawed, spitting some wine over the railing.

"But you went right for the big-ticket item."

"Well, are you?" I asked, still laughing.

"Close enough to make it fun," Michelle piped in, joining me in the laughter.

"No really," Gina said, reasserting herself. "Do you guys have a religious belief system? Or are we humans just a bunch of superstitious fools?"

"We don't have any organized religions like you have here," Everett said, "but we follow a similar moral code comparable to your 'golden rules'—do unto others kind of thing—and we do believe there is something beyond our physical death."

"After all," Michelle chimed in, "not to bore you, but its basic physics. We are all manifestations of energy, all remnants from that big bang almost fourteen billion years ago. That energy can ultimately be converted, but never destroyed. It vibrates during different times at different frequencies and our respective reality depends on the frequency at which we are vibrating. When we pass, it's just another frequency."

"And whatever you want to believe caused that big bang," Everett continued, "it provides for our uniquely varied existence no matter where we call home, in our present form and all future ones."

"So, you guys can die?" Gina asked, clearly fascinated by the direction of the conversation.

"Sure," Michelle said, "but we live over four-times as long as the healthiest humans, and disease as you know it has been eradicated from our world. Not to brag but we also have a better grasp of using the universe's energy to repair our bodies."

"We're also not violent like you folks," Everett added. "Our technology has developed to the point where all of our basic needs are taken care of, so there is no reason to harm another."

"Now that's sounds like arrogant bullshit, and maybe just a little bit boring," I said, more aggressively than probably warranted. "There's no passion? No jealousy? You never covet your neighbors' anything?"

"Well we do covet your Ass!" Michelle shouted.

"Claire," Everett said with a wink. He gazed out over the property searching for her.

It was weird hearing Claire described as property that could be coveted. She was a friend.

"Back home, we have our own ancient myths about creatures on your planet that were not quite human and not quite horse," he continued.

"They say it was one of our visiting ancestors' earliest experiments gone awry," Michelle said matter-of-factly. Then, reading our minds, "Oh yes, we've been coming here for an exceptionally long time."

"It's how our star system got its name from the ancient Greeks," Everett said. "Centaurus."

"Those genes obviously continue to flow through to the present day. Makes sense that it would manifest in a hybrid," Michelle said pensively. Then she turned to me, gave me the once over and smiled. "We did a much better job with the monkeys."

That last comment made me uncomfortable for a lot of reasons that I thought would be better left for another day. The lawyer part of my brain wanted to bring the conversation back to them.

"So, your people, or whatever you call your collective selves, never have reason to fight with each other?" I asked.

"Honestly, no," Michelle responded, "but when you live as long as we do, sooner or later you all get the same breaks as everybody else. We're pretty patient about most things and don't feel the need to take it from another. It all balances out in the end."

I have always been one of those guys who hates standing in a line more than three people deep, so patience was never one of my strongpoints. I was growing impatient just listening to their peaceful coexistence pablum, and I was clearly giving off that vibe.

"What about the people on the other fifty-thousand inhabitable planets?" I asked. "We can't be the only ones who feel like we do."

"Actually," Michelle chimed in, "with a few notable exceptions, you pretty much are."

"And that's what I love about humans!" Everett said, pointing to me. "You're all so passionate, as misguided as it often is. Right or wrong, love and hate spur you on. You are willing to fight, even die, for what you want, and you all play the short game. That's why everything from celebrations to commiserations is done with such lust, such fire, like there is no tomorrow." He thought about it a moment more. "Nothing captures it better than an Irish wake."

"And what about lust? Physical desire? Or love?" I asked, appreciating the Celtic reference. "Doesn't everyone want to date Prom Royalty? Sooner or later that has to cause friction even among your laid-back masses!"

Everett and Michelle turned and gazed at each other in silence. I could imagine the numbers whirring through their heads. I could see the mutual affection in their eyes.

"We see beauty in everything. In everyone. Not in the physical form, which is so malleable," Michelle said. "Our connections with each other go so far deeper than what you are suggesting."

At that moment, Michelle reached out and took Everett's hand. For the length of a subliminal message, I saw two identical androgynous faces, ageless, flawless, with slightly oversized, Nordic blue eyes and flowing blond hair. They were beautiful. It was gone with the next blink of my eyes.

"Whoa! Did you guys just see that?" I could hear Claire's voice rising from the yard below us. "Not a big fan of the human form but that was impressive!"

By the time my eyes located Claire, standing off in the shadows by the shed, Everett and Michelle were standing beside her. They didn't spill a drop from their wine glasses. Gina and I joined the party at our more humanly pace and, by then, all three were already deeply engaged in a conversation. Michelle and Everett were staring at Claire with the same wonder on their faces as I had for them. Michelle was gently stroking Claire's neck. As we arrived, our momentum caused the group to turn and slowly amble towards the gate to the back property, Claire leading the way.

"What's with the numbers?" Claire said to Everett.

"Simple binary mathematics," Everett responded. "Thought at its purest, fastest."

I didn't know about Claire, but I was lost. Must have been all those hedge funds managers she was forced to listen to in the mountains all those years.

"But we can speak every language found on this planet," Michelle added, finishing Everett's thought. "As well as several others in this galaxy."

"Can you think in English?" Claire said. "I'd like to try something."

Everett and Michelle again shared a knowing glance.

Claire abruptly startled and broke into a cantor. She quickly circled the group.

"Wow!" She said as she passed by us. "I can hear it all, but it's so fast, like squeaky high-pitched gibberish. I can't understand any of it."

Michelle held up her hand as if focusing. Everett closed his eyes in concentration. Claire slowed to a walk and rejoined us.

"Much better," Claire said. "Now I'm catching up. Pretty awesome stuff!"

I was beginning to feel like a blind person standing before Van Gogh's Starry Night, I knew I was in the presence of something special that I could never fully appreciate. Gina was a bit more direct with her frustration.

"Out of respect for those of us clairvoyantly challenged," Gina said impatiently, "can we all switch back to speaking?"

Michelle walked over and put her arm around Gina's shoulder. "Don't worry, sweetie. Your day will come."

"Tell them about the strangers," Claire said to Everett.

"I was just getting to that," Everett responded. He looked over at me, his face suddenly turning serious. "Not sure if you've seen them, but there's been some postings on the Nextdoor App about a small group of strangers being seen out and about the area. At first, I wrote it off as being the usual small-town paranoia. When they first started the App up around here, there were regular postings under the headings 'Men in Black.' I don't need to tell you how unsettling that could be!"

"There's still an occasional post about you walking through the back roads during the early morning hours," Michelle added. "You appear to have a very quick and suspicious walk!" She laughed. "And some of the neighbors think you're bribing the animals with treats for nefarious reasons!"

"Recently, someone posted something about seeing a group of men standing around a dark SUV over by our sewage processing plant by the county road," Everett said, gesturing east in the direction of the plant. "Too stylishly dressed for the usual engineers in the area."

"Mrs. Crabtree, over on Hoot Owl Lane, is a regular contributor who is really into her conspiracy theories," Michelle added. "Everything is a potential terrorist plot. This time it was to blow up the community shithouse!"

Lenahan had explained to me shortly after we arrived that since the people in my area were outside the official Berthoud town limits, they were not hooked into its municipal sewer system and so, as the area developed back in the 80s, a group of local property owners formed a loosely based association, got rid of their individual septic tanks and built their own communal sewerage plant. Now the local properties in our development all had their sewerage lines flowing into main piping arteries that ran beneath the large gullies that separated the back of the property lines. From there the arteries all lead east to the small plant on an isolated piece of commonly owned, fenced in property, just off a nearby county road. It was about a half mile east from the back of our property.

I made a mental note to really start accessing the App and to run it all by Lenahan.

We all returned to the back yard where the sky started to darken, and the air got cooler. Gina went up on the deck and retrieved the wine and snacks and I grabbed the chairs and brought them down to the yard. In that short time, Everett and Michelle had gone back to their home and returned with a large metal fire-pit and some wood and were already in the process of stoking a fire, which Everett ignited with his silver knick-knack. I set the chairs around the pit, strategically leaving an open section large enough for Claire. For the first time since I met her, I watched as she scuffed the earth beneath her with her hooves, slowly circled a few times in place like a dog and then, starting with her front legs, slowly lowered herself to the ground, facing the fire pit. The sound of her body when it contacted the ground and the dust that arose around her on impact, attested to her mass and weight. I wouldn't want her landing on me.

As the fire kicked in, the light from the flames danced on Claire's shadowy form and changed her dark brown eyes to reflecting red coals. She seemed to be hypnotized by the fire and her head began to bob ever so slightly, as if she was listening to the song in someone's head.

Everett and Michelle leaned back in their chairs and stared up at the night sky. Gina refilled everyone's wine glass. We all sat in silence, Gina and I with an ever-increasing appreciation of the stars above. I focused on the lopsided moon.

"Your moon is on the wane," Everett said to no one in particular.

I silently prayed that Everett wasn't into euphemisms.

CHAPTER THIRTY-TWO
THE LULL BEFORE-PART THREE

When I returned from my walk Saturday morning, Lenahan's SUV was in my driveway. I found him on the deck around back, having some coffee and croissants with Gina. Maeve and Blue were sleeping together by the side entrance to the porch.

Claire stood off in the far corner of the yard, grazing, her ears twitching away as she listened in on the conversation both aurally and telepathically. She nodded ever so slightly as I appeared on the deck. Lenahan motioned for me to sit at the table. Gina poured me a coffee.

"I was just telling Gina that DC has been reporting some interesting chatter on some of the wires they've been monitoring," Lenahan said.

"About Valachi?" I asked.

"Not specifically, no," Lenahan responded, "but these guys are always aware that someone's listening in, so they tend to speak in euphemisms."

I tore open a croissant and slathered on a heart stopping amount of 'Kerry Gold,' wondering how many ways the mob could talk about killing someone. Valachi never spoke on the phone, period. However, Valachi and Pearsall never minced words when that subject came up in their presence. "I want him gone," by either of them always seemed to do the trick.

"Anyway," Lenahan continued, "the latest buzz seems to be following a sports motif."

"Any particular sport?" I asked.

"Softball," Lenahan replied. "The word is that a local Denver team is bringing in some big bats from Chicago for an upcoming tournament and flying in new managers from the East Coast."

"Any word as to when this tournament is to take place?" I asked, my stomach clenching.

"That's all we got for now," Lenahan said. He studied my not-so-poker face. "Look, it doesn't mean shit. There's no reason to suspect that they even know where you are. I've kept a tight lid on you guys. Complete radio silence."

I didn't know whether he was trying to convince me or himself. I suspected he was 0-for-2.

"Should we be packing our bags?" Gina asked.

"No," he said resolutely. "If they want to play ball, I want the home field advantage."

Lenahan finished his coffee and called for Maeve. Blue followed them both through the house. As he opened the front door, he turned back to us.

"Listen, until I get a better handle on this," he said to Gina, "maybe you should stay close to home. And both of you keep your girls locked and loaded."

I never thought of a gun in the feminine gender. Given its shape, it seemed counter-intuitive. But then again, I never understood why guys gave their cars female names. Another great mystery in a mysterious life.

Gina and I stood on our porch and watched man and dog back out of our driveway. Gina looked a lot calmer than I felt.

"This doesn't mean we have to cancel the cook-out?" She said rhetorically.

I had completely forgotten that Gina had invited Helen, Bobbi and Eddie for a Labor Day cookout before Helen and Bobbi had left for Greece. They were due to arrive back in the states later today, and Eddie was going to pick them up at Denver International Airport. The barbeque wasn't until Sunday.

"No," I responded. "Lenahan said we should stay close to home. Didn't say we couldn't have friends over. Anyway, it will take our minds off the bullshit."

"We should also invite Lenny," Gina added, "and Everett and Michelle."

"Why not," I said. Then I remembered that the grill was still in its packing crate in the garage.

"We'll need to go into the store to pick up some extra burgers, buns and beers," she said. "Don't worry, I have our special burgers already set aside."

"Okay," I said, not sure how I felt calling my food "special burgers," having been educated in Catholic School where "Special Education" was for the academically challenged kids. "But I'm going with you and we're bringing Blue and the girls."

I had only been in the Town of Berthoud once since I arrived in Colorado, and that was the night Gina and I ransacked every ATM we could find to get the money to purchase Claire. I had no visual memory of the trip.

Girls and dog in hand, we headed into town, which turned out to be about fifteen minutes away by car along one long and circuitous county road that ultimately ran east to west and crossed 287, a four-lane artery that ran north and south and connected the two larger towns of Loveland and Longmont, themselves about twenty miles apart. Gina, now comfortably familiar with the area, drove and played tour guide, announcing the points of interest along the way, including a nest of bald eagles. Having just barely gotten used to my immediate surroundings, and with warnings of softball teams fresh in my head, I was feeling a touch agoraphobic as I sat in the passenger seat, my hand resting restlessly on the imprint of my concealed nine-millimeter. And that wasn't a euphemism.

The farther east we traveled from the foothills, the less rural our surroundings became. Once we crossed 287, I started to see more active signs of human life. We passed modern looking, mini-strip-malls with car washes, auto parts places and drive-thru coffee shops. In the distance, I could see what used to be farmland giving way to cookie-cutter housing developments. Suddenly there were sidewalks, with older wooden and brick houses appearing close enough to resemble Long Island suburbia. I saw the occasional young families with small children walking their pets or solo young adults jogging or riding their bikes. Gina pointed to an older tiny mall that we passed on our right, with an anchor grocery store called 'Hayes' right next to the seat of town government, and told me we would circle back for our shopping there but that she wanted to show me the 'Old Town' first.

Old Town would have been right at home on the cover of a 1950s Saturday Evening Post, right down to an A&W drive in. It bore all the original, quaint hallmarks of flyover Americana that the wealthier east coast suburbs so desperately try to emulate and so epically fail. There were traditionally gridded blocks with smaller, well-maintained houses with white picket fences bordering well-groomed lawns. Bicycles and red wagons served as lawn ornaments and recurring combinations of Old Glory, Colorado and Denver Broncos flags, with the occasional yellow Gadsden, 'Don't-Tread-On-Me,' hung from their wrap around porches, with their mandatory chain-linked, two-seater, wooden swings. The truly 'main' street was lined with ancient Maple, Oak and Birch trees that provided welcome shade against the hot Colorado sun, and made it possible to see without the ubiquitous sunglasses.

To our left was a beautiful, grass covered town square with a bronze marker identifying Fickel Park. Dotting its perimeter were life-sized, patina-bronze monuments of elk, moose, bear and other once dominant wildlife, whose vibrant action poses expressed its creator's appreciation and respect for the creatures, so as not to be mistaken for a catalogue of the conquered. Multigenerational families enjoying the holiday weekend, with their lawn chairs and picnic blankets, clustered around strategically placed grills throughout the bucolic setting. Busy tennis courts and baseball diamonds could be spotted in the distance.

Next came the string of mom-and-pop storefronts with enough pedestrian traffic to justify its mandatory sit-down coffee shop, hair salon, hardware and liquor store, with a tattoo and curiosity shop thrown in for good measure. I could see the ornate, swinging wooden signs above doorways of other proprietors jutting out like pendants along some of the side streets. A moment later we had passed into what was once the industrial end of the town with its life-giving railroad tracks, which was now converted into microbreweries, antique shops, and restaurants, along with the diminutive town museum, post office and library. A skateboard park and Habitat for Humanity punctuated the tour before reaching a round-about that either sent you east, out into the rest of the world, or returned you to the safety of the town. I wondered how many rotations it took the inhabitants the first time they broke free of the comforting gravity of their community. All that was needed was a large sign in the center of the round-about declaring "Beyond Here Be Dragons!" Today I was happy that Gina was taking the 180-degree return exit back to Berthoud.

Shopping in Hayes was refreshingly anachronistic. Gina explained that it was a family owned business going back generations. There were fully stocked shelves along spotlessly clean aisles with a sufficiently limited selection of anything you could need. The fruits and vegetables were locally grown and smelled deliciously fresh. Their bakery, deli and butcher counters followed suit. There were more employees than customers and, given their ages, I could see that most of them rightfully considered this more than a first job, stepping-stone to bigger and better things. In short, I could tell that they gave a shit.

Groceries in tow, we headed back towards home, and this time I listened to Gina's repeat performance as tour guide and appreciated everything down to the corn fields and bald eagle nesting sites I spotted along the way. I had expanded my comfort zone.

By four p.m., Gina and I were ready for tomorrow's guests. As I tightened the last bolt on my Weber six burner grill, Claire came up from where she was grazing in the back property and approached me in the back yard.

"Bobbi's back from Greece and has lots of news from your brothers."

CHAPTER THIRTY-THREE
WINTER DREAMS

Gina followed her usual routine Sunday morning, putting Blue through her paces with an hour of roadwork, her nine tucked safely in its holster. Then she dove into her final prep for the barbecue in a way that would have impressed Gordon Ramsey.

I followed along at my more leisurely pace, nine and goodies in my canvas sack, dispensing the latter upon demand to the waiting, domesticated creatures along the route. The dawn was still pleasantly cool as the first orange rays peaked over the eastern horizon. My weather App predicted a glorious day.

When I reached the back-and-barren stretch, a quick, unexpected movement on my periphery—one-hundred yards to my left—released a flood of adrenaline into my system, causing me to reach for my weapon. By the time my mind and eyes had properly focused, a large, young buck elk, with only a few points on its antlers, had leapt the five foot high fence to my left and touched down momentarily in the center of the road, ten feet in front of me, before clearing the fence to my right with its next leap and heading off in long bounds through the high grass towards the foothills. Each leap across that road was six-feet high and had to cover 20 feet. The animal's effortless movement evoked memories of that night at the ballet in Lincoln Center over 30 years ago. Eat your heart out Baryshnikov.

The buck was larger than Claire and moved with a confidence and freedom that only a hunter's bullet could erase. I watched as it quickly disappeared into the foothills, praying it never suffered that fate. I released my weapon back into the sack, wondering if I could ever take another's life.

When I reached the last stop along the route—the magnificent Arabian, Mystique—I found a beautiful, brand-new, turnout blanket hanging over the fence. It was royal blue and bore the trademark 'Horse Ware Ireland Rambo Supreme.' I knew nothing about horse blankets, but I had shopped in enough high-end men's stores to recognize quality, craftsmanship and expense, and this ticked all boxes. It had a handwritten note pinned to it which read: "Winter comes quickly and hard in Colorado. Give Claire our love. Pam & Tique!" I thought back to Claire's story about the neighbor who cared for her those days during Mrs. Reynolds' illness, and remembered the small, classy woman I had seen putting Tique through her paces that first day and did the math. I held back the last handful of apples from Tique to get her attention and said, "You tell Pam we said thank you." Tique nodded her head, mouthed the sliced apples from my now open palm, and then raced away for her lap around the perimeter.

By the time I returned to the homestead, Claire was waiting anxiously at the side gate.

"An Irish Rambo!" she squealed. "Only the best of the purebreds, an owner's trophy horse, ever gets one of these!"

I realized that I had a lot to learn about Equine haute couture. I also knew that once Gina got wind of this world, I'd be building Claire a closet extension to her 'Wee Lair.'

"C'mon, help me try this baby on," Claire said, as she led me to her barn.

"Really? Isn't it still kind of warm for it?" I said.

"I just want to see how it fits," Claire said. "I've never had a coat before."

Having never experienced a Colorado winter, I didn't appreciate what the coat meant to Claire.

I never even knew horses wore coats. Claire interrupted my thoughts.

"During those horrid winters back in the mountains," Claire said, "it would get so cold that I had icicles hanging from my face and my eyelashes would freeze together. And while my coat would thicken, we are not like horses, we don't have a waterproof undercoat. So, a night on the mountainside out in the freezing rain, snow or sleet would take its toll. Frostbite bent the tip of my ear," she said, rotating her right ear for effect.

"And I was luckier than most," she added. "I was forced to carry some of my less fortunate cousins down from those mountains after some of the more violent storms."

"Though we never seemed to lose a human," she added, distractedly.

"Did you lose any close friends?" I asked.

"Didn't have any really," she said, "we were all too focused on our own survival to worry about the next mule."

She thought a little more about it, replaying her memories.

"Well," she added. "There was one that I mentioned. An older Jack named Mr. Rogers."

"What's a Jack?" I asked.

"A male mule," she responded, now in full memory mode. "He was the only mule that showed me any real kindness during my stay there."

She hung her head for a moment. "I never even got to say goodbye to him," she said wistfully.

Feeling her sadness, I clumsily tried to change the subject.

"So, what about this coat?" I said a little too excitedly, holding up the blanket. "Are you going to tell me how to put it on or not?"

She stared at the coat for a moment.

"Nah," she said, softly, "maybe later."

With that, she slowly ambled away towards the back of the property, where she found a spot by the far edge of the pond and stood motionless, gazing at her reflection in the water. All she could see was loneliness.

CHAPTER THIRTY-FOUR
THE MAGNIFICENT SEVEN

I knew my nervousness the remainder of that morning was more than a macho-based worry that I may not perform well at the grill. I was anxious to learn of whatever messages Bobbi had received from my ethereal siblings and how the different branches of my expanding team from Beyond the Looking Glass were going to get along with its newest interplanetary members. And even though Lenahan seemed perfectly comfortable with both Bobbi talking to the dead while he added to its ranks, Claire, Everett and Michelle were clearly pushing the envelope. I remembered what my sister always used to say to me when we were children whenever I was facing some seemingly insurmountable problem: "Leap and the net will appear," a maxim which I later learned she had cribbed from the American naturalist, John Burroughs. She was also always the first to laugh when, after taking her advice, I inevitably landed on my ass. Still, she did teach me to always move forward even when you were scared shitless.

Gina was busy setting up an old, oversized, barnyard table she had found in a local antique store called The Farmer's Wife, and completed the ensemble with nine very different chairs she had scavenged from throughout the house, including my chair from my office and a round headed stool she used at her make-up counter. Given the idiosyncrasies of our guests, the lack of seating uniformity seemed à propos.

We had stocked both fridges with enough cold beer and wine to grease the diplomatic wheels of the most contentious gatherings that weren't more than fifty percent Celtic, in which case there was just not enough alcohol on earth. Gina set out bowls of chips, dips and pretzels on every open side table, along with an oversized bowl of chopped carrots for Claire and declared herself ready.

I distracted myself with my intergalactically-refurbished lawn mower, having manicured the space among the remaining high grass that Claire had been steadily clearing in the backyard. It now formed a nice crop circle, large enough to host the table as well as those extra outdoor chairs and smaller tables from the back deck. I had placed the grill on the cement patio off the basement sliding doors so I could easily access the kitchen, fridge, and if necessary, bathroom, and still readily interact with my guests while grilling.

Claire, for her part, stayed off by herself at the far end of the property, grazing. Blue followed her around, grooming her legs comfortingly whenever Claire stopped long enough in one spot.

I had asked Everett and Michelle to arrive a little early so I could feel them out about the possibility that their secret may not withstand the scrutiny of my other gifted guests.

That moment, they literally appeared in the circle before me with Michelle carrying the fire pit and Everett carrying some kindling and another demon bottle of Macallan.

I took the bottle from Everett and placed it on the table as far away from where I would be sitting as I could. Michelle set the fire pit down by the chairs from the deck like it was made of Styrofoam.

"Listen guys," I began, "there's something you should know."

Before I could say anything more, Everett stopped me.

"Relax," he said, "Claire's already filled us in on the others. It'll be all right."

"We've been dying for the right opportunity to be able to finally open up," Michelle said. "This may be our best shot." She thought a bit more and added, "and if doesn't work out, Everett will just shrink the lot of them and stick them in a Hamster cage at home."

I could feel my chin hit my chest. They both burst into laughter.

"Are all lawyers as gullible as you are?" Everett said.

"No," I responded, recovering, "only the ones with Mr. Ed, Theresa Caputo and Mork and Mindy as friends!"

"Touché!" Michelle shouted.

"Seriously," Everett continued, "all of us have our secrets, even your friend Lenahan."

"Jesus," I said, looking off to the back pasture, "once Claire trusts someone, she's an open book!"

"Yeah, at least we've never killed anybody," Michelle said, matter-of-factly, "couldn't if we wanted to."

Before I could follow-up on either of Michelle's comments, Blue came running out of the back-pasture barking eagerly as she raced up the side of the house to the top of the driveway. A moment later she flew back down the hill, retracing her path with Maeve inches behind her in hot pursuit. They tumbled into the grass in a ball and then reversed roles with Maeve as the rabbit.

"Leap and the net will appear!" I said out loud.

Lenahan was the first to turn the corner into the backyard, carrying a colorful bouquet. Close behind him came Helen and Bobbi, each holding bottles of Ouzo and Retsina, respectively, with Eddie following up the rear carrying a large wicker basket.

"Beware of Greeks bearing gifts!" Helen shouted, as she and Bobbi placed their bottles on the table. Eddie came over to where we were standing and presented his basket full of Greek pastry delights.

"Oh, they look delicious," Michelle exclaimed appreciatively.

Gina exited the sliding doors drying her hands on a dishtowel and proceeded to welcome the group with hugs and kisses. Lenahan presented her with the bouquet.

"That will be perfect for the table," Gina gushed, "thank you Lenny." She gave him a quick peck on the cheek, took the flowers and then entered the house, returning a moment later with them nicely arranged in a tin vase artfully hammered into a miniature, old-fashion milk can, which she then placed with a grand gesture as the centerpiece on the table.

Lenahan spotted the single malt.

"Macallan!" he said, raising and inspecting the bottle. "Who is the whisky anorak?"

"That would be me," Everett said.

"Do they have this shit up on Mars, or wherever it is you call home?" Lenahan said, deadpanned.

"Ssssooooorrrrrryyyy!" Bobbi sang from behind Helen, who was shaking her head in disbelief. "Your brothers said I better give Lenny the heads up!"

With all the various ethereal and psychic connections, trying to keep a lid on these secrets was just damned impossible.

"Oh, I like him," Michelle said, pointing to Lenahan, "and her!" pointing to Bobbi.

I wondered what was faster, Lenahan's bullet or Everett's shrinking ray.

"Nah," Everett said dismissively, "we wouldn't flush our toilets with this swill, even if we had toilets and an ass to shit out of!"

Lenahan laughed hardily and Everett joined him. Gina appeared from the basement with a handful of shot glasses. Lenahan cracked the bottle and began filling each glass like an Irish bartender, in a continuous pour, while Gina passed them all around. When everyone had one topped off, Lenahan, the tallest in our group raised the glass high over the surrounding circle.

"What should our first toast be?" he asked.

"To talking mules!" Claire said as she appeared through the gate and entered the circle.

Lenahan almost dropped his shot.

Bobbi was the first to toss her shot down the hatch and break the silence. "Your brothers never mentioned telling Lenny about Claire," she said apologetically.

CHAPTER THIRTY-FIVE
THE QUICKENING

After throwing back my shot of Scotch, I left the bottle with the group of outliers to assist them in working out amongst themselves whatever information they were willing to share, voluntarily or involuntarily, while I busied myself at the barbeque grilling the meat and sides. Gina brought out the various cold salads she had prepared and distributed them on the table, along with some bottles of wine and a couple of glass pitchers of ice water.

I watched from my spot at the grill as most of the group slowly walked through the high grass in the back property along paths that Claire had grazed down to manageable levels. From my vantage point it almost resembled a Labyrinth. Lenahan was animatedly engaged in his conversations with Claire and Everett, while Michelle and Bobbi walked a few feet behind them, stopping, every once in a while, to break into such convulsions of laughter that they were actually forced to embrace just to hold each other up. Eddie walked silently on the far side of Claire, lost in his own thoughts, with one hand stroking her neck as they proceeded. Bobbi stopped and began to point to a couple of distant spots on the edges of the back property, then swept her arm to a spot where the two lines seemed to connect—somewhere between the house and back fence. Michelle followed Bobbi's movements and nodded her head vigorously as the two women broke off from the pack and began walking to the spot Bobbi had identified.

I didn't notice Helen until she was standing right beside me.

"Need a hand with anything?" she asked. "I'm really great with a grill, and this carnivore feast must be wreaking havoc on your new sensibilities."

"You know, you're right, I'm feeling just a bit hypocritical," I said, handing her the tongs. "These are all about done," I pointed to the burgers, franks and chicken cutlets roasting on the grill, "you can help me get them onto that large serving platter."

I retrieved the platter and in less than a minute Helen had the food neatly stacked in three sections. She grabbed the tin foil roll from beside the grill and expertly covered the steaming food and tightly tucked the foils around the edges.

"There you go," she said as she double checked her work. "Can I take it to the table for you?"

"Sure," I said, handing her the platter. I followed her to the table and shifted some of the plates to make room for the food.

"So," I said, glancing at the others, "why aren't you down there with the rest of the group?"

Helen smiled. "This is Bobbi's world," she said, gesturing. "I'm simply happy to be a part of it."

"I know the feeling," I said. "If you told me that I'd be having this barbeque six months ago, I would have said you were fucking crazy."

I took a long look at my new friends and smiled.

"You can't make this shit up," I added.

"I hear you. It's a refreshing bizarro world, where I'm the 'normal' one, after a lifetime being considered the freak of the family," Helen said.

I heard the pain in her statement and thought about how my sister must have felt growing up in our alpha-male, ultra-hetero family. Relativity leads to enhanced perspective.

"Normal?" I said, trying to lighten the mood. "What about the waitresses at your place?" I noted my Pavlovian response at just thinking about them, or maybe it was the smell of the meat, neither one healthy for me. "You can't tell me you don't have something supernatural going on at The Oracle."

"That's all Bobbi's doing," Helen laughed. "That Strega is a fucking enchantress. Bobbi brought the Sirens in when I opened the place. They were new undergrads at the local university at that time. All three are now getting their doctorates in quantum physics, whatever the fuck that means."

"Must be great for business," I said, wistfully.

"The men line up outside every morning, sun, rain, sleet or snow. I could feed them dog shit and they wouldn't notice," Helen said, laughing, "but I share the wealth. I pay the girls well, provide them health care and other benefits, and let them live in an apartment, rent free, in the back of the house. They brighten up the place."

We both considered her last statement for a moment longer.

"And what about you?" Helen finally asked.

"What about me?" I said, in my most lawyerly tone.

"What's so special about you, that you can gather the mythical, mystical, ethereal and extraterrestrial all in one place?" She asked.

"Not my doing, sweetie," I responded, the wordsmith in me instantly impressed with her double alliteration. "I'm just along for the ride."

"That's not what Bobbi says," Helen countered confidently.

"What do you mean?" I said.

"Think about it," Helen responded. "This entire group has been floating independently around the periphery of the Colorado universe for years, never crossing paths and unaware of the others' existence."

"Yeah, so?" I said, with a touch of my Bronx accent.

"In just a couple of months, you've somehow brought us all together in orbit around you," Helen said, delaying a moment to let it sink in.

"You're the fucking Wizard of Berthoud," she said, laughing. She turned and headed for the back property. "I'm going to gather the others so we can get this meal started. I'm fucking starving."

Wisdom comes from the most unusual places.

I thought about how, with rare exceptions, I had spent my life selfishly doing what was best for me, and to extent it benefitted Gina it was a bonus. I certainly didn't give a shit about anyone else. I had abandoned my blood family, my profession, my life, and as a result it had led to deaths of my brothers, and probably others along the way. I rationalized it in each moment, by telling myself it wasn't my fault, that outside forces beyond my control had carried me along and imposed their will upon the world around me. Collateral damage. But the truth was, I had made those choices, and they all had consequences.

And now, those choices had led me here to this very strange place and this selfless circling of wagons around me of friends I never asked for. I couldn't let my choices destroy them too.

CHAPTER THIRTY-SIX
MANIFESTING THE NET

Gina called me inside to help her with the condiments, buns, and beers. When we returned, the group, sans Claire, was all sitting around the table. My office chair sat empty at its head. Another sat empty at its opposite end. Claire stood directly behind the chair at the head of the table.

Throughout my life, I had avoided taking the chair of power at the family table. When we were young, my grandfather sat there, my grandmother at the opposite end. When Spaghetti passed, it was my father, with my mother at the opposite end. When he passed, it was my oldest brother, with my sister at the opposite end. It just became ingrained in my psyche that whoever assumed the throne did so at their peril. I always preferred what I called the Jesus spot, as close to center point of either side of the length of the table, which often provided protective bodies on both sides and put me beyond an easy reach of those in authority at either end. That proved particularly useful for a kid with a mouth too fast for his brain and a father whose hands were too fast for his kid's mouth.

Gina and I always had round tables. At first, I thought it was because they easily fit in small apartments and not much bigger houses. When we finally hit the Valachi motherlode, we maintained the practice with a small, metal-framed, four-seater in the kitchen and a dining room table that could easily have accommodated the full Arthurian court. We even had a round table in our present dining room. I rationalized my practice by believing it gave everyone around it equal access to the food in the middle. Funny how Gina's breach of family protocol hadn't registered until this moment when I saw the group sitting around this table. I felt like the first kid left standing in a game of musical chairs.

Gina slid into the seat at the foot of the table without a second thought.

Helen stood up to help me with the extras, and I eyed her now empty chair.

"Don't even think about it," she said, ominously. "That's your seat at the head of the table!"

Bobbi and Michelle were seated immediately to the left and right of the table's end.

"C'mere, Jimmy," Bobbi said, tapping the empty seat with her hand, "we've got something to show you."

"You can do all that after we eat," Lenahan bellowed from his seat to the right of Gina.

"Now sit your human ass down and let's get started," Michelle added.

I did as I was told and the table instantly transformed into a buzzing, laughing, swallowing and belching cacophony among passing food, drinks and the occasional smacked hand. The group was fully engaged with one another, like a family. I felt like King Moonracer, the winged lion on the island of misfit toys. I stared across the length of the table at Gina, who was laughing hysterically at something Everett had said to Lenahan, causing the latter to mock-reach for his gun. Eddie ducked down below the table to complete the pantomime. Helen was busy tossing some of her scraps to the two appreciative dogs. Gina met my eyes across the table and subtly raised her wine glass in a toast. I smiled and returned the gesture.

"You can save me a very large bowl of that roasted asparagus," Claire whispered into my ear from behind me, "but for now, why don't you have some of those 'special burgers' Gina has put aside for you?"

When there was no more roasted meat to eat and wine and Ouzo to drink, Gina, with Helen's assistance, brought out the strong coffee and Greek pastries, and the party pushed back their chairs and calmed into a sated state while they awaited their second wind. I took that moment to address them.

"Listen up, you motley crew," I said in my best, buzzed, outdoor voice, "Gina and I want to thank you all for joining us today."

"To our hosts!" Lenahan shouted and began to tap the table with his fork while the others followed suit. Claire, busy with her asparagus, thumped the ground with her hoof behind me.

"Wait a minute!" Bobbi yelled, standing and raising her hands to calm the crowd. "Jimmy, your brothers are here!"

She stood for a moment in silence, focusing on a spot at the edge of the circle. Eddie, Helen and Lenahan tried to follow her line of sight. The others, including Claire, all closed their eyes and turned their faces towards Bobbi. The hair on my arms started to rise.

"They said Valachi's coming for you," she said, softly, "during the darkness of the new moon."

"Let him come!" Lenahan stood up. "I'll be waiting for him."

"Can you arrest him?" Gina asked.

"Fuck that," Lenahan responded, "this ends here."

"They said he's bringing lots of friends," Bobbi added, anxiously.

"Then we'll all be waiting for them," shouted Eddie. "I've got a gun."

"Me too," said Helen.

Everett and Michelle were awkwardly silent. Finally, Everett stood up.

"We can't impose violence on the humans," he said, apologetically, "not even these scumbags."

"But we can do just about anything else," Michelle added.

"Well, I have no problem imposing violence on the right human," Claire said rearing up and stomping the ground with her front legs.

"I can't let any of you do that," I said, raising my hands to calm the crowd, "these guys are playing for keeps."

"Not for nothing Jimmy," Gina countered, "but we don't have a lot of options here."

"Lenahan can keep you safe," I said to her.

"And what about you?" she shouted, clearly angry. "This is no time for heroes."

"I can keep you both safe," Lenahan said, a cold-blooded confidence in his voice, "we'll just wait for those bastards here."

"I'm not going anywhere," added Claire, "if they come on this property it's a one-way trip. It will be their abattoir."

"And we may not be able to kill them," Michelle said, "but we can fuck with them like they've never been fucked with before."

"Your brothers just said you really don't have a choice," Bobbi said. "I'm not sure what they mean, but they just said that we, all of us here at the table, are your 'net.'"

"One more leap," Claire whispered, now definitely in my head, "then it's over."

CHAPTER THIRTY-SEVEN
GETTING LEYED

Lenahan was in full strategic mode as he moved the coffee cups and plates to the far ends of the table.

"I wish I had a map of the area," he said.

"Shit," Bobbi said, "that's what I wanted to show Jimmy before lunch. Is your car open?"

Lenahan nodded. Bobbi stood and with unexpected speed disappeared around the side of the house and returned a moment later with a Mary Poppins' sized purse. She dropped it on the table and rummaged through it, withdrawing, with a flourish, a large folded map. Michelle helped her open it up onto the tabletop. We all closed in to review it.

It was a two-sided map. On the front side was a complete scaled map of the state of Colorado. On the flip side was a close-up map of the Berthoud area of Northern Colorado, with Loveland at the top of the map and Longmont at the bottom. All the town and county roads were visible in decent detail. Someone had hand drawn lines on both maps that intersected west of Berthoud.

"While we were away," Bobbi explained. "I spent some time charting the Ley-Lines that run through Colorado." She pointed to a few of the lines crossing the full state map. Then she flipped it over.

"As you can see," she continued, pointing to the local map, "two of those lines intersect right here on the back of your property," she pointed towards the spot in the distance, "and then continue on towards the mountains."

"What are Ley-Lines?" Gina asked.

"We don't call them Ley-Lines," Michelle interjected, "but there are magnetic energy lines that circle the earth. And this is a pretty accurate representation. We settled here because of them."

"We use them for navigational purposes when we are traveling back and forth," Everett added, "but we didn't realize you had the technology to detect them."

"Technology has nothing to do with it," Bobbi said. "I can feel them."

"What do these Ley-Lines have to do with stopping Valachi?" Lenahan asked, impatiently.

"Well, first of all," Bobbi responded, "it explains how we all ended up in this spot."

"How?" Gina asked.

"This is an energy vortex, which strengthens all of our individual abilities. We were all separately drawn to this area," Bobbi replied, "and now that we're all here, those of us that have a gift, can all basically tap into each other's minds separately, or all at once, like a bunch of receivers. Here let me show you."

She scurried around the corner of the house.

"She's in," Everett said, "switching to English."

"Got her," Michelle responded, "me too."

"Wow," Claire added, "I keep switching back and forth between the three of you. It's making me dizzy."

"Holy shit," Michelle shouted, "I think I see your brothers, Jimmy. Where did the one with the red hair come from?" They all started to laugh, even Claire, in her unique way.

"Oh, charming," Michelle said, "he just flipped me the bird."

"He hasn't evolved yet," said Bobbi as she came back around the corner. "Not sure if he's going to," she laughed.

"Well that's quite a trick," Lenahan said, "but how does that help us deal with Valachi?"

"Can you jam their cell phones without jamming us?" Bobbi asked.

"We can jam everything they got," Everett added, removing his silver toy from his pocket. "Any cell phone or radio within miles will be dead."

"They'll be traveling in the dark and unable to communicate with each other," Michelle said.

"So how am I going to know what's going on?" Lenahan asked, "I'm a little short on telepathy."

"I'll stay with you. Out there, pointing to the back property," Michelle replied. "Everett can do recon for us."

Lenahan gave Everett the once over. He shook his head.

"I don't know," Lenahan said, "I don't think he's built for recon work."

Everett stood next to Lenahan and gestured to the pond.

"You see that duck?" Everett asked, pointing. Before Lenahan finished nodding Everett was back beside him holding the frantic duck. Everett tossed the duck into the air and it flew back towards its mate in the pond.

"That works for me," Lenahan said. "What about you little lady?"

"Oh, you don't want to fuck with her," Gina said and then laughed.

Lenahan nodded and studied the map. He pointed to the gulley along the back of the property and ran his finger to where the sewerage plant was located off the county road.

"That's where they scouted, that's where they'll come in," Lenahan said, "direct, hidden access, only one set of fences to get over and no animals to get past."

"Speak for yourself!" Claire said. "If I get to them, they're going to beg for a bullet."

Lenahan laughed and continued to study the map.

"They'll send a second group in through the front of the property as backup, and to make sure no one escapes the house." He pointed to a location on Beverly between the front of our house and the county road. "They'll probably park here, on the first curve in the road, where there's a lot of cover, and then walk the rest of the way. They'll station one guy on each corner of the property, right inside the fence line."

Lenahan looked around the table and focused on me. "You and Eddie can handle the front until I get done in back," Lenahan said, "I'll send one of the wonder twins out to you if I need to get you word."

"What about me?" Helen said. "I can handle a gun as well as the rest of them."

"You and Bobbi are going to be the last line of defense. Bobbi will be coordinating with the others. If Bobbi doesn't give you the all-clear, you and Gina shoot anyone that enters the house."

"What about the dogs?" Eddie asked. "They're going to go nuts as soon as anyone hits the property. It will tip them off that we're on to them."

"I'll keep them stashed at my place until this is over," Lenahan said.

"Can you stash Gina there as well?" I asked.

"Not a chance," Gina shouted.

"There's your answer," Lenahan said, "shit, if I wasn't such a chauvinist, I'd have her out front with Eddie," he laughed, "she's a better shot than you."

He turned back to Bobbi. "When exactly do the brothers say they're coming?"

"The new moon is a three-day stretch, starting this Tuesday night," Bobbi replied.

"Then I guess we'll all be back here Tuesday," Lenahan said, turning to me. "Can you pick us up at The Oracle? We don't want a bunch of cars in the driveway."

"Why don't I pick you up?" Everett suggested. "They may have someone watching for their car."

"No wonder the government has such a hard time catching you guys," Lenahan said, shaking his finger at Everett, "always thinking two steps ahead."

We spent the rest of the afternoon hanging out together, emptying our wine supply and trying to ignore the problem coming down the pipe. The not-quite-humans spent some of their time fine tuning their connections and on occasion would purposely break Lenahan's balls by standing together as a group saying nothing and then one of them would point to Lenahan and they would all burst out laughing. Lenahan would invariably respond by pointing his finger at each of them, one at a time, shaping his hand like a gun and dropping his thumb hammer, before blowing imaginary smoke from his fingertip.

Helen helped Gina and me with the clean-up detail and Eddie spent a lot of time talking one-on-one with Claire out by Geppetto's studio. Everett got the fire pit going and soon we were all sitting around the fire, spent from the day of food, sun and alcohol, watching the night sky as the stars illuminated seriatim in their respective positions.

"You ever going back?" I said to Michelle, pointing towards the sky.

"Someday," she said wistfully, "as soon as you humans can get your shit together."

"Oh good," Gina said giving her an alcohol fueled hug, "that means we have you forever."

Bobbi seemed to become a little more withdrawn as the night wore on. By the time the party started to wrap, I could tell something was bothering her. I walked her out to Lenahan's SUV to return the basket they had come with.

"What's going on?" I asked.

"Your brothers told me that one of us is going to die," she said, her eyes brimming with tears.

CHAPTER THIRTY-EIGHT
SILENCE IS GOLDEN

By Tuesday afternoon, Lenahan was leading Helen, Eddie, Gina and me in a firearms primer as the five of us sat around our dining room table. He watched as we each disassembled, cleaned and reassembled our weapons and then inspected the finished product. Eddie was the first to complete his tasks with his M9 Beretta. Gina finished a distant second and Helen just edged me out with her Glock 19 Compact.

Lenahan had his full-sized Glock tucked in a shoulder holster but also was cleaning what he described to us as being a short barrel, CMMG "Banshee" 9MM AR9, with a Defcan 9 suppressor. It had a top-mounted laser scope, and something called a "rip-stock." To me it resembled a futuristic sub-machine gun that would not be too 'girly-man' for Arnold Schwarzenegger. His weapons all seemed color coordinated with his black ensemble.

In the center of the table were a stack of five Obsidian 9 modular silencers and thirty boxes of 9MM 147GR JHP ELITE ammunition. The idea that we might be firing fifteen-hundred rounds before it was all said and done was daunting.

There were also boxes of various aftermarket, oversized magazines that would work in each of our weapons. Gina and I were given five ten-round, extended magazines which we filled with ammo. My thumbs were aching by the time I finished loading them.

Lenahan fitted each of our weapons with the appropriate suppressor. We all then went out to the back property and took turns firing a couple of magazines each at a makeshift firing range Lenahan had cobbled together in Geppetto's workshop. The suppressors reduced the sounds of our weapons to that of two drumsticks clacking together. More importantly it hid the muzzle flash, which Lenahan explained would protect our locations in the dark. This was getting all too real.

Claire kept to herself in her Lair, meditating in its shadows. Bobbi had accepted Everett and Michelle's invitation to spend some time at their place, where they gave her the full tour of their wonderful little toys and keepsakes. They all returned to our home in time for dinner, which Helen and Eddie prepared for the group.

The mood around the dinner table was somber and introspective. While I couldn't tell what might have been communicated among the telepathically gifted, the spoken words were few and utilitarian. No one seemed to want to make eye contact, for the chance they would be forced to engage.

We had moved the barn table and chairs into the basement's living room, so that we could minimize our chances of being spotted while we were eating, from either the street or the back of the property. We left the sliding glass door fully open so Claire could make an appearance there if she wanted. Gina had parked our Toyota in the driveway to let our visitors know we were at home.

Gina and I would occasionally return to the main floor and walk around the kitchen area and dining room in case there were spotters watching the house. The lights in the front of the house were off. We left the television tuned to a station playing popular shows from the last century and whose flickering light could be seen through the glass sliding doors that opened onto the back deck. We dropped the floor length wooden blinds, half shuttered, to prevent anyone with a set of binoculars from getting too clear a look. Lenahan had stuffed two winter skully-hats with paper toweling and pinned them to the headrests of our matching recliners in such a way that from a distance their silhouettes would mimic the top of our heads against the glare of the television lights. Then he shut off the Ring cameras using his iPhone, telling us he didn't want any recording of what was to come.

As the twilight descended into total darkness, Lenahan gave us all a final pep-talk.

"Okay," he started, "maybe tonight we are all going to be incredibly lucky and the only thing we will suffer will be some lost sleep and mosquito bites. But until then...."

He turned to Eddie and me.

"You two stay together and low behind Gnome Island, one covering the eastern side of the property, including the driveway, the other the western open field between the front fence and the house. I'm hoping I get to them before any of them get to you. But if you must engage, keep firing until they stop, and don't let anyone get between your positions so that you have to fire in each other's direction."

He turned to the women. "Helen, you and Bobbi will be upstairs with Gina. Helen will stay low on the third-floor landing facing the stairs and the front door. No one gets up those stairs. If you hear anyone on the back deck, shift position and wait for them to enter the living room area. Keep firing until they are down."

"Bobbi, you are going to be in the locked bedroom suite with Gina."

Bobbi waved him off, "I got it, I got it."

Lenahan paused for a moment, "But Gina, Jimmy and Eddie don't 'have it.'"

Bobbi looked around at those of us named. "Sorry, my bad."

Lenahan patiently continued, "Bobbi, you have to keep the lines of communications open with Claire and the wonder twins. What anyone sees we all need to know about in real time. And whatever happens, don't let Helen or Gina shoot the good guys."

Bobbi smiled and nodded.

"Any last words from the brothers on the other side?" Lenahan asked. Bobbi glanced at me, then shook her head. Everett and Michelle exchanged a look.

Lenahan then picked up a large red canvas satchel and handed it to Gina.

"This is a full hospital-grade, emergency medical supply kit. You're a nurse. If something bad happens, do your best. Otherwise sit tight and if someone kicks in the bedroom door you keep shooting until one of you are dead."

He turned to the last two members of our team.

"Everett, get out to the pond side of the back gully and wait there. As soon as you see anything, jam all communications for as far out as you can and let Michelle and the rest of us know how many are coming, from where, and what they are carrying. I'll take care of the rest."

Everett nodded and then disappeared. The vertical blinds on the sliding doors danced as he passed.

"Any word from Claire?" Lenahan asked the gifted.

"She's out there somewhere in the back," Bobbi answered. "You won't see her until you need to."

Lenahan turned to Michelle, "I'm going to start out there by myself. I'll be lying in the high grass just over by the pond. When you get word from Everett, come find me."

He turned back to Eddie and me, "Give me ten minutes and then you two go around the west side of the house. Then tuck in behind those Gnomes."

With that, Lenahan disappeared into the darkness. Helen and Bobbi made their way up the stairs. They were holding hands. Gina stopped to give me a quick kiss.

"Try not to shoot your foot off," she said, barely hiding her nervousness.

"I'll see you on the other side," I said, and squeezed her hand.

I waited until she was out of sight before turning back to Eddie.

"I'll take lead," he said.

"No arguments from me," I responded.

I looked over at Michelle, who stood by the sliding doors, eyes closed, totally focused on what we would never see or hear. I didn't bother to say anything and followed Eddie out of the door, my gun pointed earthward, pockets filled with magazines and finger off the trigger. I mimicked Eddie's movements as he swung wide of the house and moved quickly from tree cover to tree cover, reflecting training you don't get from video games. I then followed him over a part of the side fence and ran the final distance in a crouch before landing hard on a spot beside him on the house side of Gnome Island. He had already crawled up and was peaking over the top at the road in the distance. I took the time I needed to catch my breath and take one last look at the house, praying for a night of just mosquito bites. When I turned to join Eddie at the crest of the island, he was gone.

CHAPTER THIRTY-NINE
THE STORM-EVERETT'S STORY

The first two hours along the northern border were boring, and I filled my time checking in with Bobbi, Claire and Michelle just to break up the monotony. Michelle took a glance out towards the front of the house and reported back that Jimmy was at Gnome Island and Eddie had picked another spot out of view, but that no movements were otherwise detected. I missed the numbers. Slowing our thoughts down to human speed was getting a little annoying.

I didn't know why Bobbi didn't share the last message from Jimmy's dead brothers with Lenahan. Such a human weakness, their consuming fear of death. But it is one of the many weaknesses Michelle and I have come to cherish about them. They all showed up today, when they didn't have to, knowing that it could end badly. I was honored to be part of it.

At around midnight I heard some movement coming west along the gully and reported it to Michelle. When a pack of coyotes appeared just east of the property line, I leapt the back fence and stayed pinned to the ground among the high grass as they passed, holding my breath as the last one in the pack stopped to sniff the air right below me. I wondered if we smelled different to them than the humans. I would assume we smelled better.

Another muffled sound coming up the gully behind them sent the coyotes scampering west towards the foothills. Before I could hop back over the fence, four men moving in their own pack appeared in the gully just east of the back-property line. They were all carrying weapons like the one Lenahan had with him and they were also wearing night vision goggles. They were whispering to each other in a language I recognized as Albanian. The lead man spoke into his headset in English and said that they had reached the property and were about to advance. There was a cold professionalism to his voice.

I mentally activated my hadron distributor, which successfully jammed their communications and disabled their goggles, as reflected in their immediate exchange of Albanian curses of all Japanese technology and their mothers, as they tossed the now useless equipment to the floor of the gully. The four men then quickly climbed the fence at the corner in the area behind what Jimmy called Geppetto's Studio, looking to take advantage of its cover from the vantage point of the house. The leader directed the others to split up and advance on the house, one along the far western property line following the edge of the pond, and the other two up the center of the property. The leader would advance straight along the eastern property line, starting along the east side of the studio building.

The other three men ran, one at a time, along the back fence to take their positions. I communicated it all to Michelle, Claire and Bobbi, and then quickly leaped back over the fence into the gully before the last of the men reached my position. To my eyes, they all seemed to be moving in slow motion. I could now feel Michelle's presence in the high weeds just south of the pond and heard her repeat my message to Lenahan.

Staying low, I turned and raced along the gully until I reached the sewerage plant, the same escape route Michelle and I followed the night we truly met Jimmy. There, I found their SUV, lights off, engine running with the keys in it. I shut it down, used the hadron to shrink it to the size of an iPhone and slipped it in my pocket, feeling the warmth of its engine. By the time I returned to the back of the property, I could only see the two Albanians stealthily moving along the center of the property, but I could listen in on the others' thoughts. They had almost reached the bat house and were closing on the area near the end of the pond where Lenahan lay in wait. Then I saw the third man, closing around the edge of the pond. Michelle appeared further down the Gulley, watching, entranced. Without warning, a swarm of tiny brown bats exited their nest, drawing the attention of the assassins. Within seconds, the three men dropped without making a sound as chunks flew off the backs of their skulls and a frothy, red mist floated in the air as they disappeared into the high grass. Then the wind came....

THE STORM—CLAIRE'S STORY

I had spent the day alone, thinking about all that had happened since I had come to live with Jimmy and Gina. I replayed Jimmy's memories and could feel his guilt and pain over the loss of his brothers, and his other lessor acts of human selfishness. I could tell that he didn't want us involved in cleaning up his problem, or to put any of us in danger, especially now that he knew one of us would die tonight. He never quite accepted that it wasn't his call.

That's why I stayed away. Out of sight, out of mind. He had enough on his plate to worry about. I would manage on my own and would help as I could. I spent that time alone listening in on all their thoughts, one after the other, to distract me from my own.

Helen stayed focused on the time she died. She kept asking her Uncle Gus to watch out for her and Bobbi. But boy is she tough. There are ancient warrior blood lines flowing through her. I kept hearing the word Thermopylae. Fearless.

Eddie kept reliving military battles from his past that he fought in some hot, desert area. He had some code burned into his soul and he did whatever he had to do. Humans have a limitless ability to be brutal if need be. He was anxious. He had the same energy as the hunting dogs the humans took with us into the mountains. Pulling at his leash. He just wanted to be let loose.

Everett and Michelle felt removed from the others. Emotionally distant but intellectually engaged, like they were watching everything happen around them without fully participating. They knew that this was not their battle, but they were determined to help however they could. They are truly fascinated by the rest of us, especially me.

Gina relied on her religious faith. She spent her day silently praying. She believed that there is someone watching out for all of us, and that someone has kept her and Jimmy safe so far. She trusted that power to continue to protect us. She was also determined to not let the bad guys win. I hoped she was right.

Lenahan was all-business, all-day. He had formulated a plan and was sticking to it. He engaged the others in this plan solely to distract them, to give them back some sense of control. He was hoping the extraterrestrial wonder twins, Bobbi and I, could give him an edge but he didn't depend on it. He was going to kill every one of them on his own or die trying.

Bobbi was feeling the pressure. She was talking constantly with her spirit guides and her grandmother, asking for their guidance and help. Looking for an advantage. In the end, her grandmother, whom Bobbi kept calling a Strega, had given her one. Bobbi just had to get it right, while keeping everyone else on the team on the same page. But she was feeling powerful.

Jimmy's mind was everywhere. He was worried about each of us. He thought for a moment that he should just give himself over to Valachi, but he knew that Valachi wanted Gina as well. No loose ends. Jimmy was willing to die to keep that from happening.

When the darkness outside my Lair matched the darkness within, I left it and headed back along the eastern property line towards Geppetto's Studio and waited in the shadows of the eastern side of the building, where even the starlight couldn't reach. I knew from Everett and Michelle that the bad guys were coming in from that corner of the property. I stood completely still and quieted my breath and waited. I saw a man stepping around the back of the building into the lane before me. My right front hoof struck his skull before his mouth could open to scream and he dropped like a slaughtered elk. Then the wind came....

THE STORM-MICHELLE'S STORY

I could really use a joint right now to calm me. Everett and I have crossed all the boundaries we were not to cross, but one. And we don't care. After all this time being on our own, devoted only to our mission, it is exciting to be part of something on this alien world that is bigger than ourselves.

These humans are amazing. Each so different and so complicated. Each driven by their own passions, each burdened by their own demons. And evolving so quickly. In the time Everett and I have been on earth their technology has advanced far faster than their biology. But then there are those like Bobbi that show us that human development is almost at the stage needed to break free of this planet. And Claire was truly amazing. My ancestors were right. This experiment is worth it.

That is why Everett discontinued his mission. He now lets the humans go wherever they can and see whatever they need to out in space. They are still violent and unpredictable, but maybe that's what they'll need to survive out there until they can catch up with the rest of us. They have a way to go but I'm confident they'll get there. Good luck to them.

But what is going on right now is so primal. I am drawn to the pending violence that is coming. I will walk right up to the line. I want to feel it.

So tonight, Everett and I are out there, watching, helping our new friends.

I waited back in the house until Everett told me that it has begun, then joined Lenahan out in the field, trying not to leave a trail in the high grass as I pass. I gave Lenahan all the information and then he asked me to get out of the danger zone.

I almost laughed. He didn't realize that I could snap him like a twig, and then kill all the others before he took his last breath, if it were permitted.

So, I played my role, and gave Lenahan what he needed to succeed, kept all the others posted, and then retreated to the gully where I saw Everett. We both watched as the bats appeared and the heads of each of the three killers approaching the house exploded before they could even raise their weapons. Then the wind came....

THE STORM-EDDIE'S STORY

I missed this. The comradery, the silent preparation, the excitement, the finality.

My new life in Hygiene was almost perfect. I loved Bobbi for taking me in after I returned from Afghanistan. I had nowhere else to go. My life in the military was over, leaving me with a pension and PTSD.

Three tours as a Ranger, clearing that God-forsaken country of the medieval Taliban, the last tour as part of the British-led Helmand Province campaign and Operation Khanjar in 2008 and 2009. We took those bastards by surprise and they fought like hell, but we drove them out, killing every one of them not smart enough to escape to their rat holes high up in the mountains. Then it was home, a medal and an honorable discharge. Thank you, Sergeant Allison, for your valuable service. Don't let the door hit you in the ass on the way out.

I returned to my family's hometown of Lafayette, Colorado, went to work as a mechanic in a local repair shop and settled into my life of 'quiet desperation.' But then the nightmares came, along with the liquor and drugs I needed to make them go away. They all soon led to the loss of my job. So, there I was. Fucked and addicted.

I refused to become a burden to my family, so I took to living on the streets. I traveled to Boulder, where the panhandling was enough to feed my habit without having to rob the condescending snowflakes that lived there. Then one day Bobbi and Helen pulled up in their red Mercedes at the corner I was working.

"I've been looking for you, big brother," Bobbi said.

"Get in the car," Helen ordered. "Leave that half-pint behind for the next shift."

They brought me back to Hygiene and with a roof over my head, some good food, all kinds of new age energy healing and a lot of tough love, they got me clean. The nightmares stopped. Helen taught me how to cook and I found that I loved the creative outlet it provided. Soon I had taken over the kitchen at The Oracle.

The Sirens were a visual bonus.

Growing up in my house with all the females blessed with their unique powers, especially Bobbi, made every day just a bit crazier for us mere mortals. The military was a wonderful escape from that world. But after all the sorrow and killing, I was happy to be back in Bobbi's orbit, and these last few months had bumped the craziness level into the stratosphere, with friendly extraterrestrials and talking mules. I was blessed by it all.

But as I said, I missed this. The battle. Guys like Lenahan. Brothers you go to war with and who take no prisoners. When I learned what was coming from Bobbi, I was all in.

I laid on the house side of Gnome Island for about two seconds, peaking over its ridge, and heard Jimmy land heavily beside me.

Rangers don't sit and wait for the enemy. We take our fight to them. Lenahan had said that this guy Valachi was going to be waiting at the car down the road. He told us to sit tight and that he'd take care of it. But he would have enough on his plate in the back property, so I figured I'd pay Valachi a visit and save Lenahan the trouble.

When Jimmy turned back towards the house, I made my move. When I got to the end of the driveway, I slipped into the wooded edge of the next eastern property and made my way to the apex of the curve in the road where Lenahan said he expected Valachi and his second crew to park. I sat about ten feet off the road there and waited, counting the seconds to keep me focused. It didn't take long.

Just about midnight a black SUV with its lights off cruised slowly down the road and pulled onto the dirt twenty feet away from my position. I could see from the dim interior lights that an older man with a pushed-in face, was riding shotgun. He must be Valachi. A large black man was driving.

Two young men, who looked Baltic, quietly exited the back of the vehicle. They were carrying Israeli Negevs with suppressors. The black man then said something to the older man and exited the driver's side. I could see he was carrying a 45 caliber Glock 21, also with a suppressor. The two men fell in behind the black man and they headed towards the house, hugging the wood line. I thought about surprising them, but knew I was out gunned, so I left them for Lenahan and Jimmy to deal with.

I waited for the men to disappear around the next bend and then circled around the back of the SUV. I was five feet away from Valachi, whose ugly mug looked smug as shit, confidently staring down the road in expectation of the quick return of his hit team. I quietly chambered a round and started to exit the woods. But the old fuck was out of his car with his own gun on me before I could raise my weapon and fire. Then the wind came....

THE STORM-HELEN'S STORY

When Uncle Gus passed, and wouldn't let me remain with him in heaven, I felt like an orphan. Even if I could have reached out to them, the rest of my family had disowned me long before I entered the Witness Protection Program. I knew that I would survive because Gus had left me everything, which was laundered through WITSEC. But I was alone, again.

I tried to reach Gus the only way I knew how, through mediums. Long distance is better than nothing. Of course, most of the mediums I went to were charlatans. They meant well, said all the right things, and made much of bringing forward all these dead relatives I had never heard of. But no Gus, so I knew they were full of shit.

When I met Bobbi in that small esoteric shop on Pearl Street in Boulder, I was instantly charmed. She called me by my real name and told me Gus had been waiting all morning for me to arrive. She also told me I was cute. The rest, as they say, is history.

By our second date, Bobbi moved in with me. She helped me put the finishing touches on my new restaurant and then picked out its name. Then she found the Sirens, and I was off to the races.

The day we found Eddie panhandling on that corner, I got it. He was family. First hers, and now mine. He was her opposite. Quiet and brooding. But after we cleaned him up, he was appreciative, loyal and hardworking. And he was a natural around the kitchen. His presence made Bobbi happy, and that made me happy. Plus, I never worried that anyone was going to rob the place.

I thought about all that as I sat on the upstairs landing, knowing Eddie was out in front protecting this house and that Bobbi was inside the room behind me, keeping everything going for everyone else. I thought about Jimmy and Gina, government orphans like me. We were siblings in WITSEC, and I was going to do everything I could to protect them.

For the first two hours I lay in the dark on that landing, gun pointed, waiting for something to happen. Then I heard Bobbi chanting in the room. I couldn't hear what she was saying. The muffled sounds of gun shots outside drew my attention. Then the wind came....

THE STORM-GINA'S STORY

I first met Jimmy when we were both turning twenty, his birthday was a month before mine. He was working in the evenings as a security guard at the private women's college where I was studying nursing. I was from a small town in upstate New York. He was the quintessential New Yorker, not the fake kind you see on *Sex and the City*, but more like the characters that appear on *Law and Order*. He could have played the cop, criminal or lawyer.

He was a terrible flirt, and I was quite frankly frightened of him. However, he was also relentless, so after a month of daily requests, I finally agreed to a date with the intent of it being our one and only. We were supposed to see the movie *Rocky*, but his clunker-car broke down and so we walked to a local pub and had dinner instead. Then he began to talk, and I couldn't help but listen.

Jimmy was rough around the edges, but he had a certain honesty and drive about him. He came from a blue-collar family and spent a lot of his teen years working construction. He was finishing up school at the local City College, was doing well, and he had plans. We've been together ever since.

Jimmy kept every promise he ever made to me. He became a lawyer, got a great job, made great money and hated every minute of it. I was making decent money as a nurse, and I got to spend it all however I wanted. If God had blessed us with children, our lives would have been perfect.

When the Valachi job came along, I was worried. Jimmy never hid the fact that Valachi was a Mafioso. He just told me that he was handling all his legitimate business matters. I trusted his judgment. I still do.

Life went from good to great. We had it all. A beautiful house, beautiful cars, and all the money we could ever spend. And Jimmy came home at night. Every night, except if he had to get one of his new friends out of jail.

But if the boss's town car showed up in the driveway, Jimmy had to get in it. And he did. But he always came home. He was a survivor.

The night the FBI raided our home was the worst night of my life, until tonight.

As crazy as this sounds, everything that has happened while here in Berthoud has been truly magical in every sense of the word, and I wouldn't trade my present life or our past one for anything.

I thought about all of this today while we went through the prepping and planning and even the dinner. I worried about Jimmy and I wished I was out there with him. Instead of him. But I was praying that he had one more magic trick in his bag that would bring him safely back to me when the sun rose.

Bobbi and I sat in my bedroom suite with the door locked and Helen on-guard outside. I had my handgun locked and loaded and sat in the rocking chair that faces the door to the suite. Bobbi sat cross-legged on the King-Sized bed, her eyes closed in concentration as she fielded contacts from all our gifted friends, and on occasion would repeat what she heard to keep me informed. For the first two hours it was relatively quiet. But around midnight, Bobbi sounded the call-to-arms from the others. I sat in the rocker, feet on the ground and hands on the gun resting on my lap, waiting for the other shoe to drop.

That's when Bobbi opened her Mary Poppins bag, removed a small package of bottles containing herbs, oils and other unidentifiable ingredients. She also removed a black candle. She took it all into the en-suite where she lit the candle and began to add everything, part by part, into a bowl she had placed in the bathtub. With the addition of each new ingredient, Bobbi called out something in a language I had never heard before. It was a guttural singsong. A chant. I heard the words Bora and Chinook. Her voice rose louder and louder with each step in the process. She was beginning to scare me more than what was out there in the darkness. In a panic, I was about to call for Helen. Then the wind came....

THE STORM-LENNY'S STORY

This wasn't going to be like the last time. I wasn't going to have what was left of my career threatened and my life torn apart because some scumbag was finally getting what was coming to them.

Jimmy and Gina were good people. And I had grown accustomed to the Bizarro world Helen and Bobbi had drawn me into, which now included a talking mule and a cute couple from space. Life was just getting interesting for me.

Once Michelle gave me the recon from Everett, I had the upper hand. I had their plans, their numbers and their routes. I had picked a spot by the head of the pond where I knew they would be forced into my crosshairs as they entered the open field by the bat house. My eyes were totally adjusted to the dark. My laser site would do the rest. Then I would just have to hunt down the last one on the far side and get out front before the other crew figured it out and came in through the front door.

As the three of them approached, the universe tossed me a softball when the bats appeared from their box on the hill. As the men gazed skyward, I slowly released my breath, stared into my scope and fired. The third man was dead before the first one hit the ground. I then stood up to run over towards the east side of the property, to nail the last one. Then the wind came....

THE STORM-JIMMY'S STORY

I almost shit myself when Eddie left. I crawled further up to the crest of the island and looked around but could see nothing. He was gone. At the eastern tip of the driveway I saw movement. I almost stood up to see if I could spot Eddie out there, but then I saw the three figures moving as a group into my field of vision by the end of the driveway. The movement of the largest of three looked familiar. When I realized that it was Dan, I slid down below the crest and almost ran for the house. Then I thought about Gina, and everybody else who was putting their lives on the line for me tonight. I quickly visualized everything Lenahan had taught me, quietly chambered that first round, and crawled back up to the crest, found the group now ten feet closer on my driveway, took a final deep breath, aimed and fired.

By the time the click-clack sound of the suppressed bullet reached my ears, the man in the middle of the group dropped dead to the gravel below him. Beginner's luck.

Dan deftly stepped to his right and fired back in my direction and while I couldn't hear his weapon discharge, the tall red hat of a Gnome that materialized on the mound before me exploded into a hail of plaster shards. When I looked back, Dan was gone, but the third man in the group took off to my right and headed in a desperate sprint towards the western end of my property. I started to fire rapidly with a slight lead in his direction, but it took nine rounds before I finally got lucky again and saw him crumple to the ground. His limp and awkward form slid across the grass until it came to a full dead stop against the remnants of a tree stump. He didn't get up.

"Well, fuck me!" I heard Dan Pearsall say from directly behind me. "Who taught your sorry ass to shoot like that?"

I turned around and pointed my gun at Dan, whose own gun was hanging down by his side. He was smiling at me, his teeth almost luminescent in the darkness. I pulled the trigger and nothing. The magazine was spent, the slide locked.

"What are you going to do now Jimmy? Throw it at me?" Dan began to laugh like he didn't have a care in the world. I had heard that laugh one too many times in my life. This looked to be the last one. He raised his gun and pointed it at me.

"Bye-bye, Jimmy." he said.

Then the wind came....

THE STORM-BOBBIE'S STORY

I couldn't get the dead brothers' message out of my head. "One of you will die."

I spent all of Monday in my bedroom at The Oracle in deep meditation, calling upon anyone from the other side able to help me. The gift I share can be used only to help others, so there was no use looking to save myself.

When my grandmother, Roberta, appeared to me, I begged her for guidance. She was a powerful Strega back in Triora, Italy. Our family was one of the few to survive the Italian witch trials in that region during the Renaissance. She had always assisted me in the past.

I was desperate. I was willing to call down hell fire to kill everyone who posed a threat to my newfound family of misfits. But my Nona quickly reminded me that we can do no harm. She did, however, offer me another way, to use nature against them to give us an advantage. I wrote down her spell and spent the rest of the day gathering the necessary ingredients and tools while committing the words of the spell to my memory. I had tried to stay clear of that part of my heritage in the past, except with the Sirens, but I was willing to give anything a try tonight, and I had nothing to lose.

After Gina and I were locked in the bedroom, I did a mental head count to make sure everyone was safe and that anyone who could tune in were all dialed into the same channel. Michelle and Everett were at their posts and courteously sharing their observations and thoughts with me in English, and Claire was hiding in the darkest part of the property. I waited for midnight and when Michelle and Everett showed me the four men on the back property, I went into the bathroom, and channeling Roberta, called upon the ancient Chinook and Bora winds to come down from the mountains and do their worst.

The responding winds struck with such force I could hear the deck furniture being tossed over the rails outside. The windows creaked under the pressure and I was afraid I had made a major mistake. I couldn't hear anything over the roar of the winds.

I tuned into Claire and saw the dead man lying before her with a crushed skull. I tuned into Michelle and watched as the three other men dropped in the field and then was treated to an almost dizzying sense of speed as she and Everett raced to the front of the house. I saw the wind strike the tall black man with such force that it knocked him over, but not before his gun fired. The man tumbled eastward towards the front of the house where he came to rest with a hard thud against Jack the Spruce. As the wind passed, he tried to get back to his feet and fire his gun. But before he could do so, one of Jack's branches reached around and pinned his gun hand, just before he was riddled with a hail of bullets silently flying from the open front door. And there stood Gina still pulling the trigger on a now empty clip.

Jimmy was lying on Gnome Island holding his left hand over his chest, dark blood seeping from beneath his fingers. Lenahan arrived by his side and Jimmy told him that Eddie had gone after Valachi. Everett disappeared in that direction. Lenahan yelled for someone to bring the first aid kit and tried to lift Jimmy to a sitting position only to see that the bullet had gone right through him. So, Lenny gently lay Jimmy back onto the ground just as Helen appeared with the Red Bag in tow. Gina and Lenahan began to work frantically with large swaths of gauze to stem Jimmy's bleeding.

I tuned into Everett and saw Eddie standing over an old man's dead body, his skull crushed by the wind-swept, slamming metal door of his SUV. Eddie helped Everett return the man to the shotgun seat in the car. Then Everett told Eddie to drive it to the house and left him there.

I could see Jimmy's brothers appear on Gnome Island over Jimmy while Lenahan applied pressure to his wound and Gina performed CPR on his chest. And then I saw Jimmy standing beside them.

The oldest brother told Jimmy, "It's not your time." The redhead said, "You got more things to do." And the youngest one said, "You have to find our sister."

Everett appeared and stared down on Jimmy's dead body. Lenahan released his hands from the wound and gently pried Gina away. Jimmy's spirit gazed painfully at the now sobbing Gina and said "I'm sorry honey. I tried."

Then Michelle turned to Everett and commanded. "Do it!"

Everett looked up at Michelle, his eyes brimming with tears. "You know the directive."

"I don't give a damn about the directive. Do it, or I will," she shouted.

Everett removed his hadron distributor from his pocket and pointed it at Jimmy's wound. A golden energy beam struck Jimmy's chest with a palpable force that caused his limp body to jerk upwards from the ground. Everett kept the beam on the wound and as we all watched, the wound started to close.

Jimmy's brothers each hugged the spectral Jimmy before turning away and fading into the darkness.

Then Jimmy's bewildered spirit disappeared.

The once dead Jimmy now coughed and tried to sit up. Lenny gently helped him lean back against Gnome island. Gina hugged both Everett and Michelle like she was trying to crush them.

"Ffffuuuuucccccckkkk that hurt," Jimmy moaned, as Gina dropped to her knees, threw her arms around him and started to cry.

Just then Eddie arrived in the driveway with Valachi's SUV, his corpse in the front passenger seat. I didn't see his soul anywhere.

"Holy shit!" Lenahan said. "You bagged the bastard!"

"Wasn't me," Eddie said, "and there's another one back on the driveway. I might have rolled over him for good measure."

Just as Eddie turned off the headlights, Claire appeared at the side gate.

"Going to need a little help here," she called. Everett looked over at the gate and nodded. Within seconds Michelle and Everett had moved all the bodies Claire had dragged up from the field into Valachi's SUV. They weren't gentle. Lenahan and Eddie carried Dan's body over and placed it in the driver's seat, slamming the door.

Jimmy pointed over his shoulder toward the western side of the front property.

"There's another one out there somewhere."

Michelle quickly retrieved it and tossed it like a rag doll through the hatch back in with the others.

Eddie said, "Now what do we do with them?"

"I'll tow the damn thing up to Crater Lake and back it in the deep end before sunrise," Lenahan said.

"No need for that," Everett said as he pointed the hadron distributor and hit the SUV with a red beam. In seconds it was the size of a cigarette pack. Everett handed the miniature to Lenahan. "Now you can just drive up there and toss it in the lake."

I broke the connection and came running down the stairs and gave everyone, including Claire, the tightest hug I could. Thank you, Roberta....

EPILOGUE
LOOSE ENDS

I was really hoping I would come back from the other side with some really cool superpowers, but all I got was some residual pain in my chest and what felt like my Macallan hangover on steroids.

And the whole dying process is so disorienting. First, you're holding your hand on a hole in your chest you cannot believe is there, thinking "how did that fucker make that shot?" Then there's the pain. Serious burning pain. Then you're trying to keep from falling asleep, like when you are going into surgery and the anesthesiologist is asking you to count backwards from ten. Then the cold. Then nothing.

The next thing I know I'm standing there with my brothers who are treating me like I've fucked it all up again. Not one "how was your trip?" from the lot of them.

But it was a mixed blessing to see my brothers that one last time. I finally got to say goodbye, but I had to say goodbye. It's funny, but they appeared to me as they once looked at the best times of their lives. I could only hope the process took a couple of pounds off me before my arrival, because you know they'll be talking shit about me for eternity.

The gang all gathered at our home for a celebration the very next Saturday. We moved the barn table back outdoors and into the circle. Gina cooked an amazing vegetable Lasagne with loaves of home-made garlic bread that even satisfied the carnivores. She made a special oversized order of roasted vegetables with a dash of garlic—to keep the flies away—for Claire. Helen's delicious desserts were literally the icing on the cake.

The wine flowed freely and there was a lot of laughter to drive away any residual demons from that night. The dogs slept peacefully together on the back deck.

Lenahan explained that the common consensus from D.C. about Valachi's sudden disappearance was that one of the other families must have taken Valachi and Pearsall out, just in case they lost at re-trial and decided to sing their way out of significant jail-time. They joined Jimmy Hoffa in the pantheon of enduring mafia mysteries. Lenahan also mentioned in passing that he had done a little midnight kayaking on Crater Lake before the new moon had waned too much and thought he heard a splash. Enough said.

Everett then presented me with what he referred to as my 'coming home' gift. I now have a beautiful 'Hot Wheels' sized version of a Ford SUV sitting on my office desk. It makes a great paperweight. I'm glad I didn't get the bloody one.

Bobbi reported that my brothers had all elevated to the next level on the other side, but not before they gave Valachi and Pearsall an Irish welcome party. She didn't go into details.

As the night wore on, Lenahan kept begging Everett for a ride on his spaceship, and Bobbi and Helen made Michelle an honorary Lesbian.

Gina just gazed around the table from person-to-person-to-mule, eavesdropping on their various conversations, her face glowing. I couldn't have loved her more.

After the celebration, when everyone had left, Claire asked me to walk her back down to her Lair.

"I've got a favor to ask," she said.

"Just say the word. Anything. It's yours," I responded.

"I've been playing with the enhanced version of my abilities that turned out to be an unexpected bonus to all of us being hooked into each other's heads that night," she said. "I've been able to reach out much further than ever before."

"That's awesome," I said, still feeling just a little jealous after being short-changed in my afterlife experience.

"I've found Mr. Rogers. He's alive," she said, "but he's being put up for the next slaughter auction."

The next day I purchased a used pickup truck and a double-occupancy horse trailer.

Early Monday morning, I arrived with Gina at the livestock auction house in Western Colorado. This time I was flush with cash. Throughout that morning the theme song from that cloyingly sweet PBS children's show kept running through my head. Gina had finally forbidden me from singing it one more time. Five thousand dollars and three hours later we were backing our old truck and new horse-rig into our driveway, which is quite a feat for the uninitiated. Eddie and Claire were waiting eagerly at the top gate.

Before we came to a stop, we heard this magnificent mix of whinny and bray coming from the horse trailer, the acoustics of the metal enhancing the volume. Claire immediately responded in kind. I got the chills from the exchange.

Eddie helped me lead an anxious Mr. Rogers out of the trailer. He was taller than Claire and he was clearly undernourished. His coat was what the Irish call salt-and-pepper in coloring and his face resembled one of my great-uncles who had an aquiline nose whom we called 'The Badger.' Unbelievably, to the extent that word still carried any meaning for me, his right shoulder bore a white tattoo of a heart with a 'J' inside, which confirmed to me that he was where he was supposed to be. Fuck Valachi. Welcome home Mr. Rogers.

He proudly cantered right over to the gate where Claire waited, and she immediately began to nuzzle him. I got the gate open while Eddie removed his harness and the two mules raced in full gallop together down the hill, past the Lair, through the back gate and across the soccer field where they performed a few synchronized laps around the bat house and then finally came to rest at the land crest at the far end of the pond. There they faced each other and began to groom each other's manes, gently. Lonely no more.

The next thing on my to-do list was to drive around to Lucian's house and speak with his folks. I brought Gina with me to reduce the creepiness factor and put his parents at ease. I explained that since we were now the proud owner of two mules, I could use Lucian's invaluable ranch-hand experience and assistance helping me around the place whenever he was free after school or on weekends. I told them I would gladly pay him fifteen dollars-an-hour, cash, for his time. They readily agreed. He whooped like a cowboy.

Our next task was really Gina's idea, and it was good that we waited until we had gotten Mr. Rogers, because it kept Claire distracted while Gina and Lenahan pulled it off.

A week after Mr. Rogers' arrival, Gina appeared at home in the Toyota, Lenahan riding shotgun. I called to Claire who was out in the field with her new best friend, and they both cantered up to the front gate. She must have been too involved with her soul mate to bother reading my mind.

Before Claire could say anything or get into our heads, Gina and Lenahan opened the back-passenger doors of the Toyota, and two beautiful twenty-something young women exited, and stood nervously looking around. Claire abruptly reared up and repeated the sound she had made when she heard Mr. Rogers, but only louder.

The older blonde, standing beside Gina, suddenly recognized her mule.

She raced up to the gate and threw her arms around Claire. The younger one followed on her heels shouting "Claire, Claire!" and soon joined her weeping older sister and Claire in the emotional scrum. Claire arched her neck over each of their shoulders in turn, rubbing her face and chin on their backs, and softly repeating their names, 'Scarlett' and 'Savanna.' Mr. Rogers respectfully grazed on the periphery.

We gave them their space out in the back property, watching them reconnect from our seats on the deck. There was that hybrid foal, and two little girls from so long ago, reunited at last. By the end of the day we had two more permanent additions to the group. Our new-fangled family just seemed to keep growing organically like that.

The final thing on my to-do list took the most planning of all and again required Lenahan's governmental intercession. On October 1st, after nine hours in the air I arrived at the Virgin Atlantic section of Terminal 3 in Heathrow Airport. Gina had stayed behind to manage the home and entertain our revolving guest-list, but I knew she wanted me to do this alone. "Put on your big boy pants and go!" she said.

I located my single piece of luggage at the appropriate carousel and was then carried along in the strong current of disembarking passengers through a large doorway to the area where the public waited. There were a few personal drivers standing among the large crowd carrying signs with the name of their expected arriving passenger. My eyes were drawn to one particular sign on a rainbow background which read: "BROTHER—DON'T KNOW HIS NAME—HE'S A YANK IN THE WPP!"

It was held by four beautifully manicured and bejewelled hands belonging to two very well turned out women of similar size and age, one of them clearly my sister, the other soon to be. Rest in peace brothers.

And yeah, I kept my new name. I finally had become Jimmy Moran, the Wizard of Berthoud.

ACKNOWLEDGMENTS

It took a long life to get here, so I have many people to thank:

First and foremost, I thank the Love of My Life, Lisa (*ne* Wallen Witch), who saw past all the imperfections in that drifting security guard at her college so long ago and embarked on an epic journey that made *The Odyssey* look like a trip to a candy store. Your love and strength got us through all the tough times. Your joy made the good times magical. You never quit. I dedicate this novel to you.

To my sisters, Veronica and b (and the Frank family), whose generous support and sage guidance, through the good times and bad, landed me in the position to write this novel. You are right, Colorado is truly magical. Leap and the net will appear.

To my children, my true legacy, who have, time and again, brought joy to my life. Luke, you are the most fearless person I have ever known. Your amazing talent as a writer inspired me to write this novel. Your time is near. The Denver Fire Department is lucky to have you. *Fortis Fortuna Adiuvat.* Jackie, ice water flows through your veins, and you have never met a challenge you could not overcome and dominate. You are unstoppable and your unending list of personal and professional accomplishments could not make me prouder. You are destined to be a Fortune 100 CEO. *Nunquam Secundum.* Mark, you have always demonstrated a wisdom beyond your ken. I value the unvarnished counsel you have continuously provided me over the years. Your insightful intelligence and even temperament when the pressure is overwhelming will guaranty your success. The NYPD is blessed by your personal values and integrity. *Vitae Caeruleae Regnant*. To all three of you, *Sapere Aude*.

To my grandchildren, Lucian, Scarlett and Savanna, who all appear by name in the novel, The Dude and Nona love you. To the newest one *in utero*, and all that follow, we can't wait to meet you. Always remember, there is magic in the world.

To my daughters (by love and marriage) Georgina and Sara, you have both brought so many wonderful blessings to our family. I love you. Hang in there, G, she's worth the effort. Matt M, thank you for your continuing support of Lucian (knuckle-sandwich).

To my three brothers Eddie, Bernie (Bones the Ginger) and John, sorry I killed you off (Freudian slip). Growing up I was never alone, and you always had my back. Thank God for the statute of limitations. To Mary, Denise and Tara, thank you for putting up with them and me. Thank you, Taylor, J-M, Evan, Eamon, Mac, Brendan, Nolan, Eddie and Kathleen, for politely tolerating the eccentricities of your mad uncle. Your respective gifts and accomplishments continue to enrich the Clan. Evan, always remember your first time in Berthoud, and please tell your mom I borrowed her name.

To my parents, grandparents and Irish ancestors, near and distant, who provided me with such a rich oral tradition and the blarney to share it. To Dutch, Mamma C, and the Collins Clan, who loved me like a son and brother during my formative years and nurtured my creative bent.

To all the Wallen Witches and their spouses and children, and their spouses and children, especially Brian and Matt, you have enriched my life countless times over the years. Thank you, Dina, for reading the early version of TWA (love the shirt). Beau, I still want to be you when I grow up.

To the real Jimmy Moran, your authentic bravery and strong character inspire me. I am honored by your friendship and the joining of our families. Love to Liz and Dana (and Kevin).

To John Frawley and each member of the Frawley Clan, thanks for keeping your cousins out of trouble. It was a multi-generational, full-time job. I love you all.

To my Aussie/Brit family, Nigel, Sarah, David, and Liz, good on you all!

To Helen LaLousis, your unwavering friendship and support over many lifetimes inspired your namesake in the novel. I love you.

To my brilliant law partner, Robert Meloni, *My Cousin Vinnie* could not do you justice. You taught me to love the law again. We have shared one hell of a run together. Love to Adrienne, Sofia, Isabella, and finally Raff, the jewel in your crown. To Liz Morin, *ma jolie fille* and legal legacy, and Tanner and Big Jim, much love.

To Mark "Lenny" Lenahan (lifelong friend and confidant), "Brother Mike" Moulton (ditto for the later years), Bobbi Allison-Roell (true sorceress) and Eddie Roell (mule companion), Mark Lafayette (stellar lawyer), the Honorable George Silver (brilliant jurist and wonderful friend), Everett and Michelle Coffelt (loyal existential extraterrestrials), Pam Ervin (my mule whisperer), daughters Jill and Amy (and Tique), Randy Trahan, realtor extraordinaire, who procured the midpoint to Gorias, Finias, Murias, and Falias, and everyone else whose names appear in my novel. I love you all. This is my humble way of honoring your friendship and inspiration.

To Amy, Mike, Delaney and Charles Honaker, thank you for sharing Claire. To Silja, Darren and Anya (and April) Knoll, thank you for your friendship, finding Mr. Rogers (and Honey) and introducing me to the Colorado Horse Rescue, a noble organization, and to the sculptor and mule maven, Cammie Lundeen. To Lynn, Lenay McQueen and all six of your beautiful children, thanks for the Christmas Carols, the cookies, the early morning greetings and for inspiring the Lucian character. To Megan, Kyle, Julia, Kole and Emma (and Nova) Schnell, thanks for your neighborly kindness (and for Stella and Rosie).

To Dick (MacGyver), Sally (and sister Sue) Smeeding, Drew, Kelly, Quinn, Aida and Felix Johnson, Erving and Peggy Olheiser, Eric Armstrong and Ezarick and Aryan, Eric and Ann Pederson (Gus and Beans), Linda (from Queens), Asha (future author) and family, thanks for holding down my perimeter.

To Jim and Kathy Fronsdahl, Walmart posse and close friends, for your invaluable feedback, last-minute editing of the novel, and welcomed emotional support, all much appreciated.

To Gary and Cathy Greer (the "Geppettos") thanks for making this house so magical.

To Ferd Beck, the McCaffrey Clan's Merlin. Your sager imprint has been multi-generational, and you are indelibly woven into McCaffrey lore. Thanks for the Latin lessons, *sapiens*.

To Colin Broderick and Ricky Ginsburg, two amazingly talented writers who continue to inspire me.

To Dr. Nick Atlas, the last true Renaissance man, Modern Mystic, and author, thanks for your careful read and invaluable insights. You are da man!

To my talented colleagues at the NoCo Writers Group, never quit writing. Thanks for the feedback.

To all those professors at Lehman College who nurtured my creativity back when Moses was in short pants, especially Walter Dubler and Clement Dunbar III, thank you.

To Pat Francis, for believing in *Revelations*. To Tina Piras, for being my biggest fan (and for putting up with Franco).

To Donald Zuckerman and Stephen Furst (R.I.P.), for loving *Spark of Faith*.

To the Vaughan family, especially Big Jack and Connie, I never would have sat for the bar had it not been for your divine intervention. Young Jack will always be my first best friend. You are my family. My love to you all.

To all members of my Riverdale ("Da Bronx") community, I miss you, especially my Tyndall roommates and guests, the PWWC – Ralph D, Mike M, Mike H, Eddie M and Tommy McQ (R.I.P.), BC (really Yonkers), Yin-Yin, and the folks at Dino's Pizza (Sal and Flora, best eggplant parm in the world) and Riverdale Bagels (Enzo, Chrissy & Cathy, pure ambrosia), nothing will ever compare. And I could never forget you, Donna, Michelle and Patrick, each integral members of the Clan. Elvis has left the building. To all of the heroes of 9/11, including, without limitation, Thomas "Rocky" O'Hagan (childhood friend), William McGinn (Riverdale neighbor) and Orio Palmer (Spellman classmate). You will never be forgotten.

To all the members of the Berthoud (Estates and Town) community, including Mike Brackett, Debra and Bill Farmer, Sean, Bekki, Simon and Hannah Garcia, Andrea and Conner Maxwell, Jay, Rebecca and Katie Elkins, Alex, Kimmy and Harley, Quinn and Beaker (RIP)("the Cerberus triplets"), Raymond and family, Earl and Denise, and all of those other neighbors whose animals are mentioned by name, thanks for putting up with me. I am an acquired taste.

To my publisher, Reagan Rothe, thanks for the shot. May this be the first of many. To my design guru, David King, thanks for your patience, I know I reached your last nerve.

Special thanks to Dan Pearson, the man, the myth, the legend (and one wonderfully scary dude). I never forgot the offer. Much respect and love.

And finally, special thanks to Claire and Mr. Rogers (R.I.P.) for sharing your story with me. Your intrinsic nobility has made me strive to be a better human being. I love you both (and Honey).

ABOUT THE AUTHOR

Photo courtesy of Georgina McCaffrey

Tom McCaffrey is a born-and-bred New Yorker who, after a successful career working as an entertainment attorney in Manhattan, relocated with his wife to a small town in Northern Colorado to follow a road less travelled and return to his first passion, writing. Despite the local rumors started by Claire the mule, he denies being in the Witness Protection Program.

NOTE FROM THE AUTHOR

Word-of-mouth is crucial for any author to succeed. If you enjoyed *The Wise Ass*, please leave a review online—anywhere you are able. Even if it's just a sentence or two. It would make all the difference and would be very much appreciated.

Thanks!
Tom McCaffrey

Thank you so much for reading one of our **Humor** novels.

If you enjoyed our book, please check out our recommendation for your next great read!

Parrot Talk by David B. Seaburn

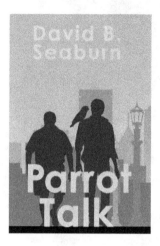

"...a story of abandonment, addiction, finding oneself—all mixed in with tear-jerking chapters next to laugh-out-loud chapters."

– Tiff & Rich